Sign up to
when I rele...

Join my Patreon (patreon.com/jackbryce) to get early access to my work!

ISBN-13: 9798303991415

# MAGE of WAYCROSS

### Book 3

## A SLICE OF LIFE FANTASY ADVENTURE

JACK BRYCE

*To the Dukes.*

# Chapter 1

"Louisville, here I come," I muttered to myself as I joined the westbound traffic on I-64.

I had never been a fan. I liked Kentucky well enough, don't get me wrong, but I wasn't a city guy to begin with, and Louisville just didn't do it for me.

When I came to my exit, I entered the city and

navigated my red Ford pickup truck through the crowded streets. I hadn't been to Louisville in a while, and the contrast between the fast-paced energy here and the quiet, easy rhythm of Waycross was jarring. It was like stepping into another world — a world I used to know but had left behind.

Even though Louisville wasn't the biggest city in the States by a long shot, it still felt suffocating after spending so much time out in the open countryside. I couldn't help but think about how Brooke dealt with this every day. It made sense now, why she'd sounded so worn out on the phone.

I parked on the street outside her apartment and sat there for a moment, hands resting on the wheel. I'd come because she needed me, and I hoped she would let me help solve this damn thing.

Brooke was independent — too independent sometimes. She should have quit the job when last we talked, but she went back in. And now, she sounded close to burnout.

Taking a breath, I stepped out of the truck and

headed toward the entrance. I went through the lobby and headed straight for the elevator. I'd been here before, and I knew my way. I rode the elevator up to her floor. When I knocked on her door, I could hear shuffling from the other side, a pause before she unlocked it.

When the door finally opened, Brooke stood there looking like she hadn't slept in days. Her pretty blue eyes were tired, her black hair pulled back in a messy ponytail, and her office clothes were wrinkled like she'd been wearing them for way too long.

"Hey," I said, trying to keep my voice light as I took in the sight of her.

She forced a smile, leaning on the doorframe. "Hey... you got here fast."

"Of course I did," I said, stepping inside as she moved out of the way. "You sounded like you needed me."

Brooke shut the door behind me and sighed, leaning against it like she didn't have the energy to stand on her own. "Yeah. Yeah, I do."

I glanced around the apartment. It was clean, but there was a kind of chaos to it — the kind that came from too much going on and not enough time to deal with it all. Papers were strewn across the table, her laptop was still open, and there were signs of an all-nighter everywhere I looked. Otherwise, it was modern and sleek — but also sterile. When I had first seen it, I was pretty sure that Cody would hate it.

Now, I was beginning to suspect that Brooke hated it, too.

"You okay?" I asked, turning back to her.

She let out a tired laugh, shaking her head. "No, not really."

I stepped closer, reaching out to brush a strand of raven hair behind her ear. "Talk to me. What happened?"

Brooke pushed off the door and walked toward the kitchen, waving a hand toward the mess of papers on the table. "Work happened? Ugh, *everything* happened." She stopped, staring down at the stack of files with a look of defeat. "I've been trying to fix this project for days, Sean. I stayed at the office all night trying to get it right, but every time I think I'm done, something else blows up, and Peter Mantle just shoves it all my way... not even a word or the slightest offer of help."

"You could've called me sooner," I said. "I could have taken Cody off your hands, Brooke. I'd have been happy to."

She turned, her eyes heavy with exhaustion. "That's sweet, Sean, but I didn't want to bother you with all this. You've got enough going on without me dragging you into my mess."

"Brooke," I said, my voice firm but soft, "you're never a bother. You know that, right? You don't have to go through all this alone."

She looked down, her arms wrapping around herself like she was trying to hold it all together. "I know, but... I feel like I should be able to handle it. You know... *by myself*. This is what I worked for, right? The big career, the deadlines, the pressure. I should be able to deal with it, but... I don't know anymore."

I moved closer, placing a hand on her shoulder. "We talked about it last time, Brooke. You need a break. I thought you were going to take it?"

She laughed again, but there was no humor in it. "I don't... Ugh..." She threw up her hands and shook her head.

I knew the problem here. Oh, I knew it well enough because I knew Brooke. She was a warrior, and she didn't want to give up. I admired her for that. Her spirit was one of the things that drew me in.

But there is a limit to what's healthy… I wanted to get to the bottom of it, to have her reach the only conclusion.

"Why don't you take that break, Brooke? What's stopping you?" I asked.

Brooke shook her head, her voice tight. "Because if I step away, I'm scared everything's going to fall apart. I've worked so hard to get where I am. If I slow down now, what does that say about me? About everything I've built?"

I studied her for a moment, seeing just how much she'd been pushing herself. "It doesn't say anything bad about you. It says you're human. It says you're smart enough to know when to step back before you burn out."

She met my eyes, and for a second, I saw the fear and doubt in them — the fear that if she stopped moving, everything she'd worked would crumble. "But what if it's too late? What if

I've already burned out?"

I took a step closer, lowering my voice. "It's not too late. You're still here. You're still fighting. But you need to let someone help you, Brooke. I respect your independent spirit — you know I do — but we're humans, right? We can't cut it alone."

She looked at me for a long moment, then dropped her gaze, her shoulders slumping. "I don't know how to stop, Sean. I don't even know what I'd do if I did."

I moved my hand from her shoulder to her back, pulling her closer. "You'd figure it out. You're strong, Brooke. You always have been. But even the strongest people need help sometimes. That's why I'm here."

Brooke leaned into me, her forehead resting against my chest. "I hate feeling like this," she whispered. "I hate feeling like I'm failing."

"You're not failing," I said firmly. "You've done more than most people could ever do. But you don't have to keep doing it all on your own."

She pulled back slightly, looking up at me with a tired smile. "I don't deserve you."

I shook my head. "Yeah, you do."

For a moment, we stood there in silence, the weight of everything between us hanging in the air. Finally, she let out a long breath, her eyes softening just a little. "I'm glad you came."

"Me too," I said, brushing a thumb across her cheek. "We'll figure this out, Brooke. Whatever you need, we'll figure it out."

We sat down on the couch together, Brooke sinking into the cushions with a heavy sigh. Her exhaustion was visible in every part of her, but it was more than just the physical kind. The weight of everything she'd been carrying was written all over her face.

"I don't know what I'm doing anymore, Sean," she said, her voice soft but filled with frustration. "I feel like I'm just... drowning in work. No matter how hard I try, there's always more. And Cody... God, I haven't had any real time with him lately."

I could hear the guilt in her voice, and I hated that she felt this way. Brooke was a damn good mother, but she was being stretched too thin.

"You've got a lot on your plate, Brooke," I said, leaning forward a bit. "But you're not doing anything wrong. You're trying to balance a crazy workload with being there for Cody. It's not easy."

She shook her head, pressing her palms to her temples. "I feel like I've already messed it up. I've been so focused on work that Cody's with the nanny more than me. I come home, and I'm too tired to even sit and play with him like I used to. I don't want him to feel like I'm abandoning him."

I let out a breath, feeling for her. "He doesn't feel like that, Brooke. Cody loves you. But you can't keep pushing yourself like this. It's wearing you down."

"I know," she said, dropping her hands into her lap. "But it's like I don't know how to stop. The deadlines, the pressure... I keep thinking, 'If I can just get through this week, things will calm down.' But they never do. There's always something else waiting for me. And I just... I feel like I'm failing. At everything."

"You're not failing," I said firmly. "You're trying to do everything at once, and no one can handle that forever. You're a great mom, Brooke, but you're human too. It's okay to need help."

She bit her lip, her gaze dropping to her hands. "But how do I just... take a break? If I step away, I'm scared everything's going to fall apart at work. I've worked so damn hard to get here, Sean. If I take my foot off the gas now, what was it all for?"

"That's the thing," I said, leaning toward her. "What *are* you doing it for?"

She let out a bitter laugh. "Yeah…"

"Let me help," I said. "Let me take some of the load off your shoulders. Why don't you let me take Cody for the day? I'll take him out, keep him occupied, and you can focus on getting some of your work done. Or just take a break and rest. Whatever you need."

She looked at me, a flicker of doubt in her eyes. "Really?"

"Yeah," I said. "Sure. We'll do something fun, and you'll have a few hours to yourself to figure things out."

Brooke hesitated, glancing down at her hands. "But... I don't want to dump him on you."

"I'm his dad, Brooke. You're not dumping him."

She stared at me for a long moment, then sighed. "It's just... I feel so guilty. Like I should be able to do it all. Handle the job, take care of Cody, be there for him... I should be able to manage."

"You shouldn't have to," I said gently. "No one can do it all, all the time. Cody needs you at your best, not burned out and running on empty."

She swallowed hard, her eyes shining with exhaustion and something close to relief. "I don't know what I'd do without you."

"You don't have to find out," I said, reaching over to squeeze her knee gently. "So, what do you say? Let me take Cody for the day. You take some time for yourself. Rest, clean, work out, whatever you need. But give yourself a break from work."

She nodded slowly, her voice small. "I think... I think I really need that."

"Good," I said with a smile. "I'll pick Cody up, and we'll have a great time. You just focus on getting yourself back on track."

Brooke let out a long breath, her shoulders sagging with a mixture of relief and exhaustion. "Thank you, Sean. I don't say it enough, but... thank you for always being there. For him. For me."

I smiled, brushing a thumb across her cheek.

"You don't have to thank me, Brooke. I'll always be here for both of you. You're never alone in this."

She leaned her head against my shoulder, closing her eyes for a moment. "I'm so glad you're here."

# Chapter 2

After Brooke gave me some coffee and we talked a bit more, she told me Cody was outside on one of the playgrounds with the babysitter, who was already overdue to go home. I headed down after finishing my coffee, and Cody's face lit up as soon as I stepped out of the apartment building and waved him over to the truck.

He came bounding down the steps with all the energy a kid his age could muster, his backpack bouncing behind him.

"Dad!" he shouted, running straight into me for a hug.

I grinned, ruffling his hair. "Hey, buddy. You ready to grab some breakfast?"

"Yeah!" he said, practically vibrating with excitement. "I'm starving! Can we get pancakes?"

I chuckled. "You bet we can. Let's get going."

I said goodbye to the babysitter, paying her extra for the trouble. Then, we climbed into the truck together, and Cody kept up a steady stream of chatter as I drove to a diner I knew wasn't too far from Brooke's place. It wasn't Waycross, but it had that same cozy vibe I liked. When we pulled up outside, Cody unbuckled his seatbelt in record time and hopped out, racing toward the entrance.

As soon as we stepped inside, the smell of bacon and fresh coffee hit me, and Cody's eyes went wide as he spotted the menu board.

"Dad, they have chocolate chip pancakes!" he said, tugging at my sleeve as we waited to be seated.

I laughed. "Alright, alright. Let's get you some chocolate chip pancakes."

The waitress led us to a booth by the window, and as soon as we sat down, Cody picked up the menu, his eyes darting across the options even though he already knew what he wanted.

"You're really going for those pancakes, huh?" I teased.

He nodded, barely looking up from the menu. "With extra syrup! And maybe some bacon."

"With chocolate?" I raised an eyebrow. "Well, it's your party."

Cody grinned, setting the menu down. "Yeah, you're right. Definitely bacon."

When the waitress came back, I ordered the usual for myself — eggs, bacon, and toast — and let Cody handle his own order, which he proudly rattled off like a pro. Once our food was on the way, Cody leaned back in the booth and started talking a mile a minute, filling me in on everything I'd missed since I last saw him.

"School's been kinda boring," he said, poking at the saltshaker in front of him. "But we did this cool science experiment with magnets. And I got an A on my spelling test!"

"That's awesome, buddy," I said, genuinely impressed. "An A? You've been working hard."

He beamed. "Yeah! And Miss Harper, my teacher, said I could be in the spelling bee next month if I want to."

"You should do it," I encouraged. "You'd crush it."

Cody shrugged, but I could tell he liked the idea. "Maybe. Oh! And I've been practicing baseball, too. The coach said I'm getting better at pitching."

I smiled, leaning forward. "You missing the open fields back in Waycross? We can practice there more next time you come out."

"Yeah, I miss it a lot," Cody admitted, his expression softening a little. "It's so much more fun there. I like playing with Tink and going to the farm with Daisy. It's fun."

"I miss having you there, too, bud," I said, patting his arm. "We'll get you back out there soon."

Our food arrived then, and Cody's eyes lit up when the waitress set his stack of pancakes in front of him. He wasted no time digging in, loading up each bite with syrup and chocolate chips. We ate in comfortable silence for a bit, and I could tell he was happy — just happy to be spending time with me, away from the usual rush of life in the city.

After we finished breakfast, I wiped my hands on a napkin and leaned back in the booth. "You up for a trip to the park?"

Cody's face lit up again. "Yeah! Can we play catch?"

"Of course," I said with a grin. "Let's go."

We left the diner and headed to a nearby park that had a little bit of everything — open fields, a playground, and even a small wooded area at the edge. Cody bounced out of the truck as soon as we arrived, already holding his baseball glove.

We tossed the ball back and forth for a while, Cody laughing every time he caught a high throw or tried to show off by pretending to pitch fastballs. He was getting better, I had to admit. His throws had more control than the last time we'd played.

"Nice one!" I called out as he threw another

straight pitch. "You've definitely been practicing."

He grinned, puffing out his chest a little. "Coach says I'm getting pretty good. I'm trying to throw like you showed me."

"Keep at it," I said, tossing the ball back. "You'll be a pro in no time."

After a few more rounds of catch, Cody spotted the wooded area at the edge of the park and pointed toward it.

"Can we explore over there?" he asked.

I glanced over and nodded. "Sure, let's check it out."

We wandered into the woods, Cody darting ahead, exploring like it was the wilderness and not some small park in the city — I loved his imagination. He picked up sticks, tossed rocks into a small creek, and pointed out birds as they flitted back and forth among the branches. The whole time, I could see how much more relaxed he was, just being outside and having the freedom to run around.

"This is cool," Cody said as he crouched down to inspect a patch of moss. "But it's not as big as the woods in Waycross."

I smiled. "You're right about that. It's just a little patch of trees compared to what we've got back home."

Cody stood up and dusted off his pants, looking up at me. "I wish we could stay in Waycross more. I like it there."

I ruffled his hair. "Maybe we can make that happen."

As we headed back toward the open fields, Cody kept chatting away, telling me all about his plans for the summer and how he wanted to do more camping, fishing, and exploring when he came out to visit. I couldn't help but smile. The more time I spent with him like this, the more I realized how much he needed these moments — time to just be a kid, to play, and not have to worry about anything else.

And I was more than happy to give him that.

The bowling alley wasn't far from the park, and Cody couldn't wait to get inside. He hopped out of the truck before I'd even unbuckled my seatbelt.

"Bowling! I haven't been in forever!" he said, practically bouncing with excitement. "I bet I can beat you this time, Dad!"

I laughed, getting out and locking up the truck. "Oh, we'll see about that. You've got some pretty tough competition."

We walked inside, and Cody's eyes widened as he took in the sights and sounds — the crash of pins, the flashing lights above the lanes. He rushed to the counter, and after we got our shoes and picked a lane, he grabbed a ball that looked almost too big for him, but he grinned like it was no problem.

"I'm going first," he announced, hefting the ball onto the lane.

"Alright, hotshot," I said, sitting down and watching him line up his shot.

Cody took his time, concentrating hard. He pulled the ball back and sent it rolling down the lane. It started to veer off, but then it straightened out just enough to knock down a few pins. He turned back to me with a huge smile on his face.

"Did you see that, Dad? I got five pins!" he shouted.

I grinned, giving him a thumbs up. "Not bad, not bad. But I'm just warming up. Watch me now…"

Cody plopped down next to me, watching as I got up to take my turn. I bowled a decent shot, knocking down seven, but I could already see him calculating how he could beat me.

"You're going down," he said confidently, watching as I tried — and failed — to pick up my spare. "That was close, Dad. But not close enough."

"Oh, you think you're already done, huh?" I teased, sitting back down.

"Yep! I'm definitely gonna win," he said, already standing up for his next turn. This time, he sent the ball a little straighter, and it knocked down eight pins. He spun around, beaming. "See? I told you I'm getting good!"

"I'm impressed, buddy. That's better than last time for sure," I said, nodding in approval.

The game continued like that, Cody laughing and celebrating every pin he knocked down, and me pretending to groan whenever I missed one. By the time we reached the halfway point, Cody was in the lead, his confidence growing with every roll.

But after one of his turns, when he sat back down, I noticed his smile dim a little, his excitement fading just a bit.

"What's up, kiddo?" I asked, nudging him gently. "You've been quiet for a minute."

Cody shrugged, staring down at the bowling ball in his lap. "I wish we could do this stuff more often."

I tilted my head, sensing there was more he wasn't saying. "What do you mean, bud? We do fun stuff all the time."

He glanced up at me, then looked away again. "Yeah, but... not with Mom. She's always busy. She doesn't have time for this anymore."

I sighed, feeling the weight of what he was saying. "She's been working a lot, huh?"

"Yeah," he said quietly, fidgeting with the ball. "She's always at work, and when she's home, she's tired. She doesn't play with me like she used to. It's like... she's too busy for me."

I leaned forward, trying to figure out how to make him understand. "I know it feels that way, but it's not because she doesn't want to spend time with you. Your mom's been working really hard, but she loves you more than anything. She's just trying to make sure everything's taken care of."

Cody frowned, picking at the edge of his bowling shoes. "But why does she have to work all the time? I miss her."

I put a hand on his shoulder, giving it a gentle squeeze. "She doesn't want to work this much either, Cody. She's just got a lot on her plate right now. But things are gonna settle down, and she'll have more time for you again. You've just gotta hang in there for a bit longer."

He bit his lip, thinking about it. "I guess. But I miss doing stuff like this with her, you know? Like going to the park or playing games at home. She doesn't even watch movies with me anymore."

"I get it, bud. I miss that stuff too," I said, nodding. "But you're not alone. We can still do all the fun stuff. Anytime you want. And when things calm down, she'll be back to doing it with you, too."

Cody was quiet for a moment, then looked up at me with hopeful eyes. "Do you think we could all go camping again? Like we did last summer?"

I smiled, ruffling his hair. "I'm sure we can make that happen. We'll plan a trip soon, just like old times."

Cody's face brightened a little, and he nodded. "Okay. I'd like that."

"Good," I said. "Now, how about we finish this game? I'm still coming for that high score of yours."

He grinned, jumping to his feet. "You don't stand a chance, Dad."

We dove back into the game, Cody laughing and teasing me every time he knocked down a pin. By the time we finished, he was in full bragging mode, claiming his victory like he'd just won the Super Bowl.

But even though he'd had a blast, I could still see that hint of something lingering in his eyes — the longing for his mom to be part of these moments again.

As we left the bowling alley, I knew I'd have to figure out a way to help make that happen.

# Chapter 3

When we got back to Brooke's apartment, it was getting close to evening. Cody was still buzzing with excitement, bouncing up the stairs like he hadn't spent the entire day running around.

As soon as we walked through the door, Cody dropped his backpack and ran straight to Brooke, who was sitting on the couch with her laptop. She looked up, a smile already forming on her face as she saw him coming. She still looked tired, but definitely a little better than when I left her.

"Mom! We went bowling, and I won!" Cody practically shouted, hopping onto the couch next to her. "Dad said I'm getting really good! And we went to the park too, and I found this huge stick — like bigger than me! Oh, and we explored this cool forest area! You should've seen it!"

Brooke smiled wider, shutting her laptop and setting it aside. "Wow, sounds like you had quite the adventure today, huh?" she said.

Cody nodded eagerly. "Yeah! Dad said we could go camping this summer, like we did last year. Can we, Mom? Can we?"

Brooke glanced over at me, and I shrugged with a smile, letting her take the lead on that one. She ruffled Cody's hair, pulling him in for a hug. "We'll see, okay? We'll figure it out."

Cody grinned and jumped back off the couch, racing to his room. "I'm gonna get my camping stuff ready!" he called out over his shoulder as he disappeared down the hall.

Brooke chuckled softly, shaking her head. "He's

got a lot of energy."

"Yeah," I said, stepping into the living room. "We had a pretty full day. I think he's just excited to tell you everything."

She smiled again, but it didn't quite reach her eyes this time. "I'm glad you guys had fun. He needed that."

"We all did," I said, sitting down next to her. "He misses spending time with you, you know."

Brooke's smile faltered for a moment, and she sighed. "Yeah, I know. I feel like I'm missing everything."

"You're not missing everything," I said softly. "He still talks about you nonstop."

Before she could respond, Cody came barreling back into the room with an armful of stuffed animals and blankets. "Look! This is my camping gear!" he declared, dropping everything at Brooke's feet.

Brooke laughed, the sound lightening the mood. "That's quite the setup. But first, how about we get you ready for bed?"

"Aww, already?" Cody whined, his face scrunching up in disappointment.

"Yeah, buddy. It's been a long day," I said, standing up and giving him a gentle nudge toward the bathroom. "Brush your teeth, and we'll read a book after, alright?"

Cody groaned but obeyed, dragging his feet as he headed to the bathroom. Brooke leaned back against the couch, her eyes following him with a soft look. "He's really growing up, isn't he?" she said quietly.

I nodded, watching Cody disappear down the hall. "Yeah. He's a good kid."

"He is," she agreed, her voice tinged with pride. Then she sighed, rubbing her temples. "I just wish I could be there more. I hate that I've been so wrapped up in work."

I reached over, brushing a hand over her arm. "You're doing what you can, Brooke. And he knows you love him. That's what matters."

She gave me a small, grateful smile. "Thanks, Sean. I needed to hear that."

We were silent for a bit, each of us reflecting on the current situation. Then, Cody's voice echoed down the hall. "I'm ready!"

Brooke and I exchanged a glance, sharing a

quiet laugh as we both stood up. Together, we walked down the hall to help Cody get settled in bed, the tiredness in all of us finally starting to catch up.

Cody was already under the covers by the time we got to his room, his favorite stuffed animal tucked under one arm. "Can we read two stories tonight?" he asked, looking up at me with wide eyes.

He seemed so happy that we were here together again. "Two, huh?" I said, pretending to think about it. "Well... since you had such a big day, I guess we can make that happen."

Brooke leaned against the doorframe, watching as I sat on the edge of the bed with a book in hand. Cody smiled up at both of us, his excitement finally giving way to the exhaustion of the day.

As I started reading, Cody's eyelids grew heavier with each word, and by the time I was halfway through the second story, he was already out cold, snoring softly.

I closed the book and stood up quietly, glancing over at Brooke. She gave me a tired smile, her eyes soft with gratitude.

We stood there for a while, just watching Cody sleep. His chest rose and fell in a soft, steady rhythm, his little hand clutching his stuffed animal tightly. Brooke's hand hovered over his hair, smoothing it gently. The look on her face was one of pure love, the kind only a mother could have for her child.

Finally, Brooke leaned down and kissed Cody's forehead, her voice barely above a whisper. "Sleep tight, sweetheart."

I watched quietly, letting her have the moment. Cody was at peace. Seeing him like that made something in the room feel lighter, if only for a few minutes.

Brooke straightened up and looked over at me with a soft smile. I returned it, nodding toward the door. Together, we slipped out of the room, careful to close the door quietly behind us.

Back in the living room, Brooke sank into the couch with a sigh, her shoulders slumping as the exhaustion she'd been carrying all day finally caught up to her. I sat down beside her, neither of us speaking right away, just soaking in the quiet.

"You're really good with him," Brooke said after

a minute, her voice quiet. "He's been missing that."

I glanced at her. "He just needs time, Brooke. Time to be a kid, you know? That's all he wants. And he still gets that from you too, even if it doesn't feel like it right now."

She pressed her lips together, looking down at her hands. "I feel like I'm barely holding on. Between work and Cody, I don't know how much more I can juggle."

"I see it, Brooke. And it's not sustainable. You've got too much on your shoulders," I said. "That's why I'm here. I'm not just Cody's dad for the fun stuff. You don't have to feel like you're doing this on your own."

She looked up at me, her tired eyes meeting mine. She pulled her knees up to her chest, resting her chin on them, her expression heavy with the weight of everything she hadn't said yet.

For a long moment, she didn't speak. Then, finally, she let out a shaky breath. "I can't keep going like this, Sean," she said quietly, almost like she was scared to admit it out loud. "I'm constantly stressed. I wake up thinking about work, I go to bed worrying about it… and Cody's stuck in the middle of all of it."

I leaned back, giving her the space to say what she needed to. This was the moment I'd been waiting for her to reach — when she could finally get it all out.

She rubbed at her temples, her voice thick with exhaustion. "Since our last conversation, I've been thinking about quitting. I mean, really thinking about it. But I just…" She shook her head. "I just went back in. I mean, if I leave my job, what are we going to do? I depend on that income, and without it…" Her words trailed off as she shook her head, clearly overwhelmed by the idea of it all.

I nodded, waiting for her to look at me. When she did, I spoke. "Brooke, just end it."

She let out a bitter laugh. "But how? Quitting means losing the benefits, the stability… everything. I can't just walk away, can I?"

"You can," I said gently, "if it's what you really need to do. There are other ways, Brooke."

Her eyes softened but doubt still lingered. "But how do we make it work? I can't manage without my paycheck. What if I'm making things worse?"

I could see the exhaustion in her eyes, the struggle of trying to figure out a way out of this mess. Luckily, I had a solution.

I reached into my jacket pocket and pulled out a small pouch. "I've been meaning to show you something," I said, holding it up.

Brooke looked at it curiously, her brow furrowing. "What's that?"

I loosened the drawstrings and poured the contents into my palm. A handful of old coins — gold and silver — shone faintly in the low light of the living room. Brooke's eyes widened as she leaned closer to get a better look.

"These," I began, "are coins I found in the crypt I told you of. Real gold and silver, worth a decent amount. More than enough, I think, to give you a little breathing room."

Brooke's eyes darted between the coins and my face, her expression a mix of disbelief and confusion. "Wait, what? You found these... where?"

"Remember that crypt I mentioned a while back?" I said, rolling one of the gold coins between my fingers. "This is what I found there.

It's the real deal. These coins could give you the cushion you need, Brooke. You wouldn't have to worry about quitting your job or what comes next. You'd have time to figure things out."

She stared at the coins, her mouth slightly open in shock. "Sean, I... I don't know what to say. That's... a lot. Are you serious?"

"Yes," I said, setting the coins down on the table between us. "Look, I know how hard you've been working, how much you've been struggling to balance everything. You don't have to keep pushing yourself to the brink. This could give you time — time to figure out what you want, what's best for you and Cody, without feeling trapped."

Brooke hesitated, biting her lip as she stared at the pile of coins. "I don't know, Sean. This is... it's so generous, but it feels like too much. I don't want to take something like this from you."

"You're not *taking* anything from me," I said firmly. "I'm *giving* it. This is for you, for Cody. It's just money, Brooke. I'm not offering it to you as some kind of charity. I'm offering it because I care about you, and I don't want to see you burn out."

She looked at me, her eyes shining with

emotion. "Sean… that's…"

"Take it. It'll be enough," I said, my voice steady. "It'll buy you time, and that's all you need. You're smart, Brooke. You'll figure it out."

She swallowed hard, glancing back at the coins before finally meeting my eyes again. "I don't deserve this. I don't know what I'd do without you."

I smiled, shaking my head. "You don't have to deserve anything. You just have to take care of yourself and Cody. Let me help, Brooke. Please."

She nodded slowly. "Okay," she whispered. "Okay. I'll take it. Thank you, Sean… Thank you."

Brooke stared at the coins a moment longer, then something in her seemed to break. Her lips trembled, and before she could stop herself, the tears began to spill down her cheeks. She tried to wipe them away quickly, shaking her head, but they kept coming.

"I'm sorry," she whispered, her voice cracking. "I don't know why I'm crying. I'm just... I'm so tired, Sean."

I didn't hesitate. I moved closer, pulling her into a hug, wrapping my arms around her as she buried her face in my chest. Her body shook with quiet sobs, and I held her tighter, letting her cry, letting her release all the emotion she'd been bottling up for who knew how long. It felt familiar and safe. I knew her well, and we had often shared grief.

"It's alright," I murmured into her hair. "Let it out, Brooke. You've been holding onto too much."

For a few minutes, she cried against me, her grip on my shirt tightening as if she was scared to let go. I didn't say anything more, just held her, waiting until her breathing slowed and the tears started to ease.

Finally, she pulled back slightly, her eyes red and puffy as she wiped at her cheeks. "I'm sorry," she said again, her voice still shaky, but she gave a sincere smile. Letting it out had helped. "I didn't mean to break down like that."

I shook my head. "You don't have to apologize. You needed it."

She sniffled, nodding as she looked down at her lap. "I guess I did. I just... everything's been so much lately. I didn't realize how much until right now."

I placed a hand on her shoulder, squeezing gently. "Take some time to figure things out, make the decision that's best for you and Cody."

Of course, I wanted nothing more than for her to come back to Waycross with me. But that was a decision I could not force — something she needed to come to on her own. I knew the seed was planted, and I hoped it would bloom into something beautiful.

She met my eyes, her lips quivering again, but this time she managed to hold back the tears. "Thank you, Sean. I don't know what I'd do without you."

"Luckily, you won't have to find out," I said, giving her a small smile. "Just... call me when you need to. No matter what you decide, I'm here."

Brooke nodded, a soft smile tugging at her lips despite the tears. "I will. I promise."

We sat in silence for a moment, the weight of the day slowly lifting. Eventually, I stood up, knowing it was time to give her space to process everything.

"I should get going," I said softly. "You need to rest, Brooke. Take tonight for yourself."

She stood too, her eyes following mine as I moved toward the door. "I'll try."

I paused, turning back to her. "And remember, call me. If you need anything, anything at all."

"I will," she whispered, her voice full of gratitude. "Thank you, Sean. For everything."

I gave her one last smile, then stepped out the door, leaving her to the quiet of her apartment. As I headed to the truck, I couldn't help but hope that now, finally, she'd be able to start letting go of some of the weight she'd been carrying for far too long.

# Chapter 4

As I left the lights of Louisville behind me, the highway stretched out like a quiet, endless ribbon under the night sky. The hum of the truck's engine filled the silence, but my mind was far from calm. I couldn't stop thinking about everything that had happened today — the way Cody's face had lit up when he saw me, his boundless energy at the park, and how he'd opened up about missing his mom.

He was a good kid, and days like today told me just how much he needed space to run around, to laugh and play, to *feel* like a kid. Not caught up in the hectic pace of life in the city, where his mom was pulled in a thousand different directions.

And Brooke... I couldn't shake the image of her breaking down tonight, the way her body had trembled as she cried against me. She was so strong, always trying to hold everything together, but even the strongest people cracked under too much pressure.

She'd been close to her breaking point for a while now, but tonight had felt like a turning point. When she saw those coins, it was like a lifeline had appeared in front of her — something that could finally give her an out. I could see the weight of her job, the endless cycle of stress and exhaustion, crushing her.

And Cody... He was feeling it too. That much was clear today. He might not fully understand what was going on with his mom, but he knew enough to feel the distance, to sense that something was off. He missed her. The time they used to have together. It was weighing on him, even if he wasn't old enough to put it into words the way Brooke could.

I drummed my fingers on the steering wheel as I drove, the road stretching out in front of me. Brooke needed to make a change. We both knew that. She was finally starting to see it too. But the idea of quitting her job terrified her. And I got it. Quitting meant stepping into the unknown. It meant leaving behind the financial security she'd fought so hard for, risking everything she'd built.

But what was it worth if it was costing her so much in the process? The sleepless nights, the stress, the way she felt like she was missing out on Cody's life... it wasn't worth it. No paycheck was worth losing yourself. I just hoped she'd see that soon enough.

The coins had given her a chance. Enough of a cushion to let her take a step back, breathe, and figure things out without feeling like she was falling into a financial abyss. It wasn't a permanent solution, but it was time. And right now, time was exactly what she needed. Time to figure out what was next. Time to be with Cody, to rebuild the bond they used to have.

Time to come home to Waycross, if that's what she decided.

A small smile tugged at my lips as I thought about that — about her coming back to Waycross. I wanted her here, too. I wanted us to be a family again. A real family, not just visits here and there, me driving up to Louisville or them coming down to the house. No, I wanted more than that. But that was something she had to choose for herself. I couldn't force it.

I pushed down the gas pedal a little harder, the truck picking up speed as the miles flew by. The open countryside was a welcome sight after the chaos of the city. Here, the air was fresher, cleaner. I could already feel the tension easing from my shoulders the closer I got to home. Waycross was quiet, steady. The kind of place where life moved at a slower pace, where people had time to breathe, to think. I knew that was what Brooke needed, even if she didn't realize it fully yet.

The highway was nearly empty this late at night, just me and the open road. The stars were faint above, the moon low on the horizon. The quiet was peaceful, but my mind wouldn't settle. I kept thinking about Brooke's face as I left — how grateful she'd been, but still uncertain. She had so much to figure out, and I knew it wouldn't be easy. But at least now, with the pressure off for a while, she had the space to breathe.

As I neared the outskirts of Waycross, something caught my eye. Flashing red and blue lights lit up the road ahead, just beyond the bend. I slowed down, recognizing the familiar shape of a patrol car.

Sheriff Jacob Fields.

I eased off the gas, pulling over to the side of the road as Jacob's cruiser sat parked under the trees at the edge of town. His strobes flashed once more as I rolled to a stop.

I stepped out of the truck, the cool night air biting at my skin as I walked toward the flashing red and blue lights. Sheriff Jacob Fields stood by his cruiser, arms crossed, his face tight with worry. Even in the dim glow, I could tell something was very wrong.

"Sean," Jacob said, his voice rough, like he

hadn't slept in days. He stepped forward, the tension in his posture clear as he sized me up. "Didn't expect to see you on the road this late."

"I was heading back from Louisville," I said, eyeing him. "What's going on? Why are you posting out here at the edge of town?"

Jacob took a deep breath, his eyes shifting to the ground for a moment before meeting mine again. "It's bad, Sean. Really bad. Timothy Harton's been found dead."

"Dead?" I echoed, feeling a sinking feeling in my chest.

"Yeah." Jacob's voice wavered, his hand rubbing the back of his neck like he didn't want to say the next part. "Mauled. We think it's a bear — at least, that's the only explanation we've got right now. But... I don't know. It's brutal. Worse than anything we've seen in Waycross before. I'm out here waiting for some deputies from Blackhill to come over and help. It's more than I can handle."

"Mauled?" I asked, though the word already felt like a confirmation of what I suspected.

Jacob nodded, his face pale, the flashing lights making it worse. "I've never seen anything like it.

We thought maybe it was the same bear that's been killing his cattle, but…" He paused, shaking his head slowly. "If it's a bear, it's the biggest damn one we've ever had out here."

I felt my jaw tighten. "You really think it's a bear?"

Jacob looked away for a moment, clearly rattled. "Honestly, I don't know what to think, Sean. Bears don't usually come this close to town, and we've never had an attack like this. But whatever did this to him, it was big. Strong. It tore him apart, like… like he was nothing."

I kept my face neutral, but inside, I was already piecing it together. This wasn't a bear. It couldn't be. The cattle attacks, the way Timothy had died — this had to be the troll.

Jacob sighed, the weight of the situation clearly pressing down on him. "Most folks are gathering at Earl's right now. You know how it is — everyone's shaken up. They need to be with each other after something like this. Nobody's ever seen a man torn up like that around here."

I nodded, understanding what he meant. In a small town like Waycross, something like this shook the whole community. They'd need to be together, to make sense of it all, even if they didn't have the full story. "I'll head over there," I said, keeping my voice steady. "See if there's anything I can do."

Jacob gave me a tired look, grateful for the support. "I'll be over soon, after I check in with my deputies. We're trying to figure out how to handle this... but truth is, we're not prepared for something like this. Not here."

"I'll be there," I said, giving him a firm nod. "Whatever you need, Jacob."

He nodded back, his eyes still filled with worry. "Thanks, Sean. I appreciate it."

I turned and headed back to my truck, my mind racing.

# Chapter 5

I drove down Main Street, which was lit only by the occasional porch light. Soon enough, Earl's came into view, its front porch lit up, though tonight it seemed more crowded than usual. The rocking chairs out front were empty, but I could see shadows of people gathered inside through the windows, huddled together like they were waiting for answers. All the town's cars were parked in the lot nearby.

I parked the truck, killing the engine, and headed toward the door. The second I stepped inside, the murmur of conversation hit me. The air was thick with tension, the usual warmth of Earl's replaced by something darker, something uneasy. The bar area was packed, locals sitting or standing in small groups, talking in low voices. It was rare to see this many people gathered at once — most of the town's ranchers and farmers had come in, needing to be around others after hearing the news.

I spotted Daisy and Caroline sitting together at a table near the corner. Daisy looked up first, relief washing over her face when she saw me, but there was still that trace of worry in her blue eyes. Caroline sat close, nervously biting her lip, her eyes darting around the room as if trying to make sense of the scattered conversations.

I walked over, and Daisy immediately stood, reaching for my hand. "Sean," she said softly. "Thank God you're here. We've been hearin' all kinds of stories. It's... it's bad, isn't it?"

Caroline glanced up from her seat, her fingers fiddling with the edge of the table. In this big crowd, her usual nerves had returned. "Uh… we've been trying to, uh, piece together what happened. It's all so confusing," she said, her words coming out quickly, her anxiety clear. "Poor Timothy."

I nodded, squeezing Daisy's hand for a second before taking a seat next to Caroline. "It's bad," I said, keeping my voice low but steady. "I ran into Sheriff Fields along the way, and he told me."

Caroline swallowed hard, her eyes widening behind her glasses. "Did he say what happened?" she asked, her voice barely above a whisper.

"Jacob said it might be a bear attack," I continued. "But… I don't know. He didn't seem to believe it himself. It sounds brutal. More than what a bear around here would normally do."

Daisy's face tightened, and she sank back into her seat. Caroline, nervously twisting a lock of her red hair, leaned forward. "A bear?" she muttered. "It doesn't sound like something a bear would do…"

"I know," I said softly, glancing around the

room. "I mean, I *think* it's not a bear. That's just what people are saying right now because they don't know what else to call it. But from what I've heard... it sounds like the troll. And it's not done yet."

Daisy's eyes flickered with unease. "You're sayin' it might come for more of us, aren't you?" she asked.

I didn't want to scare her, but I couldn't lie either. "Yeah," I said honestly.

Caroline fidgeted beside me, her green eyes darting to Daisy before landing back on me as she nervously played with a pluck of ginger hair. "What do we, um, do? I mean, should we stay... inside? Or..."

Before I could answer, the conversation at the nearby table caught our attention. One of the town's older citizens, John Fletcher, was leaning forward, his grizzled face etched with worry as he spoke to a group of farmers sitting with him. His voice was low, but in the heavy silence of the bar, it carried just enough for us to hear.

"I heard it last night," Fletcher said, his tone dark. "Big, heavy footfalls out near my property.

Thought it was just deer at first, but no... this was different. This was somethin' bigger. And now, after hearin' about Timothy, I know damn well it weren't no deer."

One of the younger farmers, Pete Calvary, chimed in. "Same thing happened out by my place last week. Something was movin' through the trees, and I could hear it from my porch. Whatever it was, it was big. But I couldn't see it — just shadows."

The men around him exchanged uneasy glances, the weight of their words sinking in.

"I thought it was a bear too," Pete continued. "But now... now I'm thinkin' maybe it wasn't. Bears don't stalk like that. They don't get close like that without makin' themselves known. 'Sides, plenty of food in the forest. Ain't no reason to get close to people."

I exchanged a look with both of my women, my mind already spinning with the pieces that were starting to come together.

Fletcher's voice carried again from the other table. "I don't know what's out there, but it's somethin' we ain't prepared for. Hell, I've lived in these parts my whole life, and I've never seen a bear act like this. If it is a bear, it's gotta be the biggest, meanest one we've ever had."

The men at the table nodded in agreement, their faces grim. Another farmer spoke up, his voice low and tense. "Whatever it is, it's got folks spooked. Hell, even my dogs won't go out past the treeline anymore. They can sense somethin' ain't right."

Earl, who had been standing behind the counter listening quietly, finally stepped forward. His usually jovial face was creased with worry, his hand rubbing the back of his neck. "A lot of folks are sayin' the same thing. This ain't no ordinary animal. We've dealt with wild creatures before, but this... whatever this is, it's got everyone on edge."

I had heard enough.

I motioned for Daisy and Caroline to follow me outside, away from the noise and tension filling Earl's. The moment we stepped onto the porch, the cool night air hit us, and it felt like we could finally breathe again. Daisy was the first to speak, her voice low but urgent.

"Sean," she said, glancing around to make sure no one was nearby, "you're right. This has to be the troll."

Caroline nodded quickly, her hands fidgeting with her sleeves. "It — it makes sense, uh, doesn't it? The cattle, the... uh, the way Timothy was found."

I leaned against the porch railing, running a hand through my hair. "Yeah, it's the troll. I knew it was dangerous, but this? Now it's moving on to people." I paused, looking at both of them. "We can't wait any longer. We need to do something before it gets worse. Waycross could end up like Harrwick if this continues."

Daisy's blue eyes flashed with determination. "You're right. We can't just sit around and wait for it to kill again. What's the plan?"

Caroline bit her lip, her brow furrowed. "But, uh, how do we even go about this? I mean, we can't just... go after it like it's some wild animal, right? It's strong, and we've seen what a troll can do."

I nodded, considering our options. "It's not just about tracking it down — we need to be smart about this. The troll's dangerous, and it's not going to go down easily. But if we don't stop it now, more people will die. We need to get ahead of it."

Daisy stepped closer to me, her voice firm. "Whatever we're gonna do, we gotta do it fast, Sean. This thing's out there, and people are scared. Hell, *I'm* scared. But I'm not gonna sit around waitin' for it to come for us next."

Caroline glanced at Daisy, then back at me. "We can't do this alone, can we? We need help. Harper... he knows about these things, right? Maybe he can help us."

I nodded in agreement. "Harper knows the forest, and he's a good shot. He can help track the troll. We'll need him."

Daisy looked up at me, her expression serious. "So, we get Harper, we come up with a plan, and we hunt this thing?"

"Yeah," I confirmed. "And we do it tonight. The trail starts at poor Timothy's place, and we are going to follow it until we kill this thing. Before anyone else gets hurt."

Caroline shifted nervously but nodded in

agreement. "It's... it's risky…"

"It is," I said, my voice steady. "We can't leave it unchecked any longer."

Daisy looked between Caroline and me, determination written all over her face. "Then let's not waste any more time."

Without another word, we headed for the truck, ready to find Harper and end this once and for all.

We first went by my place to pick up the weapons — my Mossberg and Daisy's Remington — both of them with plenty of ammunition. In addition, I made sure to bring some scrap metal. Whatever I needed for the traps, I would retrieve using a portal to Harrwick, but it was smart to carry some extra, just in case I needed it on the fly.

We drove down the quiet, winding roads leading to Harper's place, the night growing darker as we left the lights of Waycross behind. Daisy sat beside me in the truck, her hands resting on her lap, while Caroline, quieter than usual, sat in the back. The weight of what we were about to do pressed down on all of us. No one said much during the drive; we knew what had to be done, and there wasn't much more to talk about until we had Harper on board.

Harper's cottage came into view, its windows glowing faintly against the backdrop of the thick woods surrounding it. Judging by the light, he was home. Then again, he usually was.

The place was just as I remembered it — small, isolated, and well-worn by time. A single light on the porch flickered, casting long shadows across the yard. I parked the truck and turned off the engine. The night was still, but I could feel the tension in the air.

We stepped out, our boots crunching against the gravel path leading up to the door. Before I could knock, the door creaked open, and Harper appeared in the doorway. He was already dressed for action — his long gray hair tied back, his M1 Garand rifle slung over his shoulder. His eyes, sharp and knowing, flicked from me to Daisy and Caroline, then back to me.

"Figured you'd be comin' by," Harper said, his deep voice cutting through the quiet. "Heard about Timothy. Damn shame." He stepped back, waving us inside. "Was a good man."

We entered the small cottage, the smell of wood and old leather greeting us. The inside was as rustic as ever — old furniture, hunting trophies lining the walls, and relics from generations past scattered around. Harper's place always felt like stepping into a different time, but right now, there was no time for nostalgia.

"We've got to move fast," I said, getting straight to the point as we stood near the worn-out table in the middle of the room. "The troll's out there, and it's killed its first human. Timothy wasn't just attacked — he was ripped apart."

Harper nodded, his face hardening. "I figured it was only a matter of time before it moved on to people. This troll's dangerous, Sean. And I agree; it's gotta be dealt with tonight, or more folks will end up like Timothy."

"We know," Daisy said quietly, her voice steady but laced with urgency. "That's why we're here. Will you help?"

"Of course," he said.

"We'll need to keep our wits about us, though," I said. "We're all angry, but that can't cloud our judgment."

The others nodded in agreement, and Caroline wrapped her arms around herself like she was bracing for what was coming. "What, uh, do we need to do?" she asked.

"We'll need more than strength to deal with this creature," I said. "We defeated the one in Harrwick using traps. We should try the same strategy with this one. It worked well."

Harper nodded. "Sounds smart. Big predators are best hunted from a great distance or using traps. Don't want to expose ourselves like we did with the goblins unless it can't be helped."

"Right," I agreed.

Harper slung his pouch over his shoulder. "I've been ready for this day, Sean. Knew somethin' like this would come eventually." He gave me a broad grin. "I'm gonna say one thing, you sure made life in Waycross more exciting."

"I'll say," Daisy and Caroline said at the same time, then shot each other a surprised look before they both broke out laughing. Despite everything, I had to chuckle along with my girls for a moment.

Then, I looked at each of them — Daisy, Caroline, Harper — all of them ready for action.

We gathered around Harper's worn wooden table to go through our plan. Harper grabbed a folded map from one of the drawers and spread it open. "Here's Timothy's place," he said, pointing to a small dot near the edge of town, close to the forest line. "I know the land out there better than anyone. If we start at Timothy's, I can track the troll's movements from there. It'll lead us to its lair." He glanced up, his eyes sharp. "We'll need to move quickly."

I nodded, taking a deep breath. "We're going to do this the same way we dealt with the troll in Harrwick. I'll use my Wood and Metal Sigils to set up traps along the trail. If we can lure the troll into a kill zone, we'll have a much better shot at taking it down." I glanced at Daisy and Harper. "While I'm working on the traps, you two cover me."

"Got it," Daisy said, her jaw set. "I'll watch your back while you set up those traps."

Harper gave a firm nod. "Will do. You just focus on laying those traps down tight."

I turned to Caroline, who was biting her lip and glancing nervously between us. "Caroline, I need you on lookout. Stay sharp, keep an eye on the surroundings, and if you see or hear anything out of the ordinary, signal immediately."

Caroline swallowed hard but nodded, adjusting her glasses. "I can do that," she said, her voice more sure than it had been earlier. "Uh… but, don't you think we should wait until dawn? It'll be easier to see, and we'll have more light."

Harper shook his head. "We don't have until dawn," he said, his voice low but firm. "Rain's coming. I can smell it in the air. Once the rain hits, the tracks'll wash away. If we want to track this thing, we've got to move fast."

"Yeah," I agreed. I could feel it too, hanging in the air. It wasn't the best, because we were all tired, but we needed to power through that.

Daisy leaned forward, resting her elbows on the table. "Harper's right. If we wait, we might lose the trail entirely. We've gotta go tonight, before it gets a chance to slip away." She glanced at me. "We're ready, Sean. We can do this."

"Okay," Caroline said. "Then we go."

I looked at each of them in turn, feeling the weight of the decision. "Alright," I said, standing up from the table. "We go tonight. We track it, trap it, and we kill it before anyone else gets hurt."

Harper grabbed his rifle and slung it over his shoulder. "Then let's get moving," he said, already heading for the door. "We've got a troll to hunt."

Daisy and Caroline followed behind him, both of them ready for what was coming. I took a deep breath, feeling the weight of the night ahead, but there was no turning back now. It was time to end this.

# Chapter 6

The forest was thick and dark as we followed Harper deeper into the woods, the sounds of the night eerily muted. We had needed to avoid the Blackhill Sheriff's men that had come to assist Sheriff Fields, as they were still processing the murder scene.

Still, we picked up the tracks easily enough in

the forest, and the moon provided just enough light to guide us along the narrow trails. The shadows seemed to cling to everything, making the trees feel like looming giants around us.

Harper moved with quiet confidence, his rifle at the ready, scanning the ground as he followed the tracks left by the troll. Behind him, Daisy and Caroline moved cautiously, keeping close, their eyes sharp and alert.

I stayed at the back, watching our surroundings, shotgun at the ready. The woods felt different tonight, like they were holding their breath, waiting for something to happen.

Harper crouched suddenly, his hand raising in a signal for us to stop. "There," he whispered, pointing to the ground ahead. "You see it?"

I knelt down beside him, squinting at the ground. The soft earth had deep, heavy impressions, like something large had passed through recently. The tracks were unmistakable — bigger than any bear, more spread out. Troll tracks.

"These are *very* fresh," Harper said, his voice barely more than a murmur. "It came through here not too long ago."

Daisy stepped closer, peering at the tracks with a frown. "It's headin' deeper into the woods, right?"

"Yeah," Harper nodded, rising to his feet again. "We're close to its lair. We'll keep following the tracks, but stay sharp. It's likely hunting tonight, which means it's not far."

Caroline shivered, wrapping her arms around herself. "I — I don't like this," she muttered under her breath. "Feels like we're being watched."

"Keep your eyes peeled," I said, giving her a reassuring look. "We'll be alright as long as we stay alert."

We pressed on, Harper leading the way through the dense trees. The tracks grew more frequent, more obvious as we neared what Harper believed was the troll's lair. Along the way, we found more unsettling signs — bones scattered here and there, some picked clean, others fresh enough to still have bits of sinew hanging from them. Droppings littered the ground, too, confirming that this was the troll's territory. It had been here for a while.

Finally, Harper stopped again, this time

crouching behind a thick patch of bushes. He motioned for us to follow his lead, and we dropped down beside him. Ahead of us, partially hidden by the trees, was a dark cave nestled into the side of a hill. The entrance was wide, the ground around it littered with more bones and tufts of animal fur.

"That's it," Harper whispered, his eyes narrowed. "The lair."

Daisy's hand tightened on her Remington, her jaw set. "Looks like this is the place."

I scanned the area, noticing that the troll wasn't anywhere in sight. The cave was empty, at least for now. It made sense. "It's not here," I said quietly, glancing at the others. "Greida told us in Harrwick that trolls come out at night to hunt. It's probably out there somewhere, looking for more food."

Harper grunted. "That buys us a little time, but not much. We don't want to be here when it comes back, unless we're ready for it."

I nodded. "We'll set some traps. Same strategy we used in Harrwick — lure it into a kill zone and take it down before it has a chance to get too close."

Daisy gave a quick nod, already adjusting her grip on her shotgun. "Sounds good to me. Where do we start?"

"I'll set up the traps along this trail," I said, gesturing toward the path leading to the lair. "This is the only funnel. So, the troll will come back through here. Harper, you and Daisy cover me from the tree line. Caroline, you'll have the best vantage point up on that ridge over there. If you see anything, let us know."

Caroline swallowed but nodded. "Okay. I'll, uh, keep watch."

We moved quickly, each of us falling into our roles. Focusing on my Spirit Grimoire, I was ready to begin work on the traps. Daisy and Harper found their positions, weapons ready, scanning the area for any sign of the troll's return. Caroline climbed up to the ridge, her silhouette barely visible in the dark as she kept her eyes on the horizon.

The air around us was tense, the weight of what was coming pressing down on us like a storm on the horizon. We were ready, though. We had to

be. There was no room for mistakes.

I was just starting to focus on my Spirit Grimoire, ready to shape the first trap, when I felt it — a faint tremble under my boots. The earth beneath us shifted, just slightly at first, but then stronger, each vibration sending a ripple through the ground.

I froze, eyes narrowing. This wasn't natural.

Daisy's head whipped up, her grip on her shotgun tightening. "Sean... what's that?"

Before I could answer, the tremors grew more intense, a low rumble like distant thunder rolling beneath our feet. Caroline, perched nervously on the ridge, gasped. She began gesturing wildly at us — only one way to interpret that.

"Sean," Daisy muttered. "Is it... is it coming?"

I nodded, cursing our luck. It would've been a lot better if we'd had some time to prepare ourselves. Now, we had to deal with it without any traps in place. It would be a lot riskier.

Harper, crouched a little ways off, lowered himself further behind the tree he was using for cover. He raised his M1 Garand and looked more than ready. The tremors grew stronger, more pronounced. The troll was moving fast.

"Take cover," I whispered to Caroline and Daisy, signaling to them with a quick motion of my hand in case they didn't hear me. "We'll ambush it."

Daisy looked at me. "You sure? We don't have any of the traps set yet. Should we run?"

"No," I said. "It's already here. We'll fall back if we fail, and I'll cover our retreat, but we have to try."

Daisy nodded, ducking behind the nearest tree, her back pressed against the bark, shotgun at the ready. Caroline scrambled further up the ridge, flattening herself to the ground, her breaths coming fast.

I could see she was nervous, so I quickly moved toward her, using the undergrowth to conceal my movements. When I came to her, she gave me look that told me she was close to panicking. "I'm scared, Sean," she muttered, her voice shaking.

I gave her a quick hug, then kissed her forehead. "Be brave, baby. We've done this before. You know what to do. Just stay out of trouble and keep an eye out."

"I — I will," she stammered, clutching her binoculars tighter, her gaze flicking nervously between the trees. Having comforted her, I quickly moved back to my position.

Harper shifted beside me, his M1 Garand rifle aimed down the trail. "Damn thing's moving faster than I thought it would," he muttered, his voice low. "Must've caught the scent of something."

"Maybe us," I muttered back.

The ground shook harder now, the tremors growing. The low rumble of the troll's footsteps echoed through the trees, sending birds fluttering into the night sky. The air felt heavy, thick with tension, every nerve in my body screaming at me to move, to act, to get ready for the fight coming our way.

Then, through the trees, I saw it.

The troll emerged from the dark, stepping into the faint shafts of moonlight piercing the branches. It was massive — larger than the one we'd faced in Harrwick. Thick, matted fur covered its body, and its hulking frame seemed even more monstrous in the dim light. Its long arms swung low, each hand ending in thick, gnarled claws. Its eyes, small and black, gleamed as it scanned its surroundings.

"Holy hell," Daisy muttered under her breath from her hiding spot. "That thing's even bigger than I thought it'd be."

"Let's keep quiet," I whispered, motioning for her to stay still.

The troll paused, its nose twitching as it sniffed the air. It let out a low, guttural growl, a sound so deep it seemed to vibrate through the ground. I watched its head swing slowly from side to side, its beady eyes searching for something — us.

Caroline shifted on the ridge, and I caught a glimpse of her pale face, eyes wide behind her glasses. "It knows we're here, doesn't it?" she whispered, barely loud enough for me to hear.

I glanced at her, keeping my voice low but steady. "Likely. But we've got the advantage. It doesn't know where we are exactly."

Harper grunted beside me, his eyes never leaving the troll. "Big bastard. You sure we don't wanna take a shot now?"

"Not yet," I whispered back. "We need to wait until it's closer."

The troll took another step forward, its massive foot crushing branches under its weight. It was only a matter of time before it spotted us, but we had to wait until the moment was right. One wrong move, and this thing could tear through the trees and be on top of us in seconds.

The troll let out another growl, louder this time, its breath heavy and labored as it moved closer. My grip tightened around my shotgun, my heart pounding in my chest as I watched the creature's every move. It was big, stronger than any troll I'd faced before, but we had the element of surprise.

The troll's eyes scanned the area again, its nostrils flaring as it caught another scent on the wind. It took a few more slow steps forward, its massive claws digging into the earth as it moved. It was almost in range.

Harper crouched lower, his finger hovering over the trigger. "On your mark, Sean."

I nodded, adrenaline pumping through my veins. "Wait for it... just a little closer..."

Daisy's breath hitched as the troll's massive

frame came into full view, its teeth bared in a snarl.

"Now!" I shouted, and all hell broke loose.

Harper was the first to fire, his M1 Garand cracking through the stillness of the night. The shot hit the troll square in the chest, and the creature let out an earth-shaking roar, stumbling back but not falling. Daisy fired next, her Remington barking as it sent a blast of buckshot into the troll's side. The beast snarled, its hulking frame twisting as it searched for the source of the pain.

I pulled the trigger on my Mossberg, sending a slug straight into its shoulder. The troll howled, its matted fur bristling as it staggered back. The shots were slowing it down, but it wasn't nearly enough.

"It's still coming!" Daisy yelled, panic creeping into her voice as she pumped her shotgun and fired again. The second blast hit the troll's arm, tearing through flesh, but it barely seemed to notice.

The troll locked its beady eyes on us, its jagged teeth bared in a snarl. It was pissed, and it wasn't about to back down.

"Move! Spread out!" I shouted, signaling for them to split up. If the troll charged all of us head-on, we'd be done for.

Harper fired another round, hitting the troll in the chest again, but this time, it only seemed to enrage the creature further. With a roar that rattled the trees, the troll lunged forward, its massive claws swiping at the air as it barreled toward us.

"Damn it!" I cursed, mentally opening my Spirit Grimoire and focusing on my Magnetic Sigil arranged with the Metal Sigil. I didn't have time to set any fancy traps, but I could at least slow it down. Concentrating, I reached into my pouch and pulled out one of the chunks of scrap metal I had brought. I was happy now that I'd had the foresight.

I activated the Sigils and cast my spell. The rusty piece of scrap metal hovered before me and, in less than a second, took the shape of several long nails, rust flaking down as I shaped them. Then, I focused my gaze on the troll, called upon the power of the Magnetic Sigil, and fired.

The nails shot through the air like a volley of arrows, spinning wildly before embedding themselves deep into the troll's thick hide.

The creature bellowed in pain, its massive body twisting as the nails pierced its flesh. Blood dripped from the wounds, dark and thick, but it wasn't enough to stop the beast. It was too thick... I needed bigger nails.

The troll shook itself, the nails rattling in its hide, but it didn't slow down.

"Reloading!" Harper barked, already slamming another stripper clip of cartridges into his rifle. Daisy was fumbling with her own shells, her hands shaking slightly as she reloaded her Remington.

The troll, wounded but far from defeated, lumbered closer, its eyes wild with fury.

Harper and Daisy didn't waste any time. The second they had reloaded, both opened fire again. Harper's M1 Garand cracked through the night as he aimed for the troll's center mass, his shot landing in the beast's chest with a sickening thud. Daisy followed suit, her Remington blasting a spray of buckshot into the troll's side. The troll staggered back, blood streaming now, but it needed a lot more.

"Damn thing won't go down!" Harper grunted, his eyes locked on the troll.

The troll bellowed, enraged by the continuous barrage. Its massive arms swung wildly as it charged forward, its huge claws ripping through branches as if they were nothing. With one powerful swipe, it slammed its arm into a tree, sending it crashing to the ground with a thunderous roar. The troll gripped the fallen tree, lifting it like a crude club.

"Watch out!" Caroline shouted as the troll swung the massive trunk in a wide arc.

I dove to the side, rolling just in time as the tree trunk crashed into the ground where I had been standing. The force of the impact sent dirt and debris flying in every direction. The troll's strength was terrifying. One wrong move, and any of us could end up crushed beneath that thing.

"Daisy, move!" I yelled.

But before she could react, the troll had its eyes on her. It roared, raising the tree like a battering ram, intent on smashing her where she stood.

Daisy's face blanched as she fumbled to reload, panic flickering in her eyes. She wasn't going to be able to dodge in time.

Without thinking, I reached out to the Spirit Grimoire again, quickly pulling from the Wood Sigil. I poured everything I had into it, my hand glowing with green light as I shaped the spell.

"Hold on, Daisy!" I shouted, throwing my palm forward.

Thick branches erupted from the ground between Daisy and the troll, twisting and weaving into a makeshift barrier of hardened wood. The troll's makeshift club slammed into the barrier and got caught in it. It was enough to buy us a few precious seconds.

"Harper, now!" I yelled.

Harper didn't need to be told twice. He took aim, steadying his rifle, and fired. The shot rang out, and the bullet struck the troll in the shoulder, embedding deep into its thick hide. The beast howled, its body jerking violently from the impact. The tree trunk fell from its grasp as it swung its head around, eyes blazing with fury, searching for the source of the pain.

Its attention shifted from Daisy to Harper and me, leaving Daisy alone.

With the troll's focus now locked on Harper and me, I knew we had to act fast. I could feel the ground trembling again as the beast prepared to charge. We needed to slow it down.

I didn't hesitate. Focusing my energy, I reached into the Spirit Grimoire, calling upon the Magnetic and Metal Sigils once more. This time, I amplified its power, drawing on more of the surrounding metal scraps in my pouch. I shaped them into a volley of longer, sharpened stakes.

"Get ready!" I shouted, narrowing my eyes on the troll's legs. "Aim for the legs!"

The moment the troll started to move, I launched the nails with precision. The metal projectiles whistled through the air, slamming into the troll's knees and ankles. The beast let out a guttural roar as the nails pierced deep into its flesh, embedding themselves into the joints. The troll stumbled, its massive body swaying as it tried to regain its balance, but the damage was done. With a final, ear-splitting howl, the creature dropped to one knee.

"It's down! Keep up the pressure!" I yelled, signaling for the others to move in.

Daisy darted closer, her shotgun ready. As she neared the troll, she leveled her Remington and fired a point-blank blast of buckshot into its side. The impact sent the troll reeling, a fresh burst of blood spraying from the wound as the beast bellowed in agony.

Harper, taking advantage of the opening, squeezed off another round, the shot slamming into the troll's head, just below the eyes, and it wailed in pain. "It's hurt bad! Keep hitting it!" he shouted.

We pressed our advantage, each of us working together like a well-oiled machine. I focused on my Sigils, pulling from both Metal and Magnetic energy, firing off more nails to keep the troll pinned down. The creature flailed, trying to stand, but the relentless assault from Daisy and Harper's gunfire made it impossible for the troll to regain any footing.

The troll, weakened and bleeding heavily, made one last, desperate attempt to lunge at me. Its beady eyes locked onto mine, and it bared its jagged teeth, roaring as it heaved its massive body toward me, claws outstretched.

But I was ready. Reaching deep into the Spirit Grimoire, I called upon my Wood Sigil and thrust my hands forward, commanding the roots and soil to respond. Thick, gnarled branches erupted from the ground beneath the troll's feet, tangling around its legs and anchoring it in place. The beast struggled, roaring in frustration as it tried to tear itself free, but the wooden restraints held fast.

With the troll trapped, I summoned the last of my strength, forming one final barrage of nails in the air above me. I made them longer and thicker, using all of the scrap metal I still had. Then, with a grunt of exertion, I hurled the metal shards toward the troll's head.

The nails flew with deadly accuracy, striking the creature square in the skull. With sickening thuds, they buried deep into its flesh, pierced its skull, and sank into its brain. The troll let out a final, earth-shaking roar. Its body shuddered violently, then collapsed, its enormous form crashing to the ground in a heap.

Silence fell over the forest, broken only by the

troll's last gurgling breath. We stood there, panting, watching as the life drained from its monstrous body. It was over. The troll was defeated.

Daisy lowered her shotgun, wiping the sweat from her brow. "Holy hell," she muttered, her voice shaky but relieved. "We did it."

Harper grunted, slinging his rifle over his shoulder. "Damn right we did."

I let out a long breath and nodded. We did it. It was messier than I'd wanted to, but we did it.

# Chapter 7

We gathered around the troll's massive, lifeless body, our breathing heavy, our muscles aching from the battle. For a few moments, no one spoke, just taking in the fact that it was finally over.

Harper was the first to break the silence, walking up to the troll's head and giving it a hard nudge with the toe of his boot. "Well, I'll be damned," he muttered, shaking his head. "Not easy to take down one of these bastards."

Daisy was still catching her breath, leaning on her shotgun for support, but she managed a shaky laugh. "You're tellin' me. I thought it had me back there. I've never been that close to gettin' squashed like a bug." She wiped her forehead with the back of her hand, her nerves still rattled from the troll's wild charge. "Sean, baby, you and those Sigils of yours... I don't know what we'd have done without you."

I gave her a tired smile. "Thanks, but we all had a part in this." I shot her a wink. "And you were holding your own just fine."

She gave me a wry grin. "Yeah, but I'm not the one tossin' nails and wood around like it's nothin'. That's some serious stuff." She glanced down at the thick branches still wrapped around the troll's legs, the aftermath of the final spell that had saved her from being flattened. "You saved my ass, you know that?"

I chuckled and gave her a quick kiss and a pat on the butt. "It's an ass I like to save," I said, and she grinned in reply.

Harper, still examining the troll, glanced up with a grunt. "Yeah, well, next time, let's try not to get that close to one of these things. They're meaner than bears, and I've tangled with my fair share of those." He crouched down, tugging at something tangled in the troll's thick fur.

With a sharp pull, he yanked out a rusted sword, old and worn, that had been embedded in the troll's thick layers of hide. He held it up, inspecting the blade. "Looks like someone tried to fight back. Didn't end too well for them, though."

Daisy leaned in to get a better look. "Whoever owned that didn't stand a chance, poor guy," she said, glancing at Harper.

"Yeah," he replied, tossing the sword aside.

"Not a lot of people fighting with swords these days," I said. "And it doesn't look old. Maybe from another world."

Caroline, who had cautiously approached after the troll fell, finally spoke, her voice still shaky. "It's so... so much bigger than I thought..." She trailed off, her eyes wide as she stared at the beast.

Daisy chuckled. "Yeah, this one is much bigger than the one we fought in Harrwick. Tougher, too,

I think."

"I — I know," Caroline stammered. "I'm just... it's so surreal." She glanced at me, pushing her glasses back up her nose. "Sean, those Sigils of yours... how do you manage to keep so much control? I'd be terrified of messing up."

I shrugged, trying to downplay it. "It's all about focus. You've got to know what you're trying to do and stick to it. But it's no different than aiming a rifle."

Caroline gave a nervous smile. "It's a lot more impressive than that, trust me."

Harper, done inspecting the troll, stood up and stretched, his back cracking from the effort. "Well, the damn thing's dead. That's what matters. Now let's see if it was hoarding anything worth taking."

Daisy, always quick to move on, had already started looking around the area, kicking through the dirt near the entrance to the troll's lair. "These things do tend to collect some shiny stuff, don't they?" Her foot hit something solid, and she knelt down to brush away the leaves and dirt. "Well, looky here," she said, holding up a few tarnished coins. "Gold and silver. They're old too. Guess we aren't the first folks to come across this thing."

Caroline joined her, crouching down to sift through the dirt. "These coins... they look ancient." She picked up a small, worn medallion, her fingers carefully brushing off the grime. "This could've been from one of the troll's earlier victims. It must've been living here for years."

Harper walked over, glancing at the items they'd found. "Maybe it hibernated here and just woke up. It's probably been here longer than we've been alive."

I stood a little ways off, watching as they continued to gather a few more items of value — coins and a few personal trinkets that might've belonged to some unlucky traveler. There was a strange weight to it all. We had won, sure, but there was something somber about sifting through the remnants of those who hadn't been so fortunate.

Harper held up a small, rusted knife, shaking his head. "This thing probably belonged to some poor bastard who thought he could fight back." He tossed it back to the ground. "Didn't do him much good."

Daisy nodded. "Well, at least we're not walkin' away empty-handed. Got a little somethin' for our trouble." She smiled, but it was clear that the battle had taken its toll on her, too. "Still... I'd rather not be doin' this again anytime soon."

"Agreed," I said, taking a step toward them. "But we did what needed to be done. The town's safe now, and that's what matters."

Harper grunted in agreement, giving the troll one last look. "Damn thing won't be terrorizing anyone else, that's for sure." He glanced at me, a rare smile tugging at the corner of his lips. "You did good, Sean. We all did."

I nodded, appreciating the compliment. "We'll head back, let the town know it's over. They've been living in fear long enough."

Daisy let out a long breath, shaking off the tension in her shoulders. "Yeah, and I'm ready to get a stiff drink after all this."

"Right there with you," Harper said, slinging his rifle back over his shoulder.

Caroline looked between all of us, her nerves starting to settle now that the troll was dead. I gave her a reassuring nod and wrapped my arm around her as I pulled her along.

We gathered up the few valuables we'd found and prepared to leave the troll's lair. This creature had been a threat for too long, and now, it was gone. We had won, and the forest and the town felt safe again.

We drove back to Waycross in silence. The truck's engine was the only sound, humming low as the weight of the battle was still on us. Everyone was exhausted, but it was the kind of tired that came with knowing we'd made it through. No one said much as we passed the darkened houses, the small-town streets empty this late.

Harper sat beside me in the passenger seat, his rifle stowed between us, still dirty from the fight. He hadn't said much since we left the troll's lair, but I could see the relief in his posture — the way his shoulders weren't as tense, the way his eyes didn't flick around as much.

Finally, as I pulled up in front of his house, Harper let out a low grunt. "Good work tonight, Sean." His voice was rough but had a sense of respect behind it. He nodded toward me, his fingers tapping the stock of his rifle. "You handled things well."

I nodded and reached out to shake his hand. "Thanks, Harper. But we all had our part in it. Couldn't have done it without you backing me up. We make a good team."

"That we do," Harper agreed. "Still, you kept us steady when that damn troll came charging. Most men would've panicked, but not you."

Daisy leaned forward from the backseat, resting her hand on my shoulder. "Harper's right. You were the one holdin' us together, Sean. I thought that thing was gonna flatten me back there." She gave a half-laugh, shaking her head. "You were cool as ice."

I met her eyes in the rearview mirror, offering a smile. "You were the one putting buckshot into its side, Daisy. We needed that just as much as anything else."

"Yeah, but those Sigils!" she shot back, a bit of admiration in her voice. "I swear, you make it look easy. I'd have no idea how to even start controlling all that power."

"Sean's right, though, Daisy," Harper cut in,

glancing back at her. "You handled yourself better than most. For a woman who claims she doesn't like being close to these things, you sure didn't flinch."

Daisy grinned, though she looked more tired than anything. "Thanks, Harper. You did pretty well yourself."

Caroline, who had been sitting quietly in the back next to Daisy, spoke up. "You all did great. When that troll came charging, I thought... I thought we were done for. But you killed it."

I glanced at her in the mirror, catching the faint worry still lingering in her eyes. "You did great too, Caroline. You kept an eye out like I asked, and that gave us the chance to act." I paused, giving her a reassuring smile. "Besides, I wasn't going to let anything happen to any of you."

Caroline gave a small, appreciative smile, but her fingers fidgeted with the edge of her jacket, still processing everything. "It just felt... so real, you know? An actual troll..." She trailed off, shaking her head as if she couldn't quite wrap her mind around the experience.

"You held up, though," Harper said, glancing

back at her. "That's what matters. You didn't freeze. You followed orders."

Caroline looked up at him, blinking in surprise at the compliment. "Uh... thanks. I wasn't sure if I was... you know, helping much."

"You were," Harper said gruffly, turning back toward me. "We all did. But like I said, Sean, you kept the whole act together. That's leadership."

I chuckled softly. "I just did what needed to be done. But thank you all." I glanced at Harper. "Thanks for sticking with us, Harper."

Harper grinned. "Ain't the first time I've had to take down something big and ugly. And I don't reckon it'll be the last." He unbuckled his seatbelt, grabbing his rifle as he opened the door. Before he stepped out, he turned back to look at me, his face serious. "You ever need me again, you know where to find me."

I met his gaze. "Same goes for you, Harper. Thanks again."

With that, Harper gave one last nod, then climbed out of the truck. He didn't say anything else, just headed toward his front porch, disappearing into the shadows of his small house.

We watched him go for a moment before I put the truck in gear and pulled away.

As we drove through the quiet streets, the tension of the night finally easing, Daisy leaned forward from the backseat, a smirk creeping onto her face. "Y'know," she began, her voice teasing, "when that troll swung a damn tree at us? I swear, you looked so calm… it was almost like you were about to engage it in some gentle conversation."

I chuckled, shaking my head.

Caroline, who had been silent for a while, perked up. "Right? Like, 'Excuse me, sir. Could you kindly not crush us with that tree? We're just passing through.'" She gave a nervous giggle, but it lightened the mood.

I grinned. "Well, at least we didn't stick around to find out its conversational skills. Didn't strike me as a gentleman, either way."

Caroline snorted. "Yeah, it most certainly did not! And we were just trying to have a civilized fight."

"Civilized," Daisy repeated with a laugh. "Right, because nothing says civilized like Sean shooting nails into its head while I'm blastin' it with buckshot."

"And me," Caroline added, grinning now, "trying not to scream every time it roared."

I glanced at her through the rearview mirror. "You didn't scream, though."

"Barely," she said with a chuckle. "But next time, can we fight something that doesn't have the strength to turn a tree into a baseball bat?"

Daisy leaned back, stretching out her legs. "Agreed. Maybe a nice, polite monster that's allergic to bullets and nails." She sighed dramatically. "Anyway, I'm ready for a drink after all that 'civilized' battle."

"You're not the only one," I said, laughing. "We've definitely earned it tonight."

Caroline smiled softly, her hand resting on Daisy's arm. "Yeah... we did. And honestly, Sean, you were amazing. Even when it looked bad."

"Well, you two were great too," I said, grinning. "We're all still here."

# Chapter 8

We dropped onto the couch in my living room, the exhaustion from the fight catching up with us. The house was quiet now, and the adrenaline was still wearing off, leaving us all a little wired.

Daisy stretched out, kicking off her boots and propping her feet up on the coffee table. "Man, I don't know about y'all, but I'm done. That thing...

what a night." She shook her head, letting out a breath.

Caroline sat beside her, still wide-eyed but more relaxed now that we were home. "I still can't believe it." She fidgeted with the hem of her shirt, looking thoughtful. "Where do you think it came from? It couldn't have just... appeared, right?"

Daisy leaned forward, resting her elbows on her knees. "Hell if I know. Harper thought it might have been there a while — hibernating." She glanced at me. "What do you think, Sean? You think it's been around Waycross for a while?"

I nodded, rubbing my temples. "Probably. It might have been living in those woods for years, maybe since before any of us were here. That lair we found... it was comfortable."

"Yeah, but... how does something like that stay hidden for so long?" Caroline asked, glancing between us. "People had to have noticed something, right? Or do you think it just stayed out of sight, picking off animals and the occasional traveler?"

"Could be both," I replied. "We haven't seen anything like this since Harrwick. Maybe it came

from another world, just like the other creatures —
the goblins. Found a quiet spot and set up shop."

Daisy huffed. "Well, it sure as hell ain't quiet
anymore. You think it was the only one, or should
we be worried about a troll family reunion in the
woods?"

Caroline bit her lip, looking a little nervous at
the thought. "You don't think there's *more* out
there, do you?"

I leaned back, throwing an arm over the back of
the couch. "I don't think so. But *if* there are more,
we'll be ready. We handled this one, didn't we?"

Daisy smirked, her eyes glinting. "Handled it?
That's an understatement. You took that thing
down like it owed you money."

Caroline nodded with a smile. "When you
started launching those nails... I couldn't believe it.
It's like you just knew what to do, no hesitation."

I chuckled. "Well, when you've got something
like that charging at you, there's no room for
second-guessing."

Daisy leaned closer, her grin widening. "So,
when you were tossing those nails, did you
already know you'd look that badass, or was it

just instinct?"

I gave her a mock serious look. "Oh, definitely instinct. I don't plan to look badass, Daisy. It just happens."

Caroline laughed, pushing her glasses up as she shook her head. "Yeah, sure, because that's normal. Most people would panic when a troll swings a tree at them, but you? You're like, 'Oh, let me just nailgun it in the face.'"

Daisy laughed. "Exactly! You didn't even flinch, Sean. Meanwhile, I'm over here like, 'Oh shit, it's about to flatten us!'" She gave me a playful nudge. "You've got nerves of steel. Admit it."

I shrugged, keeping my tone light. "What can I say? I aim to impress," I joked.

Daisy raised an eyebrow, leaning in even closer. "Well, you succeeded. I'd say you've got a fan club now."

Caroline smirked, her eyes flicking to mine. "Oh, definitely. I'm president of the 'Sean's Too Cool Under Pressure' club."

I chuckled, glancing between them. "You're both crazy, you know that?"

Daisy's grin turned mischievous. "Maybe. But

you like it." She gave me a slow, playful look, biting her lip. "And don't pretend you weren't enjoying showing off a little back there. You knew we were watching."

Caroline flushed slightly. "Yeah... I mean, you did look pretty good doing all that. Not that I was... staring or anything."

I raised an eyebrow, teasing. "Oh, you *weren't* staring? That's not what it looked like to me."

Daisy laughed, nudging Caroline. "See? He noticed. Don't be shy, Caroline, you know you were impressed."

Caroline laughed, the flush on her cheeks deepening as she met my eyes. "Okay, fine, *maybe* I was impressed. Just a little."

I gave her a grin, leaning in just a little. "Well, I'm glad I didn't disappoint."

Daisy scooted closer, her knee brushing against mine, her voice dropping into a softer, more playful tone. "Oh, you didn't disappoint, Sean. You were... something else back there."

Caroline nodded, her voice quieter now. "Yeah... you were amazing."

The air in the room shifted, the teasing giving

way to something warmer. I looked between them, feeling the tension turn into something else entirely. Daisy's hand rested on my thigh, her eyes locking with mine as a slow smile crept across her lips. "You know, Sean... after a night like this, I think we all deserve a little... relaxation, don't you?"

Caroline leaned in, her hand resting lightly on my arm, her green eyes soft but filled with that same playful energy. "Yeah... we should definitely... unwind a little."

I smiled, the tension melting away as I leaned back into the couch, both of them close, their touches light but full of promise. "I think you're both right about that," I said.

# Chapter 9

I leaned back on the couch, feeling the warmth of Daisy's body as she snuggled up against me. Caroline, with her green eyes sparkling, sat across from us on the coffee table, her gaze drifting between Daisy and me.

"Hmmm," Daisy hummed, "I reckon a hot shower might do us some good before we unwind. Scrub the dirt off and all."

I nodded in agreement, thinking back to the day's hike and the mix of sweat and dirt that clung to our skin.

Caroline nodded, a naughty light already in her eyes. "A shower sounds... nice."

Daisy giggled, her blue eyes twinkling with mischief. She took my hand, and Caroline did the same, both women pulling me to my feet. The warmth of their touch fueled the anticipation building inside me, and my heart raced at the prospect of what was to come.

We made our way upstairs, and my entire world was the sight of these two beautiful women that I shared my bed with. Once inside the bathroom, Daisy and Caroline started the shower, the steam quickly clouding the room with a sultry haze.

I found it hard to focus on anything other than them as they were doing their best to move as sensually and sinuously as possible, shooting me naughty grins as they turned to face me.

"Let us help you out of those clothes, Sean," Daisy suggested, her voice warm and inviting. Caroline nodded, biting her plump lip at the prospect.

"You'll hear no objections from me," I said with a grin.

At that, both girls rushed in. My pulse quickened as they slowly undressed me, their fingers teasing my skin as they unbuttoned my shirt and pulled down my pants.

"Looks like someone's excited," Caroline whispered huskily as she pulled down my boxers.

"Can't blame him," Daisy added with a wink.

As they continued to undress me, I found myself lost in their touch. The steam from the hot shower enveloped the bathroom, making me nice and comfortable and more than in the mood for a little shower fun.

The girls gently ushered me under the cascading water, and their mischievous laughter was like music to my ears. I watched them undress themselves slowly for me, their fingers working expertly to unbutton, unzip, and untie their outdoors outfits. The sight of their naked bodies, still a little sweaty, made my heart race with anticipation.

"You ready for some good ol' fashioned clean

fun?" Daisy teased.

I laughed, then reached out to pull both of them in with me. "Get in here," I said with a chuckle as the girls yelped.

I held them close, their warm, slippery bodies pressing against mine as they lathered soap on their hands. They took turns washing me, their hands gliding over my chest, arms, and legs, leaving a trail of tingling sensations wherever they touched. It felt heavenly to be pampered by these beautiful women who knew exactly where to apply pressure and where to caress.

"You're getting real clean now," Daisy hummed, grinning mischievously as she and Caroline rinsed off the soap from my body. I could feel the heat building within me — a desire to grab them and have my way with them, but I wanted to let it all last a little longer.

"Hmm... Let's make sure you're thoroughly clean," Caroline added, her green eyes locked onto mine, filled with lust and desire. Then, she looked at her harem sister, and they both giggled.

Before I knew it, Daisy and Caroline sank to their knees in front of me, their gazes never leaving my face. Daisy's hand wrapped around my dick, stroking it slowly, while Caroline leaned forward and began licking my balls, her tongue swirling around them with expertise.

"Ah, feels so damn good," I moaned, my thoughts blurring as I surrendered to the pleasures. Their touch sent shivers down my spine, as the pleasure continued to intensify.

"Like that, huh?" Daisy asked. "We're just gettin' started, baby."

Caroline glanced up at me, a naughty smile on her face as she continued her ministrations, her tongue dancing over my sensitive flesh as Daisy continued to stroke me, her eyes locked onto mine.

"Mmm, you like that, don't you?" she teased, her voice dripping with seduction. "I bet you're just dyin' to slide that hard cock into our tight little pussies, huh?"

"Come here," I murmured, reaching out to pull Daisy to her feet. She gave a playful yelp as I took control, and then our lips met in a passionate kiss, her body pressing against mine as Caroline took my cock into her mouth, her warm, wet lips enveloping me in ecstasy.

Daisy moaned into our kiss as I let my hands roam over her curvy figure, my fingers finding her large breasts, which I began to fondle. She broke away from the kiss for a moment, her breath heavy with lust. "Hmmm," she moaned, glancing down at Caroline sucking me off. "Look at Caroline down there, suckin' your dick. So pretty!"

"Yeah, she looks good on her knees," I agreed, my heart racing at the sight of her servicing me so eagerly. Meanwhile, my fingers slipped lower, finding their way between Daisy's legs, where they traced teasing circles around her pussy, eliciting a moan from her as I gradually increased the pressure.

"Hmm, Sean, don't stop," Daisy begged, her hips grinding against my hand, desperate for more.

I kept teasing her pussy with my fingers as the sensation of Caroline's soft lips wrapped around my cock sent shivers down my spine. Her wet tongue swirled around the head with practiced skill.

"That feels so good," I murmured, my eyes

flicking between Caroline's green orbs staring up at me and Daisy's lust-filled gaze.

Daisy's moans turned louder, and her body arched against mine as I continued to finger her slick pussy. I could feel her walls contracting around my fingers, growing tighter by the second. Her breasts pressed against my forearm, their perkiness and warmth intoxicating as I groped them with my other hand.

"Sean... if you keep this up, I'm gonna cum so hard," Daisy warned breathlessly, her voice thick with need.

"Tell me how much you want it," I demanded.

"Please, Sean... I need it. I need you to make me cum," Daisy begged, her hips bucking against my hand in search of more friction.

I felt her muscles clench around my fingers, a telltale sign that she was on the edge. With a final thrust of my fingers and a flick of my thumb over her clit, Daisy's body tensed, a deep, guttural moan leaving her lips as her orgasm washed over her.

"Fuck, Sean... oh my God!" Daisy cried out, her legs shaking as waves of pleasure coursed through

Jack Bryce

her.

"Good girl," I praised, watching as she rode out the aftershocks of her orgasm, her body trembling with the intensity of it all.

She took a moment to recover even as Caroline kept diligently sucking me off. The water cascaded over us, and steam billowed up around us, but her blue eyes were clear as day as Daisy looked up at me.

"Sean, I... I need you to fuck me now," she panted. "Please."

"Your wish is my command," I murmured, pulling my cock from Caroline's eager mouth with a wet pop.

Gently, I turned Daisy around, pressing her hands against the slick tile wall of the shower. Her ass was perfectly positioned for me, and as I slid into her warm, wet pussy, we both gasped at the exquisite sensation.

Caroline rose with a delighted sigh, pressing her naked body against mine from behind. I could feel the softness of her large breasts against my back, her nipples hardening from the steamy mix of arousal and the hot water. She whispered

106

breathlessly in my ear, "You two look so good together. Give her what she wants, Sean."

Daisy's ass jiggled tantalizingly with each thrust, her moans growing louder and more desperate as I fucked her from behind. The feeling of her silken walls gripping me tightly was almost too much to bear, building pressure deep within me.

"Oh, Sean, it's so good," Daisy groaned, pushing back against me with every thrust, urging me to go deeper.

My eyes roamed over her toned back, the way her blonde hair clung to her damp skin, her beautiful, heart-shaped ass. Next to me, Caroline's lithe fingers began dancing across her own pussy as she started to pleasure herself.

"Caroline," I panted, my voice shaking with each word, and our lips met in a kiss as she fingered herself while I pounded her harem sister from behind. She hummed softly as we kissed, her fingers eagerly seeking out her clit and rubbing it in tight little circles. The sight of both women lost in pleasure because of me only intensified the experience, making every touch and sound echo through my body.

"Please," Daisy begged between moans, "don't stop, Sean. Give it all to me."

My breath came in ragged pants as I thrust faster and faster into Daisy's wet heat, her ass rippling with each movement.

Caroline's breaths grew shallow, and I could tell she was close. The combination of their lustful gazes and the sensation of Daisy's tight walls surrounding me made it difficult to hold back my own impending release.

"Please, Sean, cum inside me," Daisy pleaded, her voice strained with need.

"Y-yes, Sean... do it," Caroline whispered between moans, her body trembling as her orgasm washed over her. She trembled against my back, and I couldn't resist any longer.

"Daisy, I'm gonna cum," I warned, my voice barely audible above the sound of the shower and our heavy breathing.

As my climax approached, I pulled out of Daisy, her pretty ass beckoning for my release. Her hips swayed playfully, and I let out a guttural groan as hot spurts of cum coated her skin. She grinned as she looked over her shoulder, jiggling her ass as I coated it with my seed.

"Beautiful," Caroline panted.

"Very," I agreed, my voice hoarse as I watched Daisy's cum-glazed butt.

With a satisfied sigh, I leaned back into the warm cascade of water, feeling both physically and emotionally spent. Daisy and Caroline joined me, pressing their wet bodies close to mine as we enjoyed the soothing embrace of the shower.

"You know," I said, still catching my breath, "if every one of our adventures ends like this, we should go on one every day."

Daisy chuckled, her laughter like music to my ears. "I ain't gonna argue with that, baby."

We all chuckled at that, losing ourselves in the warm water and the gentle embrace and kisses. By the time we were finished with the shower, we were ready to go again, and we retreated to the bedroom for a night full of loving.

# Chapter 10

The next morning, I woke up feeling sore all over. Every muscle in my body reminded me of the night before, but there was a sense of accomplishment in the aches. We had won, and Waycross was safe.

At least, for now. We still weren't sure if there would be more threats like that out there.

I dragged myself out of bed and made my way downstairs, the smell of something cooking pulling me toward the kitchen.

When I walked in, I found Daisy and Caroline already there, working together like a well-oiled machine. Daisy was at the stove, flipping pancakes, while Caroline hovered nearby, setting the table and pouring coffee.

Daisy glanced over her shoulder and grinned at me. "Well, well, look who decided to join us. Mornin', Sean. Thought you'd sleep half the day away after all that excitement last night."

I chuckled, rubbing the back of my neck. "I'm surprised I woke up at all. I feel like I've been run over by a truck. Or, you know, a troll."

Caroline smiled, looking a little more at ease this morning. "You looked like you needed the rest. We figured we'd let you sleep and handle breakfast."

"You've got a good system going," I said, nodding toward the stove. "Smells great in here."

Daisy turned back to the pancakes, flipping another one with a flourish. "Well, we figured the least we could do is feed you after you saved our butts last night."

"You did more to them than *save* our asses," Caroline quipped, and Daisy and I both exchanged a wide-eyed look at that. It wasn't every day that Caroline made a dirty joke.

She caught on and blushed slightly, glancing at me from the side. "Well, uh, we, uh, thought you'd be starving."

I grinned, taking a seat at the table as Caroline brought over a plate of pancakes. "I could get used to this kind of treatment. You keep feeding me, and I might just stick around." I winked at her, and she chuckled.

Daisy shot me a playful look. "Oh, we'll keep you fed, don't worry. Can't have you wasting away on us."

Caroline laughed softly, setting a cup of coffee in front of me. "Plus, you'll need your strength for... well, whatever comes next."

I raised an eyebrow, taking a sip of the coffee. "Whatever comes next, huh? Are you two planning something I should know about?"

Daisy smirked, her eyes twinkling with mischief. "We're always planning something,

Sean. But today? Today's just about takin' it easy." She slid the plate of pancakes onto the table with a flourish. "Now eat up before I *decide* to start planning some trouble."

Caroline sat down next to me, her eyes warm as she handed me the syrup. "No trouble today, please. I think we've had enough excitement for a while."

I grinned, pouring syrup over the stack of pancakes. "I'm with you on that. After last night, I could use a break."

Daisy sat down across from me, grabbing her own fork. "Agreed. A whole day of nothin' sounds like paradise. No trolls, no monsters... just us."

Caroline nodded, taking a bite of her pancakes. "Exactly. I don't think I've ever been so ready for a peaceful day." She glanced at me, a soft smile tugging at her lips. "Though, I have to admit, I'm still kind of curious about where that troll came from."

Daisy leaned forward, her expression thoughtful. "Yeah, it's not like trolls just pop up outta nowhere, right? That thing had to have been lurking around for a while."

I nodded, chewing thoughtfully before answering. "Like I said, it's possible it's been here for decades, just hiding out in those woods. Or hibernating, as Harper seems to think."

Daisy leaned back in her chair, stretching her arms above her head. "Well, speaking of a peaceful day, I was thinkin'... how about you come out to the farm with me today, Sean? I could use an extra set of hands. You know, feed the animals, check on the fences, all that fun stuff."

I raised an eyebrow, smirking as I took another bite of pancake. "Fun stuff, huh? Sounds like you're putting me to work after all."

Daisy laughed, her eyes twinkling with that playful spark. "Oh, come on. You're not gonna let me do all that heavy liftin' alone, are ya? Besides, think of it as a relaxing day in the fresh air. No trolls, just you, me, and the animals. You know the animals love you, right?"

Caroline chuckled, shaking her head as she reached for her coffee. "Sounds like you're just trying to rope him into doing your chores, Daisy."

Daisy winked at Caroline. "Hey, a girl's gotta

try. I figure if I make it sound fun enough, he won't notice he's actually working."

I laughed, leaning back in my chair as I looked between them. "Alright, alright, you've convinced me. I'll come help out at the farm. But if I'm doing all this hard labor, you better have something cold waiting for me at the end of the day."

Daisy grinned, clearly pleased with herself. "Deal. I'll even throw in a home-cooked meal for your trouble."

Caroline smiled, but there was a glint of humor in her eyes. "You know, while you two are out there working the farm, I think I'll head to the library today. Got a few things I need to organize, and there's some research I've been meaning to get to."

Daisy raised an eyebrow. "Research? You're not still thinking about that troll, are you?"

Caroline shook her head, laughing softly. "No, not exactly. Just... well, there are some old texts I want to look into. You know, stuff about Waycross's history. It's always been an interest of mine, even before we started dealing with... you know, everything."

"Of course you're diving into research," I teased, leaning toward her slightly. "You sure you don't want to take a day off and join us at the farm? You could use a break."

Caroline smiled warmly, tucking a strand of hair behind her ear. "As tempting as that sounds, I actually enjoy the library. It's... calming for me. Plus, someone has to make sure all those dusty old books don't fall apart."

Daisy gave her a playful nudge. "Well, you better not let the dust bunnies get ya. They can be ferocious."

Caroline giggled, taking another sip of coffee. "Don't worry, I think I'll manage. I'll leave the heavy lifting to you two."

I grinned, glancing between them. "So, it's settled then. Daisy and I will tackle the farm, and Caroline will wrestle with old books. Sounds like we all got a productive but relaxing day ahead."

Daisy reached across the table, giving my hand a light squeeze. "You're a good man, Sean. I promise I won't work you too hard." Her voice dropped just a little, her eyes glinting with familiar playful challenge. "But then again, you don't mind a little hard work, do you?"

I raised an eyebrow. "Depends on the reward."

Caroline blushed slightly, catching the shift in tone, but she smiled at us both, clearly enjoying the banter. "Well, while you two are negotiating your 'rewards,' I think I'll get a head start. If you need me, I'll be at the library, lost in a mountain of books."

"Try not to get buried," I said with a grin, watching as she stood up and grabbed her jacket.

Caroline laughed, her eyes sparkling as she moved toward the door. "I'll do my best. See you both later. Don't work Sean too hard, Daisy."

"No promises!" Daisy called after her, laughing as Caroline waved goodbye and slipped out the door.

Once the door closed behind her, Daisy turned her attention fully to me, her grin widening. "So, before we go... How about we take a few more minutes to ourselves." Before I could reply, she was on me, dragging me toward the couch...

About half an hour later, Daisy and I made our way to her farm, the walk short but pleasant, the countryside peaceful as always. As soon as we pulled up, Tink came bounding over, barking happily and wagging her tail like she hadn't seen us in weeks, even though it had only been a day.

"Tink!" Daisy called out, grinning as she knelt to greet her German shepherd. "Missed us, huh, girl?"

The dog circled around Daisy before trotting over to me, her tail still wagging like she was ready to burst with excitement.

"Hey, Tink," I said, giving her a good scratch behind the ears. "Looks like you've got plenty of energy today."

Daisy laughed, straightening up and brushing her hands off on her jeans. "She's always got energy. Makes me tired just watchin' her." She glanced over at the large plot of land behind the house. "Alright, so we've got some work to do. I was thinkin' about expanding the vegetable garden a bit this year, and we did the fences for the cows last time, but we need to look into the ones keeping the critters out of my plots. Those fences need fixin' before they get any worse."

I nodded, already rolling up my sleeves. "Let's

start with the fences. I can use the Wood Sigil to get things done faster."

"Yeah?" Daisy's eyes lit up as she smiled. "That'd be great. I swear, you make my life so much easier with those Sigils of yours."

I grinned, giving her a quick wink. "That's the plan."

We walked out to the section of the fence that was sagging the most. Some of the boards were rotting, and others were just barely hanging on. Daisy grabbed a few tools from the barn, but I knew I wouldn't need much for this job.

I focused on the Spirit Grimoire, feeling the power of the Wood Sigil surge as I activated it. My hands glowed faintly as I placed them on the broken boards, and with a slight push of energy, the wood began to shift and repair itself, merging back into one solid piece.

Daisy watched, her eyes wide with admiration. "That's incredible. You make it look so easy."

I chuckled, moving down the fence to the next broken section. "Practice, Daisy. Just like you and those cows. I bet you make wrangling them look easy."

"Well, I'd like to think so," she said with a grin, leaning against the fence as she watched me work. "But this? This is somethin' else."

We worked side by side for the rest of the morning, fixing up the fence while Tink darted back and forth, chasing birds and barking at nothing. The sun climbed higher, warming the day, but the work was steady, and the company made it enjoyable.

By the time we finished with the fence, Daisy was already looking toward her vegetable garden, her brow furrowing as she mentally mapped out the new section she wanted to plant. "I'm thinkin' we could add another few rows of carrots and tomatoes. I've been meaning to expand, but with everything going on, I haven't had the time."

I nodded, surveying the land. "We can get the soil ready for planting tomorrow. I'll help you with that, too."

She smiled, wiping a bit of dirt from her cheek. "Great idea! You're really somethin', Sean. I don't know what I'd do without you."

We moved over to the garden, where Daisy had already marked out the new rows she wanted to expand. The ground hadn't been touched in a while, so it was packed tight, but nothing we couldn't handle.

"I'll grab the tiller," Daisy said, heading toward the shed. "We'll need to break this up before we can do anything else."

While Daisy went to the toolshed, I crouched down and ran my hand over the dry soil. I hadn't done much farming before — just a few small things back when I first got to Waycross. I'd helped with a couple of gardens, some light work here and there, but nothing major. Still, I had to admit, there was something satisfying about working with your hands, especially when you knew it was all for a good harvest. It reminded me of simpler times.

When Daisy came back, pushing the tiller in front of her, I stood up and gave her a grin. "You know, we could use this," I said, nodding toward the machine, "or... we could do it the old-fashioned way. Get our hands dirty."

Daisy stopped, looking at me with a raised eyebrow, half a smile playing on her lips. "Oh, so now you want to rough it, huh? I thought you were all about speed and efficiency, Sean."

I chuckled. "Depends on the job. But I'm not above a little hard work if it means I get to spend more time out here with you. And we still have a lot of daylight."

She laughed, setting the tiller aside. "Alright, Mr. Old-Fashioned. Let's see what you've got."

I grabbed a shovel and started turning over the dirt, loosening the packed soil. It wasn't easy, but it felt good, grounding in a way that I hadn't expected. Daisy worked beside me, and we made a solid team. The sun was warm on our backs, and Tink ran around chasing birds and barking happily, keeping the mood light.

After a while, we'd worked the ground enough to be ready for planting. Daisy crossed her arms, watching the freshly turned soil with a satisfied look. "I swear, I could get used to having you around more often. You've turned a day's worth of work into a few hours."

I grinned, wiping the sweat from my forehead. "Just glad to be of service. Now you just need to decide what we're planting here."

Daisy smirked, nudging me with her elbow.

"Carrots and tomatoes, right? But if you keep up this pace, we might have room for some more. Maybe even a whole extra row of corn."

I glanced over the garden, feeling pretty good about the progress we'd made. "You plant it, and I'll be here to help with the harvest. You'll have more vegetables than you know what to do with."

Daisy grinned. "That's the plan. And don't worry — I'll make sure you get your fair share of the rewards. Maybe I can even touch you how to do it."

I smiled and nodded. "I'd like that."

# Chapter 11

The next morning, after an early breakfast with Daisy, I headed to the Waycross library to meet up with Caroline. The sun was just beginning to warm the quiet streets, casting long shadows as I made my way over. The day was peaceful, the kind of calm that only a small town could offer.

Caroline had asked me if I wanted to spend a

day with her at the library, and that sounded like an interesting way to spend a day. I wasn't as bookish as she was, but I would love to see her in the habitat she so enjoyed spending time in.

When I stepped inside the library, the familiar scent of old books and wood polish greeted me. The place was nearly empty, save for a few early risers flipping through newspapers at the tables. And honestly, the place was way too big for a town like Waycross anyway.

Caroline was already there, perched on a stool near the back, surrounded by stacks of old documents and records. She looked completely absorbed, her focus entirely on the yellowed papers in front of her, but she still gave me a warm smile when I approached, noticing me only when I was standing at her desk. She was sitting in the exact place we had first met.

"Hey, Sean," she said, brushing a strand of ginger hair behind her ear as she looked up. Her glasses caught the light, making her green eyes stand out. "Right on time."

I grinned, pulling up a chair beside her. "Wouldn't miss it. What have you got for me today?"

She nudged one of the stacks toward me, her lips curling into a soft smile. "Old town records. We're reorganizing some of the founding documents for an upcoming history exhibit. There's actually a lot of fascinating stuff in here — old letters, maps, even some personal journals from the original settlers."

I reached for one of the older-looking maps, careful not to tear the fragile paper. "I'm guessing you've already found something interesting?"

Caroline's eyes sparkled with excitement as she leaned in closer, her voice lowering like she was about to share a secret. "You wouldn't believe some of the things I've come across. It turns out, Waycross has a lot more to it than just small-town history. I had some of this stuff sent over from the archives, and there's a lot of talk of magic in the old records."

I raised an eyebrow, intrigued. "Magic? You mean, like what we've been dealing with recently?"

"Exactly," she said, her voice almost a whisper now. "There's this one journal from a man named

Elias Carnigan. According to his entries, the settlers encountered strange phenomena when they first arrived here. He wrote about seeing 'flickering lights' in the woods, hearing voices in the wind, and even having dreams that warned him of danger. It's subtle, but if you read between the lines, it sounds a lot like magic."

I leaned in a little closer, the old journal she was pointing to catching my attention. "Was this in the Vanderlees' time?"

Caroline nodded, flipping carefully to a page marked with a small ribbon. "Here, look at this entry. Elias writes about a 'presence' in the forest that guided them to a safer location, away from a danger he couldn't explain. He believed it was a sign, a guardian of some kind."

I scanned the passage, the faded ink still legible despite the years. It gave me chills. "And you think that presence is connected to the magic we've been encountering?"

Caroline leaned back, pushing her glasses up the bridge of her nose thoughtfully. "I do. I mean, think about it — the strange creatures, the troll, even the goblins. They're not from here, not from this world. But what if there's something in Waycross that's been keeping these things at bay all this time? And now, for whatever reason, that protection is weakening."

I set the journal down, taking in her words. "That would explain why everything's happening now. Maybe whatever was protecting the town is fading, and that's why we've had to step in."

Caroline smiled, her expression softening as she looked at me. "And maybe that's why you're here, Sean. To help protect Waycross."

There was a silence between us as we both thought about that, the weight of her words settling in. I glanced around at the quiet library, the peacefulness of it almost surreal considering the dangers we'd faced recently. Caroline's theory made sense in a way I hadn't considered before. And sitting here with her, working together to piece it all together, felt right. It felt like we were uncovering something important — not just about the town, but about ourselves.

She reached for another stack of papers, her fingers brushing against mine for just a second. The touch was brief, but it sent a warmth through me, and I could tell she felt it too. She didn't pull away, though. Instead, she smiled and continued organizing the documents, her movements a little more confident than before.

"You've really settled into all this," I said, watching Caroline as she delicately sorted through the fragile papers. "It's like this place was made for you. You've practically become the town historian."

Caroline glanced up at me, a soft smile tugging at her lips. "Yeah, well... I suppose I've always been a little obsessed with old books and forgotten stories. It's where I feel most comfortable, I guess." She paused, then added with a hint of fondness in her voice, "Funny to think it all started with you coming in here, asking about that dusty old grimoire you found."

I grinned at the memory. "Yeah, I remember that. I'd just moved to Waycross, still trying to figure everything out, and then I found that thing hidden up in my attic. I didn't know what the hell I was looking at, but I figured the library might have answers. You were right there behind this very desk."

Caroline's cheeks flushed slightly, and she let out a small laugh. "I didn't know what to think when you first asked about it. But I could tell there was something special about that grimoire." She pushed her glasses up, her green eyes glinting. "I'm glad I was here that day. It feels like everything changed after that."

"It definitely did," I said, leaning back in my chair. "You were the first person I really talked to in town. I had no idea that a trip to the library would lead to... all this." I gestured around. "Killing trolls in the forest."

Caroline laughed, then looked down at the journal in her lap, her fingers tracing the worn edges. "It's funny to think how far we've come since then. I remember being so nervous about helping you with the grimoire, afraid I'd mess something up or give you the wrong information. I didn't think I'd be part of... any of this. But here we are."

I nodded, a warm smile playing on my lips. "Indeed. And I like where we are."

She nodded. "Me too. It feels like I've found where I belong."

"You have," I said, my tone firm but gentle. "You belong with me, Caroline. You're a part of this — of us."

Her cheeks turned a shade pinker, but she didn't shy away from my gaze. "I'm glad you think that, Sean. I didn't think I'd ever feel this... *connected* to something or someone. But with you, Daisy, Cody... Maybe even Brooke... it's like I've found my own little family."

There was a deep sense of comfort between us as we continued organizing the old town records. The Waycross library was a quiet sanctuary, but it was also the place where Caroline's and my story had started, and it felt nice to be back here.

That evening, as the sky darkened into a deep indigo and the last bit of light faded from the horizon, I sat around the dinner table with Daisy and Caroline at my house. The warm light of candles softened the edges of the room, and the scent of roasted chicken and vegetables filled the air.

The mood was easy and light — the days just hanging around and doing mundane work and relaxing had comforted us all.

"So," Daisy began, shooting me and Caroline a teasing look, "want to tell me a little about all that boring book stuff you two got up to yesterday?"

I chuckled and shook my head. "Not exactly boring," I said.

Caroline acted hurt, pouting a little exaggeratedly and placing a slender hand on her full bosom. "Why, Daisy, you hurt me!"

Daisy chuckled and waved a fork around as she rolled her eyes. "Sheesh! Alright, tell me about that *mighty interesting* book stuff y'all got up to!"

I laughed and nodded. "That's more like it."

Caroline leaned forward, her smile softening. "Well, if you *must* know," she joked before beginning to speak in earnest, "we weren't just flipping through dusty books for the fun of it. We were looking into some old town records... things about Waycross and how it's changed over the years. It's actually pretty fascinating."

Daisy raised an eyebrow. "Changed how?"

Caroline's eyes lit up a little. "There's this whole hidden history to the town. Most people think of Waycross as a quiet, sleepy place with nothing but farmers and woods. But the truth is, a lot of strange things have happened here. Unexplained disappearances, odd weather patterns... and not to mention, people who lived here centuries ago believed the town was on a ley line."

Daisy blinked. "A ley line? Like magic?"

Caroline nodded, excited now. "Exactly. There's something about Waycross — it sits at the intersection of several of these lines. People used to believe that the town was a kind of... well, a nexus for magical energy."

"Okay, now you've got me interested," Daisy said, her fork pausing midair. "You mean this place has always been weird?"

Caroline smiled. "Pretty much. There are all sorts of old journals and diaries that talk about strange occurrences. Farmers hearing voices in the fields, travelers going missing only to turn up days later without any memory of where they'd been. And there seems to have been some kind of ritual at some point to protect the town from these magical influences."

I leaned back in my chair, smirking. "That's what makes this place interesting. It's not just random that we're all here now."

Daisy glanced at me, intrigued. "So, are you telling me we're living in some kind of supernatural hotspot?"

"Something like that," I said with a shrug. "Waycross has a lot of secrets. Caroline's been digging through records to figure out just how deep it goes."

Caroline smiled at me, a little proud. "There's so much more to uncover. Some of it even ties back to the founding families — the ones who started Waycross."

Daisy nodded. "I gotta say, Caroline, you know more about Waycross than anyone. You could probably tell a story about every little spooky corner of this town."

Caroline laughed, shaking her head. "Well, maybe not every corner, but... I do know some of the old stories. Growing up here, I spent more time in this library than I did anywhere else." She paused, her gaze softening. "My brother used to tease me about it all the time. He'd be outside with his friends, working on cars at the shop, and I'd be buried in old books about Waycross history."

Daisy leaned forward, curious. "Your brother? He's the one who runs that auto shop on the edge of town, right?"

Caroline nodded, smiling fondly. "Yep, that's him. Justin. He's been running it ever since he finished high school, practically. He's a good guy, but we don't always see eye to eye. He's very... hands-on, practical, while I'm more of a 'live in my head' type." She chuckled. "But we've always been close. Even when our parents moved to D.C., Justin stayed here to keep the shop going, and I stayed because... well, I couldn't imagine being anywhere else."

I nodded, remembering bits and pieces of the story. "Your parents don't come back to visit often, do they?"

Caroline shook her head. "No, not really. They're busy with their lives in D.C. They call every now and then, and I visit once in a while, but it's been... distant for a while now."

Daisy gave her a sympathetic smile. "I know the feeling. After my dad passed, my moms sort of scattered. One's in Arizona, another's up in Michigan... They call often, and we see each other once or twice a year, but it ain't the same as when we were all together. It's been a long time since Monica came back to the States."

"Monica's your sister, right?" I asked, leaning back in my chair. "The one in France?"

Daisy nodded. "Yeah, she's officially still co-owner of the farm. But she hasn't been here for a long time. You know how it is — her life is way too fast for Waycross. But we talk... it's just not like it used to be."

There was a pause, the easy conversation shifting to a softer tone as we all shared a quiet understanding of the distance that life could put between family members.

I cleared my throat, offering a small smile. "Sounds like our families are all a little spread out. But hey, at least *we* are all here." I gestured around the table. "We've built something good here."

Daisy's smile warmed, and Caroline nodded in agreement. "Yeah," she said softly, "we have."

As we finished the last of dinner, the comfortable warmth of the evening settled in, the sound of silverware clinking gently against plates filling the kitchen. Daisy stacked the plates, while Caroline stood by the sink, rinsing each dish before handing them to me to dry. It was a simple routine, but it felt like more — like a moment that could be the start of something permanent.

And we had been doing a lot of it together. We were really growing into a unit — a family. The bond had grown strong, and I could see that in the ease with which Daisy teased, in how Caroline's stuttering and nervousness faded when it was just the three of us, and the easy contentment that settled in my stomach whenever we spent time doing these menial chores.

I caught myself watching them both, my thoughts drifting to the future. I wanted this — wanted them in my life, every day. Daisy's playful energy, Caroline's quiet, thoughtful presence... They fit here, with me. And the more time we spent together, the clearer it became that I didn't want this to be temporary. I wanted us to be more than just friends who happened to survive the chaos together. I wanted them to be part of my life. Permanently.

Daisy glanced over her shoulder, catching me

lost in thought. She grinned, waving a soapy plate in my direction. "What're you thinkin' about over there, Sean? You've been standin' there lookin' dreamy for a good minute."

I chuckled, grabbing a dish towel to dry the plate she handed me. "Just thinking about how nice and easy this feels. Like... we've done this a hundred times."

Caroline smiled softly as she rinsed the last dish. "It does feel easy, doesn't it? Like... we belong here together," she said, revealing that she had the same thing on her mind as I did. She glanced at Daisy, then back at me, her green eyes soft behind her glasses. "I like it. It feels like... home."

Daisy's grin widened, and she nudged me with her elbow. "Well, sounds like you'd better get used to it, Sean, 'cause we're not goin' anywhere."

The warmth in her voice despite her teasing settled something in me. I dried the last plate and hung the towel over my shoulder. "Good," I said, my voice steady. "Because I want you both here."

Caroline's cheeks flushed a little at that, and Daisy's smile turned softer, more serious for a moment as she looked at me. "Good," she just hummed, but the light in her eyes betrayed how happy my words had made her.

We finished cleaning up and moved into the living room, the atmosphere still relaxed but filled with an unspoken understanding that something between us had shifted. As we settled onto the couch, Caroline broke the silence, her tone a little more somber.

"So, I heard Timothy's funeral is in two days," she said softly, adjusting her glasses as she looked between us. "The whole town's going to be there, I'm sure."

I nodded. "Yeah... I figured. We should go together. Pay our respects."

Daisy sighed, leaning back against the couch. "Poor guy. The whole town's still reeling from it. But yeah, we should definitely be there. Timothy was one of us."

Caroline nodded in agreement, her hand resting on her lap. "It feels right for us to go together."

We sat in quiet reflection for a moment before Daisy perked up, her tone shifting back to something lighter. "By the way, the town fair is coming up in a few days. I've been roped into helpin' out, and I was thinkin'... you want to give me a hand with the stall, Sean? I could use the extra pair of hands."

I grinned, the thought of spending more time with Daisy at the fair appealing. "Yeah, I'm in. What kind of stall are we talking about?"

Daisy's eyes lit up. "Oh, you'll love it. I'm doin' a farm stall — sellin' some fresh produce, maybe some baked goods. It's gonna be fun. Plus, you'll get to see the whole town come out. It's a big deal around here."

Caroline smiled, her fingers playing with the edge of her sleeve. "I've always loved the fair. It's one of those things that makes Waycross feel like... well, like a real community. Everyone comes together. Maybe I could make some baked goods and sell them at the stall as well?"

"That's a great idea!" Daisy agreed.

I nodded. "It is. Sounds like fun! Sounds like it'll be a good time."

Daisy stretched her arms over her head, letting out a content sigh. "Well, that settles it. We've got plans. Now let's get some sleep — we've got a lot to do in the next few days."

Caroline nodded, her smile soft as she stood up from the couch. "Yeah, I'm ready to call it a night."

I grinned and nodded. I was right with them — tired and ready to sleep. But time and time again, a little tussle was what followed whenever the three of us went up together. And that, too, was one of the things I wouldn't change for the life of me.

# Chapter 12

The next morning, I found Daisy already outside by a pile of boards and metal scraps, her sleeves rolled up and a bright smile on her face. She waved as soon as she saw me approach. "Morning, Sean! You ready to get this stall built?"

I grinned. "Morning. Looks like you've got quite the project for me."

She put her hands on her hips, looking over the materials with a proud glint in her eyes. "Yup, yup! We need this stall to be perfect. I'm thinkin' something simple but sturdy. You know, so it doesn't fall apart when the crowds start coming. We can drape something over it to make it look real nice-like, so long as the thing itself is sturdy."

I knelt by the pile, picking up a couple of the old wooden boards and testing their weight. "No problem. We'll get something built that'll do the trick."

Daisy chuckled, walking over to hand me a measuring tape. "I like the sound of that, baby. How 'bout I handle all the bossin' around while you handle the hard stuff?"

I laughed as I glanced up at her, and she was throwing me the biggest pair of puppy eyes she had. "Oh no," I said. "You're not getting away with that."

She grinned, leaning against the fence as I got to work. "Oh, alright. So, what's your plan, Mr. Magic Hands?"

I laughed. "Well, I was thinking I'd start by using the Wood Sigil to smooth out these boards and make them uniform. We'll still use nails, because people will have questions if I meld the boards together and this thing appears like it's made out of a single piece of wood. But I can make those nails with the Metal Sigil. I suppose it's mainly a matter of getting the right height and shape for your display. Sound good?"

Daisy gave a slow nod. "Sounds like you know what you're doin'. Maybe I should just sit back and watch the magic happen."

I laughed and gave her a slap on the butt. "Gather the materials, you lazy woman!"

She laughed. "I'm goin', I'm goin'!" she yelped as she headed off to grab the boards.

Once she'd brought the boards, I focused on them, summoning the energy from my Wood Sigil. The old planks vibrated slightly, their rough edges smoothing out and their surfaces becoming polished with barely any effort. One by one, they shifted into perfect, straight beams. Daisy let out a low whistle as she watched the transformation.

"I swear, I'll never get tired of seein' that," she said, walking closer to inspect one of the finished boards. "Makes everything look like it came straight out of a catalog."

I shrugged, feeling a bit of pride. "It's handy. Definitely beats trying to do it all by hand."

Daisy smiled and leaned against the fence again, crossing her arms. "Well, don't get too cocky. We've still got a lot to do. What's next?"

"Bring that scrap metal over here. I'll make them into nails. Combining the magic of the Wood and Metal Sigils, I can drive them in."

She nodded and hopped to it, bringing me more scrap than I would need. Then, I got to work, moving over to the pile of metal scraps. I activated the Metal Sigil, letting the pieces bend and shape themselves into sturdy nails. "Now we make sure this thing won't collapse if someone leans on it too hard."

Daisy laughed. "Good idea. We've got some folks in town who'll test that for sure. You should see the way people get when they're fightin' over the last jar of my world-famous pickles."

I smirked, glancing over at her. "You planning to have a crowd fighting over your pickles, then?"

She gave me a playful shove. "You know it! My pickles are a hot commodity. You'll see. You'll be workin' the stall with me, right?"

I nodded. "Of course. Wouldn't miss it."

"Good. I could use the extra set of hands," she said with a wink before motioning toward the frame I'd built. "Lookin' good so far. I think it'll hold up."

I stepped back, surveying the progress. The frame was sturdy enough for our purposes. "It'll definitely hold. Just needs some shelves now."

Daisy picked up one of the newly shaped beams, holding it up like she was testing the weight. "Shelves, huh? Think I'll be able to fit everything on here?"

I grinned. "If we make them wide enough, yeah. How much are you planning to bring, anyway?"

She gave me a mischievous look. "Oh, you know… just a little bit of everything. Gotta impress everyone."

I chuckled. "So, everything from your farm, then."

"Exactly," she said, handing me the beam. "And some of Caroline's baked goods as well, of course. Now, how wide are we talkin'? I don't want it to look crowded."

I measured the distance between the support beams with my hands. "Let's go about two feet wide. That'll give you enough space without making it look cramped."

She nodded thoughtfully. "Two feet sounds good. We'll have some height too, right? I want people to see it from across the fair."

I grinned. "You want this thing visible from space, don't you?"

"Maybe not *that* high," she teased, stepping back to let me finish the shelves. "But yeah, I want people to know where the best produce is."

I grinned, liking her competitive spirit. I worked quickly, attaching the shelves to the frame. As I did so, Daisy kept up a steady stream of conversation, bouncing ideas off me.

"What do you think? Should I put the tomatoes up top? Or maybe the peppers?"

I glanced over my shoulder. "Top shelf should be the stuff that'll catch people's attention first. Bright colors. So yeah, tomatoes are a good choice."

Daisy nodded, her face lighting up as she started mentally organizing the stall. "Tomatoes up top, then maybe some cucumbers and squash on the middle shelf. That way, people can grab 'em easily. And I'll save the preserves for the bottom shelf."

I raised an eyebrow. "You sure you want the preserves down low? You said those are a hot commodity."

She tilted her head, considering it. "Good point. Maybe I'll put 'em on the side. Give people a reason to stick around and look for 'em."

I smiled. "Sounds like you've got this all figured out."

"Damn right I do," she said with a grin. "I've been thinkin' about this stall for a while now. Just need a handsome and muscular man to bring my vision to life." She shot me those puppy eyes again, and I couldn't help but laugh.

I finished securing the last shelf and stepped back. The stall stood tall, sturdy, and simple but with enough space for all of Daisy's produce and preserves. "Well, your vision's ready. What do you think?"

Daisy walked up to the stall, running her hands over the smooth wood and metal with a satisfied smile. "I think it's perfect. You're a genius, Sean."

I wiped my hands on my jeans, grinning at her. "I'd better get a jar of those famous pickles as a reward."

"Oh, you will," she hummed before turning to me, her expression softening for a moment. "Seriously, though. Thanks for helpin' me with this. I couldn't have done it without you."

I waved her off, feeling a little embarrassed. "It's nothing. I'm happy to help."

Daisy's smile returned, brighter than before. "Well, you're stuck with me for the fair now. Don't think you're gettin' out of it."

I laughed. "Wouldn't dream of it."

As I made my way back inside, the quiet evening settled in. Daisy had taken my truck to drive the stall down to her place, and she had assured me that she could handle the unloading. She would be back after that, and I decided to get started on dinner and try to surprise her and Caroline, who was bound to return from the library within the hour.

But as I stepped up to the porch, I heard

grinding tires and an engine. When I turned, I spotted a police cruiser coming down the road, so I waited.

The cruiser parked, and Sheriff Jacob Fields emerged, his gray hair tucked under his worn-out hat. He waved when he saw me.

"Evenin', Sean!" he called out.

I raised a hand. "Evening, Sheriff. Out on your rounds?"

Jacob nodded as he walked up to the porch, resting his hands on his belt buckle. "Yeah, just checkin' in on folks. Wanted to see how everyone's holdin' up. It's been quiet since... well, since Timothy. Folks are mostly good — if a little shook."

"Glad to hear," I said. "Why don't you come in for a coffee? Sounds like you could use a break."

Jacob gave me a grin, tipping his hat. "Don't mind if I do. Could sure use somethin' to wash down all the dust from today. Not too long, though; the missus expects me back for dinner."

I chuckled and gestured for him to follow me inside, which he did. I led him in and got him to settle at the kitchen table while I got the coffee brewing.

As I made the coffee, he glanced around. "Nice place you got here, Sean," he said after a while, as I finished brewing. "You've really made yourself at home."

I smiled, handing him a mug. "Thanks, Jacob. People around here make it easy. You've all been welcoming."

Jacob nodded as he took a sip, savoring the warmth of the coffee. "Waycross is a good town. Folks here stick together. We've always been that way. My family's been here since the beginning, you know."

I raised an eyebrow, leaning against the counter. "The beginning? As in, the founding of the town?"

He chuckled. "Yup. My ancestor was one of the first settlers. The Fields have been in Waycross since the start, and most of us have had a hand in lookin' after the place. I'm just carryin' on the tradition."

"That's pretty incredible," I said, genuinely impressed. "So, law enforcement runs in the family?"

Jacob nodded, his mustache twitching with a

smile. "You could say that. My dad was sheriff before me. His dad before him. We've always had one foot in the law and one foot in the community. I grew up knowin' I'd take over someday, but my pa made sure I earned it. No handouts in the Fields family. I'm hopin' my son will take over someday. He did the academy, and he's a city cop." He chuckled. "I guess I'm hoping he'll miss Waycross and come work with me before I'm too old. But yeah, we've always been in law enforcement."

I smiled. "Guess it explains why you're good at what you do."

He shrugged, taking another drink. "Just doin' my part. Been sheriff for about 25 years now, and I've seen just about everything this town has to offer. But I gotta admit, lately things've been... strange. Timothy's death hit folks hard. And not just 'cause he was a good man. It's left people feelin' unsettled."

I nodded, keeping my expression neutral. He didn't know about the troll, and I didn't think now was the time to tell him — if ever there would be. "The whole town's feeling it."

Jacob sighed, setting his mug down. "Yeah. Tomorrow's funeral is gonna be tough. The man didn't have any family left, but the whole town'll be there. We take care of our own in Waycross. Always have."

"I'll be there too," I said. "I didn't know him too well, but I want to pay my respects."

The sheriff gave me a grateful look. "Appreciate that, Sean. You haven't been here long, but you've fit in real quick. Hell, some folks around here still call me 'the new guy,' and like I said, I've been the sheriff for over 25 years."

I chuckled at that. "Yeah? Doesn't sound like anyone could forget about you."

Jacob smiled, shaking his head. "They do it just to mess with me. Small-town humor, you know? But seriously, you've made an impression. People talk, and they like what they've seen of you. Not everyone fits in with small-town life, but you... you've adapted like you've been here your whole life."

I shrugged, a little humbled by his words. "I'm just trying to help out where I can."

"Well, you've been doin' a damn good job of it.

And believe me, I don't say that lightly," Jacob said, his eyes meeting mine. "This town needs folks like you, especially now. You've got a good head on your shoulders, and you know how to handle yourself. That's more than I can say for some of the folks around here."

I raised an eyebrow. "You talking about anyone in particular?"

Jacob smirked, shaking his head. "Nah, just talkin' in general. Waycross is full of good people, but some of 'em ain't seen half the things you have. You're a good addition to this place. Hell, if you ever feel like runnin' for sheriff someday and my boy don't come around, I might just step down early and hand you the hat."

I laughed. "I'll keep that in mind, but I think you're doing just fine where you are."

Jacob chuckled. "Yeah, well, the day's gonna come when I'm too old for this job. I'm hopin' it's a ways off, but you never know. Life's funny like that."

We sat in comfortable silence for a moment before Jacob glanced at the clock on the wall. "I should be headin' out. Missus gonna be mad otherwise."

I grinned and stood, walking him to the door. "Thanks for stopping by, Sheriff. I'll see you tomorrow at the funeral."

Jacob nodded as he stepped outside, pausing on the porch. "Appreciate the coffee, Sean. And remember what I said — you're good for this town. Don't forget that."

I smiled, watching him head back down the road. "Thanks, Jacob. Take care."

With a tip of his hat, he stepped into his cruiser and pulled out. I felt for the poor guy, but he was doing as good a job as he could. I was happy that we had been able to deal with the threat, though; that at least saved him some trouble.

# Chapter 13

Not long after Jacob left, my phone buzzed in my pocket.

I pulled it out and saw Brooke's name on the screen. Swiping to answer, I brought it to my ear. "Hey, Brooke. What's up?"

"Hey, Sean," she greeted. She sounded better than the last time we spoke, and I harbored the hope that she was slowly overcoming her challenges. "I was hoping you'd be okay with Cody coming over in two days? I've got some stuff to finish up at work, and it'd be great if you could take him off my hands for a bit."

"Yeah, no problem at all," I said. "Looking forward to it, in fact. He can stay as long as you need. You know he's always welcome here."

Brooke let out a soft laugh, clearly relieved. "Thanks. I really appreciate it. Work's been a mess, but it's finally starting to settle down. I feel like I'm getting back control. I just need this last stretch to go smoothly."

I wasn't sure about that. It sounded like she still hadn't made the decision to just end it. Instead, she was trying to master it. I knew her like that — she was a fighter. But some fights simply weren't necessary — and this was one of them.

Still, I also knew her well enough to understand that there was no point to pushing her. Brooke came there on her own, or not at all.

"How're things going for you otherwise?" I asked, leaning against the counter as I spoke.

"Better," she admitted after a pause. "I'm finally

getting my footing again. It feels good to be back in control, you know? For a while there, I wasn't sure I'd manage to pull everything together, but I think I'm finally getting it."

"That's good to hear," I said. "You're handling more than most people would. Don't forget that."

She chuckled softly. "Yeah, well, sometimes I feel like I'm just barely keeping my head above water. But lately, it's been better. I've got a plan, and I'm sticking to it. That's something, at least."

"You've got a lot on your plate," I said. "Don't be afraid to take a step back when you need to. You've got help if you need it."

"I know," she replied, her voice softening. "I've been thinking about that. The whole job situation… it's not exactly what I imagined when I started, and sometimes I wonder if it's worth it. But I'm getting through it." She gave a laugh that didn't instill too much confidence, to be honest.

I nodded, even though she couldn't see me. "Just know I'm here if you need me."

"Thanks," she said, and I could hear the smile in her voice. "You're always there when I need it. I don't say it enough, but I really do appreciate everything you've done for me."

"Anytime," I said simply. "You know I've got your back. So, I'll grab Cody in two days?"

"Yeah, that works. I'll give you a heads-up if anything changes, but that should give me enough time to wrap things up at work. I'll come drop him off, how does that sound?"

"Sounds great!" I said. "Just let me know if you need anything else."

We said our goodbyes, and as I hung up, I let out a breath. Brooke said she was handling things better, but I couldn't shake the feeling that she was pushing herself too hard. It wasn't my place to tell her what to do, but I wished she'd consider stepping back from that damn job.

The sound of a car engine outside snapped me out of my thoughts. I glanced out the window and saw Caroline's little sedan pulling up, with my red truck right behind it. The girls got out. Caroline had a few books in her hands, and Daisy was gesturing animatedly about something as she engaged Caroline in conversation.

I grinned, stepping to the door and opening it as they came up the porch.

"Hey, you two," I called out. "Perfect timing."

Daisy smirked as she led the way inside, and Caroline and I followed her. "I know, I know, we're perfect in every way, baby," Daisy teased as she threw me a smoldering look.

I chuckled and shook my head as Caroline blushed slightly, adjusting her glasses as she followed her in. "Hi, Sean. Were you making dinner?"

"I was about to get started," I said, closing the door behind them. "You both just missed Sheriff Fields, but now I've got company while I cook."

Daisy laughed, then gave with a dramatic sigh. "Oh, is that how it is now? We're here to entertain you?"

I laughed and turned to give her butt a hard slap, making her yelp. "Woman, do you want dinner or not? I'm fine with *you* making it too!"

She grinned, rubbing her butt. "Apologies, mister! I definitely want dinner. *And* I'll keep you entertained."

I chuckled. "Well, you always do."

Caroline grinned and both girls sat down. I made a little show of pouring them both a glass of wine. The girls applauded me happily, and I finished the act with a little bow. "Ladies, your wine…"

"Thank you, *garcon*," Daisy said exaggeratedly, her pronunciation of the word mangled enough to make the entire French population wince subconsciously across the ocean. Caroline covered her mouth and chuckled — more likely than not, she knew exactly how it was pronounced.

With a grin, I went back to the kitchen counter and began chopping some vegetables for dinner. As the girls talked, I made a mishmash of fresh vegetables and tossed them all into a pan. I sliced through bell peppers, onions, and zucchini, the crisp sounds of the knife chopping filling the kitchen. The fresh scent of the vegetables started to blend as I tossed them into the sizzling pan with some oil, reaching for a few spices to kick things up a notch. I'd decided on a stir-fry, something quick and flavorful that would keep the mood light.

Also, I wasn't the finest cook, and this was nice and easy.

Daisy took a sip of her wine, eyeing the pan.

"Smells delicious, Sean," she hummed.

Caroline nodded. "Hm, it does! What are you making, Sean?"

"Stir-fry," I said, flipping the veggies in the pan with a practiced motion. "I'm thinking rich flavor. Garlic, ginger, soy sauce, maybe a little sesame oil to finish it off."

Daisy's eyes widened. "Ooh, fancy! What's the meat?"

"Chicken," I said, nodding toward the cutting board where thinly sliced pieces were ready to go. "Going to cook that up in the same sauce, then mix it all together."

Caroline watched me with a small smile. "It's like watching a cooking show in real life. You were lying when you said you couldn't cook, Sean!"

I chuckled as I grabbed the chicken and tossed it into the hot pan. It sizzled immediately, mixing with the aroma of the garlic and ginger I'd just thrown in. "This isn't difficult," I said. "I couldn't make a pie for the life of me, but I can toss some vegetables and chicken in a pan. Once you've done this a few times, you get the rhythm down."

162

Daisy chuckled, swirling her wine in her glass. "Listen to you, talkin' about rhythm in the kitchen. You got rhythm everywhere, huh?"

I shot her a grin over my shoulder. "Everywhere, baby. You know that."

Caroline blushed a little at the exchange, but she looked amused as Daisy winked at her.

"So," Caroline started, changing the subject, "have you decided on what you're bringing to the fair yet, Daisy? Besides your pickles, of course."

Daisy's face lit up at the mention of the fair. "Oh, I've got a whole plan. I'm bringing a bunch of stuff from the farm — tomatoes, cucumbers, peppers. Plus, I'm making a few jams and jellies. And, of course, the pickles."

Caroline nodded thoughtfully. "That sounds great. I was thinking of baking a few apple pies to sell with your produce. You know, something to draw people in."

Daisy beamed. "Now that's what I'm talking about! Between your pies and my farm-fresh goodies, we're gonna have the best stall there."

I glanced over at them, tossing the chicken around in the pan. "Sounds like you two are gonna be the stars of the fair."

"Damn right we are," Daisy said with a proud grin. "And with you helping out, we'll be unstoppable."

I smiled, turning back to finish the stir-fry. The vegetables had softened perfectly, and the chicken was golden and tender. I mixed them all together in the pan, pouring in a bit of soy sauce and sesame oil to coat everything in a rich, savory glaze.

The kitchen was filled with the delicious smell of the finished meal, and both girls leaned in to take a deep inhale.

"Oh, man," Daisy groaned, her eyes half-closing. "That smells incredible."

Caroline nodded in agreement. "It really does. I can't wait to try it."

I plated the stir-fry, sprinkling a bit of green onion on top for a finishing touch. "Alright, ladies," I said, handing them each a plate. "Dinner's served."

They both smiled as they dug in, and I sat down with my own plate, ready to enjoy the quiet evening with them.

# Chapter 14

The next morning, the house was unusually quiet as we all got ready for the funeral. There was a somberness in the air that hung over us, the thought of Timothy's passing still weighing heavily. I pulled on a clean button-up shirt and black dress pants, adjusting the cuffs as I stared at myself in the mirror. It felt odd dressing up like this — it wasn't something I did often — but today called for it.

When I stepped out of the bedroom, I found Daisy already in the living room, smoothing down her dress. She was wearing something simple, a black dress with a sash around the waist that clung to her in all the right places but was respectful for the occasion. Her usual bright energy was dialed back, and she looked up at me with a small, soft smile.

"You ready?" she asked, her voice quieter than usual.

I nodded, glancing toward the hallway. "Just waiting on Caroline."

Right on cue, Caroline appeared, dressed in a modest black skirt and blouse. She'd tied her ginger hair back neatly, her glasses perched on the bridge of her nose. She looked a little nervous, her fingers playing with the edge of her sleeve as she stepped into the room.

"Sorry I took so long," she murmured. "I'm ready now."

I smiled at her. "No rush. We've got time."

The three of us stepped outside, and I locked up

the house before heading to my red Ford truck. The ride to the church was quiet, the only sound coming from the hum of the engine and the occasional sigh from Daisy as she stared out the window. Caroline sat beside her, her hands folded neatly in her lap, her expression thoughtful.

When we arrived at the small church, it was already filling up. People were gathered in little groups outside, speaking in hushed tones. Everyone was dressed in dark clothes, and the mood was heavy but respectful. Having been in Waycross for a while, I recognized most of the townspeople, and a few gave us nods of acknowledgment as we made our way inside.

The church was simple, with wooden pews and soft light filtering in through the stained-glass windows. We found seats toward the back, and soon the service began. The pastor spoke kindly of Timothy, recounting his long life in Waycross, his contributions to the community, and the way he had touched so many lives. There was sadness, of course, but also a sense of celebration of the good times.

Daisy's hand found mine during the service,

and I gave it a gentle squeeze. Caroline sat quietly beside me, her head bowed in thought, her fingers tracing the hem of her skirt.

After the service, people slowly filtered out of the church, offering their condolences to each other and sharing stories about Timothy. There was a sense of unity among the townsfolk in the face of loss, and I admired that attitude.

Outside, the sun was shining. The sky was blue. Birdsong hung in the air, and the world was still vibrant and alive.

My beautiful Daisy glanced up at me as we stood outside, the sun starting to break through the clouds. "Earl's, right?"

I nodded. "Yeah. Most of the town's heading over there for coffee."

The walk to Earl's was short, and soon we found ourselves in the familiar diner. The atmosphere was more subdued than usual, but there was still the comforting clatter of dishes and the smell of coffee in the air. Some people were joking and laughing as they shared stories of Timothy, and I was happy to see that his was a life that people celebrated.

We grabbed a booth, and soon a few of the townsfolk came over to talk. Old Mr. Thompson leaned on his cane as he approached us, offering a weary smile. "You three doin' alright?"

Daisy nodded, giving him a warm smile. "We're hangin' in there, Mr. Thompson. How about you?"

He sighed, rubbing a hand over his face. "I'll be alright. Timothy… he was a good man. Hard to see him go. Never expected he'd go before me." He chuckled a little at his quip. "But we gotta keep movin', don't we?"

Caroline nodded, offering him a sympathetic smile. "It was a lovely service. I think Timothy would've appreciated it."

Mr. Thompson grunted in agreement before he shuffled back to his seat, and we were joined by a few more people, all sharing similar sentiments. The conversation was easy, despite the occasion, and soon enough, there was a small warmth to the room — a shared understanding that life moved on, and so would the people in Waycross.

Still, all of this made me think about my life here in Waycross. It was good — better than I had dared hope, but there was room for improvement. And why wait to tell the girls how I felt about them?

After all, Timothy had just demonstrated that life can be over in a snap. I didn't want that for any of us, but I also understood that it made sense to be honest — to tell the girls how I feel.

I resolved to do that. Tonight, I would tell them.

Once we got back home, the three of us sat in the living room, still processing the day. Daisy was the first to break the silence, stretching her legs out under the coffee table with a sigh. "Well, that was a hell of a day." She glanced at me with a half-smile. "Beautiful... but glad it's over, to be honest."

Caroline nodded, sitting quietly beside her, fiddling with her fingers. "It was a nice service, I agree. Timothy... he had a good life. It's comforting to think that way."

I leaned forward, resting my elbows on my knees. "Yeah, it was a good service. The whole town showing up like that, it really makes you appreciate what's important." I hesitated for a second, but then the words just came out. "And what's important to me is you two."

Daisy raised an eyebrow, her smile softening. "That's so sweet of you to say, Sean."

Caroline glanced at me, a little surprised but listening intently. I took a deep breath, meeting their eyes one after the other. "I've been thinking about this for a while. Especially today. Life's too short to put things off. You two... you're everything to me. I love you both. I need you to know that."

Daisy practically melted. "Awww," she hummed. "Sean... Oh, I love you too!"

She was on my lap in a moment, kissing me, and Caroline sat down beside me on the other side, holding my hand. "And so do I, Sean. You know I do."

I chuckled as I kissed Daisy back, then wrestled myself away from her lips — however hard that was — for another moment, since there was more I wanted to say. "Good, because I want you two to move in with me permanently. I want to share this house with you two — for it to be a place of love and family between the three of us."

Daisy blinked, clearly not expecting that, and a wet sheen formed over her pretty blue eyes. She sat up straighter, staring at me for a moment. "Wait, like... move in, move in? Full-time?" She laughed, a little caught off guard, then covered her mouth. "Oh Sean, are you serious?"

Caroline's eyes widened behind her glasses, her hands frozen mid-fidget. "I... I..." She looked down at her lap for a moment before looking back up at me, her voice soft. "You really want that?"

"I'm serious," I said firmly, glancing between them. "I want this house to be our home. No more back-and-forth, no more you staying here some nights and heading back to your own places. I want us living together, full-time, 24/7. For real. These past few days have been heaven to me. You girls brighten my life, and I want every day to be like this."

Caroline's eyes welled up with tears, and she quickly swiped at them with the back of her hand. "I-I've never... I never thought... I don't know what to say," she stammered, her voice cracking as she tried to hold back the flood of emotion. "I've never had anything like this."

Tears spilled over, and she let out a choked little laugh. "I want that, Sean. I really, really want that. I love it here. I love being with you, with Daisy." She covered her mouth, trying to compose herself, but the tears kept coming.

I pulled her into my arms, holding her tightly. "I want you here. Both of you. This is our home."

Daisy wiped her eyes with the back of her hand, blinking away the tears that threatened to spill over as she watched her harem sister get emotional. She sniffed once, looking at me with an expression that was more serious than I'd ever seen from her. "Damn it, Sean," she muttered, her voice trembling. "You really do know how to hit a girl where it counts." She swiped at her eyes again, but then gave a soft laugh through the tears. "You know I want that too."

Her voice broke, and she let out a shaky breath before throwing her arms around my neck and hugging me tight. "I don't wanna be anywhere else. I want this, too."

I wrapped an arm around her, holding both of them close. Caroline, still sniffling, pressed her face into my shoulder, and Daisy buried her face in my chest, the weight of the moment settling over all of us.

"I love you both," I said softly, my voice steady but full of emotion. "I don't ever want to lose this. I don't want to lose either of you."

Caroline sniffled and pulled back just enough to look up at me, her eyes still watery but filled with so much happiness. "I love you too, Sean. You... you've given me more than I ever thought I could have." She leaned up, pressing her lips against mine in a soft, lingering kiss.

When she pulled away, Daisy was there, lifting her head to kiss me too, her lips lingering as if to make the moment last just a little longer. "You beautiful, crazy man," she whispered against my lips, her voice full of affection. "I love you so much."

We stayed like that for a few moments, the three of us, wrapped up in each other. Finally, Caroline broke the silence, her voice still a little shaky from the tears. "I... I never thought I could have something like this. I'm so happy." She smiled, her face still wet with tears, but it was the happiest smile I'd ever seen on her. "I'm so, so, so happy."

Daisy nodded, her eyes shining as she looked at Caroline and then back at me. "Yeah… me too. I didn't think I'd ever find this kind of happiness."

I kissed Daisy's forehead, then Caroline's, feeling an overwhelming sense of peace wash over me.

Caroline, still sniffling, reached over to wipe at Daisy's tear-streaked face, causing them both to giggle a little. "I guess we're all a mess now," she said with a watery laugh.

Daisy sniffed, laughing through her tears. "Yeah, well… we're a good-lookin' mess, at least." She gave Caroline a warm smile, her usual playfulness returning now that the heaviness had lifted.

I chuckled at that. It was great to see how Daisy always managed to lighten the tone and make things easier just at the right time and in the right way. It was an impressive skill, and one that fitted her character perfectly.

For a moment, we were all silent — sharing the bliss of this perfect fraction in time when we all had everything we could want. I held my girls close, happy with what I had said and happy with how they had responded. It felt right, and it felt real.

# Chapter 15

Daisy was still on my lap when she sniffed dramatically before throwing me a teasing look. "Alright," she said. "Now that we've got the mushy stuff out of the way, we can talk about what's really important."

I raised an eyebrow, knowing what was coming. "What's that?"

She grinned, wiping the last of her tears. "The closet. Half of it's mine. No negotiations."

I laughed, shaking my head. "Half? I thought you were already taking three-quarters."

"Three-quarters, I mean," she corrected herself with a wink, her grin wide and full of life again.

Caroline giggled softly, wiping at her eyes. "I suppose we'll have to start planning the layout. Maybe add a few more shelves? Maybe a whole new house?"

I groaned playfully, shaking my head. "Fine, fine. Whatever you two want."

"Well, you can just bend wood with your mind!" Daisy said. "Don't act like it's a lot of work! Oh, and I've got a lot of boots. Maybe a little house for those?"

Caroline laughed, and I joined in. "You girls keep this up, and I'll build a little prison cell to lock you both up in when you're acting up!"

"I'll just break out!" Daisy said sticking out her tongue, and Caroline chuckled at that.

"I'll handcuff you," I said with a grin.

Daisy licked her lips and shot Caroline a wink as she wriggled in my lap, shooting me a naughty look. "Don't threaten me with a good time…"

At that, both girls broke out laughing. Their laughter was contagious, and I couldn't help but join in as I admired these two beautiful women who had just agreed to live with me. Daisy's skin-tight black dress clung to her curvy figure, while Caroline sat in her tight skirt and blouse, her red hair cascading over her shoulders, and Daisy's naughty joke sent my blood flowing.

"Really?" I said once we'd all recovered. "You like handcuffs, huh?"

"Well, I — *Yeep!*"

Without giving her time to respond, I scooped her off her feet and placed her gently on the rug on her stomach.

"Hey!" she squealed, giggling with excitement.

"Let me guess — hands behind your back?" I asked rhetorically, already reaching for the sash of her dress.

"Sean! Naughty!" Daisy replied, still grinning. I could feel her anticipation growing as I tied her hands securely behind her back using the sash from her dress.

Caroline, sitting on the couch, watched the scene

unfold with a mixture of curiosity and amusement. As I tightened the knot, she let out a soft giggle, covering her mouth with her hand.

"Looks like someone else is enjoying the show," I teased, glancing at Caroline who blushed slightly.

With her hands bound, Daisy hummed in contentment, clearly turned on by the situation. Brooke and I had done some light constraints in the past, but it had been a while, and I felt a thrill at being in control of Daisy's pleasure — it was fun to play around like this a little.

Daisy gave a happy squirm as she looked over her shoulder at me with big eyes. "Oh no," she purred theatrically and mock-innocently. "*Whatever* shall you do to me?"

I licked my lips and chuckled as I gave her pretty butt a smack. The sight of it in that skin-tight black dress was more than any man could bear. I left my hand on it, following up with a squeeze.

Daisy yelped playfully and squirmed, and the warmth of her body radiated through the fabric of her dress. Kneeling behind her, I couldn't resist the urge to lift up the hem of her tight black dress, revealing her stockinged legs and a glimpse of her black lace thong, hugging her plump pussy lips and revealing her perfect, tanned ass.

"Hmm," Caroline purred from behind me, her green eyes full of admiration as she took in the view. "You look incredible, Daisy."

She gave a happy hum in reply, and I felt my pulse quicken as I contemplated the possibilities laid out before me. Slipping my finger under the delicate lace of Daisy's thong, I could feel the wetness that had already gathered, and it was impossible not to explore further.

"Ah!" Daisy mewled softly as I slid a finger inside her, her hips squirming against the sensation. My own arousal grew, fueled by her enthusiasm.

"Caroline," I murmured, beckoning her closer.

Biting her lip, she came over and knelt down beside me, her green eyes wide as she watched Daisy squirm in front of me. As I continued to gently finger Daisy, I turned my head towards Caroline and captured her lips in a passionate kiss.

My sweet Caroline, the one with the intense

inner fire, nearly ate me alive. She kissed back passionately, aroused by me controlling her harem sister like this, and I had to suppress a chuckle at the intensity of the kiss.

It was exhilarating, the feeling of being in control of both of these beautiful women, guiding them towards their pleasure as they willingly submitted to my touch.

I lost myself in the kiss, nipping at Caroline's plump lips. Meanwhile, the soft noises Daisy made while I fingered her filled my ears. She struggled a little against her bonds as I made her writhe, and she seemed so close to finding her release.

"Ah, ah..." she panted, and just as she was about to reach the peak of pleasure, I stopped and pulled back my fingers, coated in her juices.

"Wh-what?" she stammered, her hips still grinding against the empty air. Caroline chuckled at her predicament, and I smirked, enjoying the control.

"Sean," Daisy groaned, her frustration evident as she wriggled against her bindings. "Please..."

"Please what?" I asked teasingly, raising an

eyebrow. "You need to beg, Daisy."

"Please, Sean," she panted, her blue eyes pleading with me as she glanced over her shoulder. "This is… It's too hot. I want it... I need it... Please make me cum."

"Aww, isn't that sweet?" Caroline cooed, her green eyes twinkling with amusement.

"Alright, Daisy," I relented. "I'll continue." With a grin, I slid my finger back under the lace thong. She mewled with delight as I resumed my intimate exploration, her hips bucking against my hand.

"Please, please, please," she repeated, her voice desperate and needy. But just when she was on the brink once more, I stopped again, leaving her whimpering in frustration.

"Sean!" Daisy grumbled, her face flushed with desire.

"Patience, baby," I winked at her. Shooting Caroline a mischievous grin, I pulled her to her feet. "Now, let's see what we can do about our lovely librarian."

Caroline bit her lip, anticipation dancing in her eyes as she looked at me, eager to see what I had in store for her. With a smile on my lips, I left Daisy squirming on the rug, then led Caroline around her so she could see us both easily.

"Seaaaan," Daisy mewled. "What are you doin', baby? Please! Ugh!" She squirmed a little more as I gently lowered Caroline onto the rug, her wide hips and shapely legs on full display before Daisy's bound form.

"You'll get your turn," I teased Daisy as I focused on Caroline, who trembled with excitement by now.

My fingers deftly lifted the hem of her skirt, revealing her lace panties beneath. The sight of Daisy, hot and frustrated, watching our every move added a wicked thrill to the moment.

"Sean... that ain't fair," Daisy protested, wiggling her hips in desperation. "I wanted... Hmmm... You were..."

"Life isn't always fair, baby," I replied with a smirk, my eyes never leaving Caroline's flushed face. She stared back at me, her green eyes betraying the kinky depths of this tantalizing woman.

With a practiced hand, I pushed Caroline's

panties aside, exposing her glistening folds. Bending down, I pressed my lips against her wetness, eliciting a gasp from her throat.

"O-oh, Sean…" she moaned, her fingers tangling in my hair as I tasted her sweet arousal.

"Damn it, Sean," Daisy mewled, the sound of her voice dripping with envy and longing.

Ignoring Daisy's complaints, I continued pleasuring Caroline, my tongue teasing and exploring her most intimate parts. Her body trembled beneath my touch, her breath coming in shallow pants.

"Y-yes, just like that," Caroline panted, her body tightening as I pleasured her.

"Still ain't fair," Daisy grumbled, her cheeks flushed and her eyes clouded with desire. But nothing could tear my focus away from Caroline now, not when she was so close.

Caroline's trembling intensified, her hips bucking against my mouth as she quickly reached her climax, turned on from the little play as she was. Her moans filled the room, and I drank in every last drop of her pleasure.

"Oh, Sean," she gasped, her fingers burying in

my hair as she drew up her legs. "Oh... Ahnn... I'm cumming!"

With that, her body began jerking as her orgasm swept through her. An envious mewl escaped Daisy's lips as she watched Caroline cum, and I kept lapping at her clit until she was spent and lay trembling on the rug.

"Not. Fair. At. All," Daisy whined, hands still tied behind her back.

With a grin at Daisy, I flipped Caroline onto her stomach and unzipped my dress pants. Freeing my throbbing erection, I positioned myself behind her, preparing to claim her.

"Ohhh," Daisy whimpered, her blue eyes wide as she stared at the sight before her. A blush spread across her cheeks, and she bit her lip in anticipation as I lined the tip of my cock up with Caroline's entrance.

"Yessss," Caroline moaned, still trembling from her orgasm, and as I penetrated her, her gasp of pleasure mingled with Daisy's moan of longing.

The warm, wet sensation of being inside Caroline was incredibly satisfying, and I let out a low groan as I began to thrust into her from behind while she lay on her stomach. Her body fit so perfectly against mine, the curve of her ass pressing against my hips with each movement. I could feel her muscles tightening around me, her body needing me.

"Sean, that feels so good," she hummed, her voice breathy and filled with pleasure.

Daisy watched us intently, her blue eyes wide and frustrated, biting her lip as she squirmed against her bindings. To tease her some more, I made sure to maintain eye contact with her as I continued to fuck Caroline, letting her see just how much I enjoyed it.

"Y'all are drivin' me crazy over here," Daisy said, her voice thick with need.

"Your turn will come soon enough," I promised, my voice strained as I continued to pound into Caroline.

As my arousal grew, I knew I wouldn't be able to hold back much longer. My breathing became ragged, and my thrusts grew more erratic. Just as I prepared to pull out, Caroline reached around and grabbed my behind, pulling me deeper into her.

"Cum in me. Please, Sean... just cum in me," she

begged, her voice desperate and pleading.

That was all it took for me to lose control. With a guttural groan, I released my seed deep inside Caroline's warm and welcoming pussy, still locking eyes with Daisy who watched us with wide eyes and pouting lips.

Exhausted, Caroline and I collapsed together on the rug, our bodies slick with sweat. She chuckled, and I gave her butt a smack as I grinned at Daisy.

"That ain't exactly what I had in mind when I was talkin' 'bout restraints," Daisy huffed playfully, her cheeks still blazing.

I licked my lips as I watched her lay bound there, then winked at her. "Give me five minutes, and you'll get what's coming to you too…"

# Chapter 16

The morning started off busy, with all three of us bustling around the house, getting everything ready for Cody's visit. Daisy was in the kitchen, making sure we had enough snacks, while Caroline was double-checking the guest room, straightening the bed for the third time.

"Do you think he'll like the room?" Caroline

asked from the doorway, her voice a little unsure.

"He'll love it," I reassured her, glancing over as I adjusted a picture frame. "You've made it nice and cozy for him. Besides, he's slept here before and loved it. As long as he gets to hang out with us and Tink, he'll be fine!"

Daisy chimed in from the hallway, a grin on her face. "Cody's gonna have a blast, trust me. And Sean's right: as long as he's got room to run around and play, he's not gonna be too concerned about the sheets or the pillows."

Caroline smiled softly, still looking a little uncertain. "I just want him to feel comfortable here. I want him to like it."

"He already does," I said, walking over and placing a hand on her shoulder. "You've both done a great job. He's going to feel right at home."

Daisy popped her head back into the room, her eyes glinting playfully. "Relax, Caroline! It's gonna be great. We've got snacks, a whole day planned, and most importantly, he gets to hang out with his awesome wizard dad. What more could a kid want?"

I grinned. "Yeah, but ixnay on the agicmay,

please! I'll tell him when he's ready."

"Roger Wilco!" Daisy hummed from the hallway.

Caroline laughed softly, shaking her head. "Well, I suppose you're both right."

"I'm always right," Daisy called out from the hallway before she popped her head in again. "And you, Sean, you ready for a whole day of energy? Cody's got way more stamina than you, I bet."

I grinned. "I think I can keep up. Besides, we've got a fun hike planned. Plenty of space for him to burn off that energy."

Caroline perked up at that. "He'll love that. I remember the last time he was here; he couldn't stop talking about how much he liked being outside."

Daisy gave a satisfied nod. "Yep, that's how you keep them entertained. Fresh air and running around."

We continued prepping the house, making sure everything was perfect for Cody's visit. I was happy he was coming; it was always great having Cody around, and today, we had some quality time planned. I wanted to show him more of Waycross, maybe even take him to some spots in the forest I'd found on my own.

By late morning, we were just about done with everything when I heard the familiar sound of a car pulling up outside. I glanced out the window, and sure enough, Brooke's black sedan was rolling into the driveway.

"They're here," I called out, heading to the front door.

Brooke stepped out first, looking a little tired but smiling warmly. And then Cody came bursting out of the car, his face lighting up the second he saw me. "Dad!" Cody shouted, running up to me full speed.

I knelt down, catching him as he threw his arms around my neck. "Hey, buddy! You excited for today?"

"Yeah!" he exclaimed, practically bouncing on his toes. "I've been waiting forever! What are we doing? Are we going hiking? I want to see the forest!"

I laughed, ruffling his hair. "You bet we're going hiking. We've got the whole day planned out, don't worry."

Brooke approached, a smile on her face as she watched the interaction. "He's been talking about this all week, Sean. Thanks for taking him. I've got a lot to catch up on at work."

"No problem at all," I said, standing up and giving her a nod. "How about we come and drop him off at your place in three days? I'll return him to you all tired with his energy spent."

Brooke let out a soft laugh, glancing over at Cody, who was still practically bouncing with excitement. "I appreciate it. Work's been… well, you know how it is. But today's important."

"Take your time," I said. "We've got plenty of stuff to keep us busy."

Brooke smiled, her eyes softening as she looked at Cody. "Be good for your dad, okay? No getting into too much trouble."

"I won't, Mom!" Cody promised, tugging on my hand eagerly. "Come on, Dad! Let's go already!"

Brooke laughed at his enthusiasm, then gave me a grateful nod. "Thanks again, Sean. I hope you don't mind me not staying for coffee, but I'm really eager to get all this work out of the way."

"No problem, Brooke," I said, giving her a kiss on her cheek. "You go on and do what you have to do."

I watched as she got back into the car, and Cody barely waited for her to drive off before tugging on my hand again. "Come on, Dad! Let's go! I want to see the forest!"

I chuckled, glancing over at Daisy and Caroline, who were both watching with smiles on their faces. "Alright, alright, slow down, bud. Let's get everything ready first."

As soon as Brooke drove off, Cody was bouncing on his heels, looking at me with wide eyes. "Dad, where's Tink? Can she come play?" His excitement was contagious, and I couldn't help but smile.

Before I could answer, we heard the telltale sound of paws hitting the ground, and within moments, Tink came bounding out of the field. She spotted Cody and barked once before sprinting toward him.

"Tink!" Cody yelled, dropping to his knees just as she skidded to a stop in front of him. She practically tackled him, licking his face and wagging her tail so hard her whole body shook.

I chuckled. "I guess she missed you."

Cody laughed, wrapping his arms around Tink's neck. "I missed her too! She's the best dog ever!" He scratched her ears, and she responded by trying to climb into his lap, despite being way too big for that.

Daisy walked up beside me, leaning against the porch railing with a grin. "Looks like Cody and Tink are already having the time of their lives."

I nodded, watching them with a sense of contentment. "Yeah, it's always great having him here. I missed this."

Daisy looked at me, her smile softening a bit. "You're a good dad, Sean. It's obvious how much he loves being around you."

Caroline stepped out, wiping her hands on a towel. "He does seem so happy when he's here. And…" She hesitated for a moment, then added, "Brooke seemed better today, didn't she? Not as tired."

I nodded slowly, my eyes drifting to where Cody was now trying to teach Tink how to fetch an oversized stick. "Yeah, she looked better."

Daisy, however, wasn't as convinced. "She might've looked a little better, but she's still pushing herself too hard. You can tell. There was something strained about that smile."

Caroline glanced at her, then back at me. "I noticed that too... she smiled more, but she still looked a little worn out. Like she's trying too hard."

I didn't say anything for a moment, but I knew they were both right. "Yeah. I just hope she realizes she doesn't have to do everything on her own. She's tough, but everyone's got a limit."

Daisy crossed her arms, her expression serious. "Yeah, and she's pushing hers. Hopefully, she figures it out soon."

Caroline gave a soft nod. "She's smart, though. She'll get there, right?"

I shrugged slightly. "I hope so. It's just hard seeing her like this, you know? She's always been strong, but... I worry."

Daisy's expression softened, and she rested a hand on my arm. "You're a good guy for worrying, but you've done what you can. She's gotta figure out the rest herself."

I gave her a small smile, appreciating the support. "Yeah, I guess you're right."

Caroline smiled gently, her hand still resting on mine. "It's clear you care. But today's about Cody. He's been looking forward to this."

I glanced over at Cody, who was now running around the yard, Tink happily chasing him. His laughter echoed in the air, and I couldn't help but feel my mood lift. "Yeah, you're right. Today's about him."

Daisy grinned, stepping back. "Speaking of… I think it's time to burn some of that energy of his. You ready for it, Sean, or you need some help?"

I chuckled. "I think I'll manage. We've got the hike planned, so that should tire him out." I smiled for a moment as I watched him frolic about with Tink. "Alright," I said, tearing my eyes from the show. "Let me just grab some water and the backpacks, and we'll head out in a bit."

Daisy crossed her arms, looking over at Cody and Tink. "You think they're gonna stop running around long enough to actually hike?"

I chuckled, glancing at the two of them still

tearing around the yard. "We'll see."

As I headed inside to grab the gear, I heard Daisy calling out to Cody. "Hey, kiddo! You better save some of that energy for the hike, or your dad will have to carry you back!"

Cody's laughter rang out. "I won't get tired! I can run forever!"

Daisy shot back, "Oh yeah? Bet you I can beat you to the other side of the field!"

I grinned, shaking my head as I grabbed the water bottles. By the time I came back out, Cody was bouncing with excitement, and Tink was still right at his heels. It was good to see him so happy — it made everything feel right.

# Chapter 17

After I packed and we had a quick bite, Cody and I were ready to set out. I had packed a small backpack with some snacks, water, and a first aid kit — just in case — and Tink was right by Cody's side, her tail wagging as she sensed the adventure ahead.

"Come on, Dad! Let's go!" Cody shouted,

bouncing on his heels like he couldn't wait another second.

I chuckled, slinging the backpack over my shoulder. "Alright, alright. We're going." I turned to Daisy and Caroline, who were lounging on the porch, watching us with amused expressions. "You two sure you don't want to come?"

Daisy waved us off, grinning. "Nah, you boys go ahead. We'll hold down the fort here. Besides, someone's gotta make sure the house is still standing when you get back!"

Caroline smiled softly, giving a small wave. "Have fun! We'll be here when you return."

Cody was practically hopping with excitement as I led the way down the trail behind the house. Tink bounded ahead, darting in and out of the trees, her nose to the ground. Cody ran after her for a moment before falling into step beside me, his eyes wide as he took in the sights around him.

"This is so cool, Dad!" Cody said, his voice full of wonder. "Are there any animals out here? Can we see some?"

"Maybe," I said with a grin. "If we're lucky, we might spot some deer or squirrels. And there are plenty of birds too. But you've got to be quiet if you want to see them."

Cody nodded seriously, as if I'd just given him the most important mission in the world. He walked a little more softly after that, his eyes scanning the trees and bushes for any sign of wildlife.

As we made our way deeper into the woods, I pointed out different plants and trees, showing him which ones were safe and which ones to avoid. "See that one over there?" I said, pointing to a cluster of berries. "That's called elderberry. It's good for you when it's ripe, but you have to be careful — if you eat it when it's not ready, it can make you sick. And even when they're ripe, you have to prepare them first. Cooking, boiling, putting them in a pie…"

Cody's eyes widened. "Really? How can you tell when they're ready?"

I crouched down beside him, showing him the dark purple berries. "When they're this color, they're ready. But if they're green or red, don't touch them. But don't eat the ready ones raw."

Cody nodded, taking it all in. "Got it. Purple is

good. Green and red are bad." He glanced around, his eyes bright with curiosity. "What else can you eat out here?"

I stood up, pointing to a nearby patch of clover. "That's clover. You can eat the leaves, but they don't taste like much. And over there, that's wild mint. You can use it to flavor your water or tea."

Cody knelt down to pick a few leaves, holding them up to his nose and sniffing. "It smells really good!" He grinned, shoving the leaves into his pocket like he'd just found buried treasure. "I'm gonna keep these for later."

I laughed. "Good idea. We'll make some mint tea when we get back."

We kept walking, and I showed him how to find his way using the sun. Cody soaked up everything I said, asking questions and making mental notes, his enthusiasm never waning.

"Hey, Dad," Cody said after a while, glancing up at me. "Do you know how to make a fire? Like, with just sticks and stuff?"

I grinned. "Yeah, I can do that. Want me to show you?"

Cody's eyes lit up. "Yes! That would be so cool!

Can we make one when we stop?"

I nodded. "Sure thing. But remember, fire can be dangerous if you don't know how to control it. I'll show you how to build one safely and — even more important — how to safely douse the flames and make sure you won't set the whole forest on fire."

Cody nodded eagerly. "Great! I promise I'll be careful."

After walking for a bit longer, we found a small clearing, and I decided it was a good spot to take a break. Cody dropped his backpack on the ground, and Tink flopped down beside him, panting happily.

"Alright, Cody," I said, kneeling down beside a small pile of dry sticks and leaves. "First thing you need is some rocks. If you got the time, you can try to find a little depression or even dig one to make the fire in. The pit and the stones will contain the flames, making sure the only that's gonna be burning is what you want to burn."

He grinned and nodded, and we went to work to gather some good stones. We found a natural depression in the clearing that we built a ring of rocks around. When that was done, I brushed off my hands and gave Cody a nod.

"Okay, great! Next thing we need is tinder — something that catches fire easily." I grabbed some dry leaves and bark, placing them in the center of the pile. "Then you add kindling — small twigs and branches. You want to build it in a way that allows air to flow through it."

Cody watched intently as I explained, his eyes wide with fascination.

"Once you've got it set up," I continued, "you can use a spark or a match to get it going. But since we're out here, I'll show you how to do it the old-fashioned way — with sticks."

Cody grinned. "This is so awesome!"

I showed him how to use friction to create a spark, explaining the technique as I worked. After a few moments of effort, a small flame flickered to life, and Cody's face lit up with excitement.

"Whoa! You did it!" he exclaimed, his voice full of awe. "That's so cool, Dad!"

I smiled, watching the fire grow. "Now remember, you've always got to be careful with fire. Never leave it unattended, and make sure to put it out completely when you're done."

Cody nodded seriously, his eyes still fixed on the flames. "I will. I promise."

We sat by the fire for a while, eating some of the snacks we'd brought and talking about everything Cody had learned. He was full of questions, and I answered each one as best as I could, enjoying the time with him.

But as we sat there, I felt something was up. He was thinking about something, and he needed to voice it.

I figured it was time to ask.

"Hey, bud," I said, leaning forward a bit. "You've been awfully quiet for the past few minutes. What's going on in that head of yours?"

Cody glanced up at me, then back at the fire, hesitating before speaking. "It's… it's just school, I guess."

I raised an eyebrow, curious. "School? What's going on with school?"

He shrugged, poking the ground again. "I don't know. It's just… the kids there are different. I don't really have a lot of friends, you know?"

That broke my heart, and my first instinct was

to go to that school and level it to the ground. But I tempered the lion inside. Instead, I frowned, leaning in a bit more. "Different how? You having trouble fitting in?"

Cody nodded slowly, his face scrunched up in thought. "Yeah. It's like… they're into stuff I don't really care about. And when I try to talk about things I like, they just kinda… don't listen. Or they make fun of it. Like when I talked about Tink and the hikes we do, some of the kids said it was boring to walk around in the forest."

I felt a pang in my chest, knowing what it was like to feel out of place. "I'm sorry, bud. That sounds rough."

Cody sighed, kicking a small rock into the fire pit. "Yeah. And they all seem to have these friend groups already. It's hard to… I don't know, break in, I guess. I just feel like I'm always on the outside."

I nodded, letting him get it out. "It can be tough, finding your place. Especially when it feels like everyone's already got their thing going. But you'll get there, Cody. Sometimes it just takes a bit of time."

Cody looked up at me, his brow furrowed. "Did you ever feel like that? Like you didn't fit in?"

I chuckled softly. "Plenty of times. I used to feel just like that back in Murray, in Iowa. That's where I lived when I was a kid."

He nodded. "Yeah." Then, he looked up at me. "Why did you feel like that?"

"Because my mom and dad and me, we were outsiders, and the town was pretty close-knit. It was no one's fault — just the way people are. But yeah, I felt out of place." I smiled at him. "But I found my people and my place eventually. You've just gotta be yourself, and the right friends will come around. Trust me."

Cody gave a small nod, seeming to take that in. "Yeah... I hope so."

After a moment of silence, his face brightened a bit. "I'm really excited for the fair, though! That's gonna be awesome! Do you think there will be games?"

I grinned, glad to see his mood lift. "You bet there will be. And I'm thinking you have a good shot at winning some of those games."

Cody smiled, the firelight reflecting in his eyes.

"I want to win a big stuffed animal. For Mom."

"That's a good plan," I said, nodding in approval. "She'd love that."

We sat quietly for a few more moments. It was a peaceful kind of silence, the type that didn't need filling with words. I could see his mind was still churning — the apple doesn't fall far from the tree — but he was also feeling better about it all.

"Alright, buddy," I said eventually, "time to show you how to properly douse a fire."

Cody perked up, watching closely as I grabbed the water bottle from my bag. "First thing you do is make sure you've got enough water. You don't want to just sprinkle it — soak the whole thing. And after you pour it, you'll stir the ashes around to make sure the fire's completely out. If you're out on a longer hike, don't use drinking water unless you have to. Get some from a nearby water source or use a shovel to put dirt onto the fire."

I poured the water slowly over the embers, steam rising up as the fire hissed and sputtered out. "See? Once it stops steaming, you mash the ashes and embers with soil. Then, you stir it a bit to make sure there aren't any hidden embers.

Coals and embers and partially burned pieces of wood you have to touch to make sure they're not too hot. But just briefly — if they *are* too hot, you don't want to burn yourself."

Cody nodded, looking serious as he helped me make sure it was done right. I was glad to see he took this seriously. There were plenty of fires in my youth from kids just messing around. Usually, they were easily contained or didn't spread too much, but that was plain luck.

"Good job," I said, ruffling his hair. "Now, always check twice. Better safe than sorry."

Cody smiled up at me, his earlier worries seeming to fade a bit. "I got it, Dad. Thanks for teaching me all this."

"Anytime, bud," I said, feeling a swell of pride. "That's what I'm here for."

We packed up the rest of our things, and with the fire safely out, we started the hike back home, which should take an hour or two and get us home before dark. Cody's mood had lifted, and I couldn't help but smile at the quiet strength he was developing. He was growing up fast, and these moments with him were becoming more important than ever.

As we started the hike back, the trail led us through a quiet stretch of woods, the afternoon sunlight filtering through the trees. Tink trotted ahead, nose to the ground as usual, and Cody stayed close by my side, his earlier worries forgotten for now.

After walking for a while, I decided to take him to a special place. I glanced down at him and nodded toward the trees ahead. "Hey, Cody, remember the old oak tree we saw last time?"

"Yeah! That was really cool."

"We can take a slight detour and visit it again. Would you like that?"

Cody's eyes lit up. "Yeah! Let's go there."

"Alright," I said, giving him a wink.

We continued walking for a few more minutes until we reached the ancient oak tree that had been at the beginning of this entire adventure. Its massive branches stretched wide, casting a cool shadow across the ground. This was the spot where I first discovered the Wood Sigil's power — a moment I'd never forget.

This was also where we had uncovered the dungeon leading to Jan Vanderlee's crypt, but the entrance to that place was no longer in sight. After we had cleared the place, it had simply disappeared.

As we settled under the tree, Cody leaned back, staring up at the branches. "I love this forest," he said, his voice full of awe. "I wish I could stay here."

I nodded, handing him another granola bar. "Yeah, I thought you'd like it. It's quiet, away from everything."

Cody took a bite of the bar, still looking up at the tree. "How'd you find it?"

I leaned back against the trunk, remembering that day. "I was just out exploring one day, kind of like we're doing now. Stumbled upon it. Something about this tree just felt... right, I guess."

Cody chewed thoughtfully for a moment, then turned to me. "Can we go deeper next time? Like, way deeper into the woods? Maybe go camping?"

I smiled at his excitement. "Absolutely. There's a lot more to see out here. I'll take you further next time, show you some of the other spots I've found."

His face lit up, and he nodded eagerly. "That'd be awesome! I want to see everything! Do you think there's like, secret places? Like caves or stuff?"

I chuckled. "There could be. You never know what you'll find if you look hard enough."

Cody grinned, clearly already planning our next adventure. "Maybe we'll find treasure or something!"

"Maybe," I said with a laugh. "We'll bring a shovel next time, just in case."

He laughed along with me, then went quiet again, picking at the wrapper of his snack. After a few seconds, he glanced up at me, his voice softer. "Dad... do you think we could all be together more? Like, you, me, and Mom?"

I smiled and squeezed his shoulder. "I hope so, pal."

Cody kicked at a small rock. "I don't like that we're not together. And I don't like that Mom's working so much."

I hesitated for a moment, then said, "I think

she's trying to find a way to balance it all. It might take some time, but she's figuring it out. She loves you more than anything, Cody. That's why she works so hard."

He looked up at me, his eyes searching mine. "Yeah, I know she loves me. I just miss her, you know?"

"I know," I said softly. "And I bet she misses you too, more than you know. She's doing her best, Cody."

He nodded, sitting quietly for a moment. "I just wish... I wish things were easier for her. She always looks so tired."

I sighed, wishing I had a better answer for him, wishing I could solve this with a snap of my fingers, but it was never that easy when there were other people involved. "She's got a lot on her plate right now. But you help, you know. You being you, that's what keeps her going."

Cody smiled a little at that. "Yeah? You think so?"

"I *know* so," I said firmly. "She's proud of you, Cody. Every time I talk to her, she's always telling me how smart you are, how kind you are. She's doing everything she can to make sure you have what you need."

Cody looked down, fiddling with the hem of his shirt. "Thanks, Dad. I like being here. It's fun, and it's… I don't know, it feels good."

I ruffled his hair. "I'm glad. I love having you here too."

We sat there for a little longer, Cody seeming to relax as we talked. Eventually, he asked, "So… can we do the camping trip soon? Like next time I'm here?"

I nodded. "Absolutely. We'll go deeper into the woods, explore more. We'll find a good place to camp, and we'll bring marshmallows."

Cody's face brightened again. "That would be so cool! Can we bring Tink?"

"Sure," I said. "Maybe even Daisy or Caroline. Or both! We'll make a whole trip out of it. But for now," I said, standing up, "we should probably head back before it gets too dark."

Cody hopped to his feet, grabbing the backpack. "Okay, but next time, we're going even further, right?"

"Definitely," I said, smiling as I ruffled his hair

again. "Now let's get moving. We've got to make sure we get back before it gets dark."

Cody nodded, calling out to Tink as we started back down the trail. As we walked, I couldn't help but feel proud of him. He was growing up fast, thinking about things in ways that showed how mature he was becoming. I knew he was going to be a good man when he grew up.

# Chapter 18

By the time Cody and I returned from the hike, the sun was starting to lower in the sky. We could see Daisy out in the field, bent over a basket, gathering vegetables and placing them carefully inside. Tink, after leading the way back, darted off to chase a few birds in the distance.

"Daisy!" Cody called out, waving as we

approached. "What are you doing?"

Daisy straightened up, wiping her hands on her jeans as she smiled over at us. "Hey there, Cody! I'm getting stuff ready for the town fair tomorrow. Got a lot of veggies to pick, and I've got to make sure everything's perfect for the stall."

Cody's eyes lit up. "Can I help?"

"Of course you can!" Daisy said with a grin. "Come on over here, grab a basket, and let's get to work. I could use an extra pair of hands. I wanna finish before dark, and with you guys helpin' out, I just might!"

Cody hurried over, grabbing the nearest basket and following Daisy's instructions as they started picking tomatoes and cucumbers. His little hands moved quickly, eager to help out. He was pretty deft too — he had a talent for work like this.

"What's this one called again?" Cody asked, holding up a funny-shaped vegetable.

Daisy chuckled. "That's a zucchini. You know, if you slice it up and fry it, it's pretty tasty. Ever had zucchini fries?"

Cody shook his head. "No, but that sounds terrible!" He stuck out his tongue. "Vegetable fries, ew!"

Daisy laughed, shaking a zucchini at him. "I'll change your mind yet, mister!"

He grinned. "Do you grow all these vegetables yourself?"

"Yup, yup!" Daisy replied, clearly enjoying the chance to talk about her farm. "Everything you see here, I've grown with my own two hands. Well, and a little help from your dad from time to time." She shot me a playful look.

Cody glanced over at me. "Really, Dad? You help with all this?"

I shrugged. "I try, but Daisy's the expert. I mostly just do the heavy lifting."

Cody grinned, clearly impressed. "That's so cool! I want to help more when I'm here."

"You're always welcome to help," Daisy said, handing him another vegetable to place in the basket. "There's plenty to do around here, that's for sure."

As they continued working, I stepped back a little, watching them with a smile. It was nice seeing Cody so eager to jump in and help, and I could tell he was enjoying the simple tasks of farm life. There was something about the fresh air and the rhythm of working with your hands that had a way of putting things in perspective.

A little while later, Caroline appeared, walking toward us with a basket of her own, covered in a light cloth. "I've brought some of the baked goods for tomorrow," she called out as she approached. "Thought you might want to taste test a few."

Cody's eyes widened at the sight of the basket. "Are those cookies?"

Caroline smiled warmly. "Some of them are, yes. I also made a few pies and muffins. They'll be for the fair, but you can have a taste."

Cody wasted no time, rushing over to peek under the cloth. "Can I try one now?"

Caroline laughed softly, handing him a cookie. "Go ahead. Tell me what you think."

Cody took a big bite, his face lighting up immediately. "This is so good! You really made these?"

She nodded. "I did. I'm glad you like it."

Daisy glanced over at the baked goods, her eyes narrowing playfully. "Hey, don't let him eat all of those! I've got dibs on at least one of those cookies."

Cody laughed, holding up the basket for Daisy to take one. "Here, Daisy, you can have one too!"

As the four of us stood there, the sun casting a warm glow over the fields, Daisy dusted off her hands. "You know, we've got plenty of veggies and now some baked goods. How about we all stay here for dinner tonight? I can whip something up with what we've got."

I glanced over at Cody, who was already nodding eagerly. "That sounds like a plan to me."

Caroline smiled, clearly pleased with the idea. "I'd love that. It's been a while since we all had a meal together here."

Daisy grinned. "Perfect! Let's get these veggies inside, and I'll start cooking. Cody, you're officially on kitchen duty."

Cody saluted with a grin. "Yes, ma'am!"

About an hour later, the four of us sat around Daisy's big, sturdy kitchen table, the smell of roasted vegetables filling the air. Cody was in high spirits, practically bouncing in his seat as he shoveled food into his mouth between excited bursts of conversation.

"And then, Tink ran ahead and found the trail before we even did!" Cody exclaimed, grinning as he recounted the hike. "Dad showed me how to make a fire, too! Like, with sticks and everything. It was awesome."

Daisy, seated across from Cody, nodded approvingly. "Well, sounds like you two had quite the adventure. You're gonna be an expert woodsman before long, huh?"

Cody's eyes lit up as he nodded vigorously. "Yep! Dad said next time we can go even deeper into the woods. Maybe we'll find something cool! Like… a secret cave or treasure!"

I chuckled, catching Caroline's amused smile from across the table. "We'll definitely explore more next time, bud. You did great today."

Cody beamed at the praise, taking another bite of the roasted zucchini. "And this isn't bad either, Daisy. I thought I wouldn't like it, but it's actually good!"

Daisy grinned, clearly proud of her cooking. "Told ya I'd change your mind about zucchini! That's the power of a good farm-to-table dinner."

Caroline laughed softly, passing Cody another piece of bread. "You've been quite the helper today, Cody. Picking vegetables, hiking… you must be tired."

Cody shook his head, clearly unwilling to admit any kind of fatigue. "Nope! I could do it all again tomorrow if I wanted."

Daisy leaned back in her chair, crossing her arms with a teasing smile. "Well, don't get too comfortable. We've still got the fair tomorrow, and I could use an extra pair of hands at the stall. You up for that?"

Cody sat up straighter, his excitement immediately renewed. "Are you kidding? Yeah! I wanna help at the stall. What are we selling?"

"Veggies, jams, pickles, and some baked goods from Caroline," Daisy replied. "You can help us sell them, maybe run around a bit and see all the other stalls. It's always a big day for the town, lots of people come out. Some folks from other towns like Blackhill, too."

Cody nodded, eyes wide with anticipation. "It sounds so fun! I wanna see everything."

I smiled, watching how naturally Cody fit into

our little group. It felt good, this dynamic. Daisy, with her playful energy; Caroline, with her quiet thoughtfulness; and Cody, so full of life and curiosity. It was... comfortable. I wished Brooke was here too; if she could see the effect that Waycross was having on Cody, I knew she'd be inspired.

As we ate, we started planning out the next day, going over the list of what needed to be done for the fair. Daisy talked about finalizing her setup, and Caroline mentioned adding some finishing touches to the baked goods she'd bring along. Cody chimed in with ideas about how to make the stall look "cool" and volunteered to help carry things, even though we all knew he was mostly excited to explore.

After dinner, we moved outside. The sky had turned a deep shade of blue, the stars twinkling overhead as we sat on the porch. Cody was sitting on the steps, looking up at the stars with wide eyes, Tink curled up beside him. Daisy and Caroline were on the porch, quietly talking, although they spent a lot of time simply looking at Cody, enjoying his presence.

"Dad?" Cody asked, his voice quieter now, as if the night had softened him. "The forest looks so magical at night. When we go out camping, can we go really deep? Maybe we'll find something magical!"

I glanced at him, smiling at the eager look in his eyes. "Of course. We can make a whole weekend out of it if you want."

Cody grinned, clearly loving the idea. "That would be awesome! I wanna sleep in a tent and cook over the fire, just like in the movies. And at night, I want to look around with a flashlight. Maybe we'll see fairies!"

I chuckled, nodding. "Sounds great! We'll give it a try, I promise. We'll bring the tent, some marshmallows for roasting, and maybe even catch some fish for dinner."

Caroline leaned back in her chair, a soft smile on her face as she listened. "That sounds like a perfect plan. A real camping adventure."

Daisy, who had been staring up at the stars, turned to us with a grin. "Well, count me in! I'm always up for an adventure in the woods. Especially if it involves marshmallows."

Cody laughed, clearly delighted that everyone was onboard with his camping idea. "It's gonna be the best trip ever!" He looked at Daisy. "Can we bring Tink too? I bet she can help me find magical fairies."

"Of course," Daisy said, patting Tink's head. "She wouldn't miss it for the world."

We sat there for a while longer, talking quietly under the stars, the air cool but comforting. Cody, his energy finally starting to wane, leaned back against me, his eyes growing heavy.

"I can't wait for tomorrow," he mumbled, his voice sleepy. "And for the camping trip. It's gonna be so much fun."

I smiled, ruffling his hair gently. "Yeah, bud. It's going to be great."

It didn't take much longer for Cody to get really sleepy, and so we wrapped things up at Daisy's and headed back to my place — all four of us. There, I tucked Cody in before enjoying what remained of the evening with my girls. Still, we all checked in early — tomorrow was the day of the fair, and we all wanted to be well-rested.

# Chapter 19

The morning of the town fair arrived, and the house was buzzing with activity. After breakfast, the four of us drove over to Daisy's in my red pickup truck. Within moments after parking, Cody was carrying a basket of produce to the porch while Daisy had just headed inside to make us all some coffee.

"Dad! We gotta start loading these in the truck!" he called out, running back inside for another armful of produce.

I chuckled as I watched him sprint around, his energy at full blast. "Hold your horses, buddy," I said, standing up from the kitchen table. "We've got plenty of time. We're gonna have some coffee first!"

"Coffee! Coffee! Always coffee!" he complained.

Caroline covered her mouth to chuckle at that. "He's not wrong, you know?"

I laughed. "Hey, a man needs his fuel," I joked before nodding at Cody. "Go play with Tink for a bit. We'll be ready to start loading up in half an hour."

Grinning, I headed inside with Caroline where Daisy was already making us a hot cup of coffee. We drank it in relative quiet while Cody was already burning off some of his energy with Tink outside, and we sampled a few of Caroline's baked goods before we were really good and ready to go.

"Alright," I said, finishing my coffee. "Let's hop to it!"

The girls nodded, and we got to work. Daisy stayed in the kitchen, carefully packing jars of homemade pickles and jams into crates. "Make sure we don't forget the cooler, Sean. Gotta keep some of the veggies fresh," she reminded me, handing over the first crate.

"Got it," I said, grabbing the crate and heading out to the truck. Seeing we were finally getting started, Cody made his way over, and Tink followed closely behind, wagging her tail and sniffing the air, sensing the excitement.

"Help me with this, bud," I said, pretending the crate was too heavy, and Cody quickly came to my aid, happy to contribute.

While we loaded the first of the crates, Caroline appeared at the kitchen door, holding a tray of baked pies, their golden crusts gleaming in the morning light. "These should go in the front seat," she said, smiling. "I don't want them getting squashed under everything else."

"Good call," I said, gently taking the tray and placing it on the passenger seat of the truck. "They look amazing, Caroline."

"Thanks," she said, a small flush of pride in her

cheeks. "I'm hoping they'll sell out quickly."

Cody ran back inside and grabbed another basket, his grin wide. "Dad, can I sit with the pies with Tink when we drive down to the fair? Please?"

I shook my head, laughing. "Nice try, but you're riding up front with us. Tink can stay in the back, though. We'll have to make sure she can't get into the crates, but we can cover them and keep them closed. It isn't that far anyway."

It took us a little under twenty minutes to load everything in the truck and secure it. As we finished up, Daisy walked out, wiping her hands on her jeans. "Alright, looks like we've just about got everything ready. You're a big help, Cody. I don't know what we'd do without you."

Cody puffed up with pride, then grinned at me. "Can we go now?"

Caroline stepped out behind Daisy. She had changed into a pretty dress with a floral print for the fair. It was loose-fitting and a little less sexy than what she normally wore, but a woman with her kind of curves could hardly hide anything. "He's been a great helper all morning," Caroline agreed. "I think we're almost ready to head out."

I shot the girls a wink before hopping into the truck bed, making sure everything was secure. "Alright, let's get a move on, then."

With everything packed up, Cody scrambled into the truck, sitting in the middle seat between me and Daisy, his legs swinging with excitement. "This is gonna be the best fair ever!" he declared as I started the engine.

Tink hopped into the back, her head poking up over the side as she wagged her tail. Caroline climbed into the passenger seat, carefully holding onto the tray of pies.

As we pulled out of the driveway, the truck loaded with fresh produce and baked goods, I couldn't help but smile. The day was just getting started, and with Cody's excitement leading the charge, I had a feeling this was going to be a day to remember.

When we arrived at the town square, it was already busy with other folks setting up their stalls. We parked near the edge of the square where most folks had left their vehicles while unloading. Before I'd even turned the engine off, Cody was already scrambling to get out of the truck. "Dad! We gotta start setting up! Come on!"

I chuckled, putting the truck in park. "Hold on, kiddo. Let's take it one step at a time. The fair's not going anywhere."

Daisy hopped out of the passenger seat, stretching her arms over her head as she grinned at Cody's enthusiasm. "First thing's first, we've gotta set up the stall. We've gotta put it together before we unload anything."

Cody's eyes widened with excitement. "Oh, yeah! What do I do first?"

I hopped out of the truck and nodded toward the bed, where we had packed the pieces of the stall. "Grab one of the smaller parts, bud. We'll need to assemble the frame first, so let's get everything laid out."

Cody dashed to the back of the truck, grabbing one of the lighter pieces as I reached in for the heavier ones. Daisy was already pulling out the smaller pieces to set on the ground. "Okay," she said, dusting her hands off. "Once we get the base in place, this'll go up quick."

Caroline, who had been waiting by the passenger side, came over with a smile. "I'll help with the setup too. It'll go faster that way."

"Thanks," I said, nodding at her. "It's all about teamwork."

With Cody's eager help, we started assembling the stall. I fitted the first two beams into the base while Daisy held them steady. Cody looked on, fascinated by the process. "Whoa, Dad, you built this?"

I grinned. "Yep. Well, Daisy and I did it together. It's pretty simple, but sturdy enough for what we need."

Daisy chuckled. "That's right. We needed something solid, especially with how much produce we're gonna be stacking on it today. It's gotta hold up under pressure."

Cody was watching every move I made, eager to jump in. "Can I help screw this part in?"

I handed him the screwdriver with a nod. "Sure thing. Just make sure you screw it in straight."

Cody beamed, gripping the drill like it was the most important tool in the world. He lined it up with the screws and, with a bit of guidance, got them drilled in smoothly. "I did it!"

"Nice work!" Daisy said, giving him an approving smile. "You're a natural at this."

Caroline, meanwhile, was laying out the shelves, making sure everything was ready for when we started stacking the goods. "This is going to look great once it's all put together," she said, smoothing a hand over the surface.

Once the frame was up, I attached the top beams and secured them in place. The whole stall came together quickly with all four of us working on it. Cody held the boards while I screwed them in, and Daisy double-checked everything to make sure it was sturdy.

"There!" I said, stepping back to admire our work. "Stall's up and ready to go."

Cody wiped his forehead dramatically, grinning. "That was awesome! Now we can start putting out the veggies, right?"

Daisy ruffled his hair. "Yep! Now we're ready to load it up. Great job, Cody."

Daisy pointed toward the back of the truck where we had the crates of vegetables. "How about you help me carry these to the stall? We'll start with the tomatoes."

Cody ran over without hesitation, grabbing one of the smaller baskets full of ripe tomatoes and holding it like a treasure. "Where do these go?"

I hopped out and walked to the back, lifting one of the heavier crates. "Right up front. We want everyone to see those when they walk by. Tomatoes sell themselves if they're in the right spot."

Cody nodded, carrying the basket over to the front of the stall that Daisy and I had built together. He set it down carefully, making sure every tomato stayed perfectly in place. "How's that?"

"Perfect," Daisy said, walking over with another basket. "Now let's get the peppers out next. They're bright, so they'll catch people's eyes."

Caroline, who had been busy setting up her baked goods on a smaller table beside the produce stall, stepped over to give Cody a hand. "Here, I'll help you with these," she said, picking up a basket of cucumbers. "You're doing great, Cody."

Cody grinned up at her. "Thanks! This is so much fun. I like helping."

I carried a few more crates over to the stall and started arranging them as best I could. "Cody, think you can handle organizing the zucchinis?"

"Yeah! I got it, Dad," he called out, grabbing the zucchinis from the truck. "These go right next to the peppers, right?"

"Exactly," Daisy said, giving him a thumbs-up. "You're getting the hang of this. By the end of the day, you'll be running the whole stall."

Cody's chest puffed out with pride. "I could do that! Maybe next year I can have my own stall and sell something cool."

Caroline laughed softly as she placed a tray of pies on the table. "What would you sell, Cody?"

"Maybe, like… cool rocks or something!" Cody said, his eyes sparkling with excitement. "Or maybe toys! Everybody loves toys."

"That's a great idea," I said, smiling at him.

As we continued setting up, more townsfolk arrived, their stalls popping up all around us. The square was soon filled with the sounds of laughter, greetings, and the unmistakable smell of food cooking from other stands. The fair was starting to come alive, and it was clear Cody was loving every second of it.

Daisy wiped her hands on her jeans and looked around, clearly satisfied with how the stall was coming together. "Alright, I think we're just about ready to go. What do you think, Cody? Are we missing anything?"

Cody stood back, looking at the stall with a serious expression. "Hmm…" He scratched his chin like he was deep in thought, making Caroline chuckle. "Nope! I think we got everything."

"Good eye, Cody," I said, leaning against the stall. "Now all we have to do is wait for people to start buying. And when they do, you're in charge of selling the tomatoes."

Soon enough, more people began arriving at the town square. More stalls were popping up in every direction — some selling fresh produce, others offering handmade crafts, preserves, and all sorts of local treats. The cheerful hum of conversations filled the air, and the fair was quickly becoming the lively event we'd all been looking forward to.

I was honestly pretty impressed with the turnout. Waycross was just a tiny town, but apparently, the fair drew attention from all around.

Before the clock had even struck ten, families strolled through the square, kids darting around excitedly as they explored the different booths. The scent of food cooking on nearby grills started to mix with the aroma of fresh bread and flowers from various stands. It was a classic small-town fair, and the community spirit was in full force. Everyone seemed eager to connect and enjoy the day.

Throughout the day, we took turns manning the stall while Cody mainly ran around, exploring the fair with Tink trotting happily beside him. The square was bustling with activity — kids chasing each other, people chatting, and stalls selling everything from crafts to homemade jams.

I was happy to see that Cody had no problems mixing with the local kids. Especially after what he'd told me yesterday during our hike, it was good to see he got along just fine with kids who were a little more like-minded. It was clear he simply didn't mesh well with city kids, and I had no problem with that. He and I just had a lot in common.

"He's doing well, isn't he?" Caroline asked after she'd sold another of her pies. She had noticed where my eye had drifted.

I grinned and nodded. "He is," I said. "And I'm glad for it. He's a good kid, and he deserves to be happy."

She smiled and touched my arm lightly. "Brooke will come around," she simply said, her sharp mind heading straight to the root of the issue.

"Think so?" I asked.

Her green eyes sparkled. "*Know* so," she said with a wink before she turned to a new customer.

As she did so, Daisy leaned against the side of the stall, fanning herself with a paper she found. "Man, this heat's no joke. Think we'll run out of pickles first or the jams?"

"Jams," Caroline said without hesitation, handing the customer a pie. "Everyone loves jam. Especially around here."

I grinned, scanning the square for Cody. He'd been running back and forth between the games and our stall, his energy seemingly endless. "He's gonna sleep like a rock tonight," I said, chuckling.

As if on cue, Cody came barreling toward us, Tink trotting beside him, her tail wagging. In Cody's hand was a small stuffed toy he'd clearly won at one of the booths. His face was lit up with pride.

"Dad! Look what I won!" Cody shouted, holding up the toy like a trophy. "It's a dragon! I got it at the shooting booth!"

I smiled, ruffling his hair. "That's awesome, bud! How many tries did it take?"

Cody puffed out his chest. "Just two! The guy said I was really good!"

"Nice!" I said, genuinely impressed. "You'll have to teach me your trick later."

Cody beamed, clutching the toy dragon to his chest. "You wanna come look at some other stalls now? There's one with honey, and I saw some cool crafts over there too!"

"Sure thing, let's go," I said, standing up. I glanced over at Daisy and Caroline. "You two good holding down the fort for a bit?"

Daisy waved me off with a grin. "We've got this covered. Go have fun."

Caroline gave a small nod, a smile on her face as she tidied up the display. "We'll manage!"

Cody grabbed my hand, practically pulling me along as we made our way through the crowds. "Come on, Dad! There's so much to see!"

We stopped by a few craft stalls first, where local artisans were selling handmade jewelry, wooden carvings, and hand-sewn quilts. Cody inspected everything with the kind of curiosity only kids had. He paused in front of one stall selling small trinkets carved from wood. "These are so cool! Can we get one, Dad?"

I smiled, looking over the little figures. There were tiny animals, trees, and even some carved into small mythical creatures. "You like one of these, bud? Pick whichever you want."

Cody's eyes scanned the display before he picked up a small wooden wolf. "I want this one. It looks like Tink!"

I laughed. "Good choice." I handed a dollar to the vendor, and Cody proudly stuffed the little wolf into his pocket.

Next, we wandered over to the honey stall. Cody's eyes went wide when he saw the jars of golden liquid lined up on the table. "Can we try some?"

The vendor, an older man with a broad smile, handed Cody a small spoonful. I didn't know him, so he was probably not from Waycross. Still, he was very friendly. "Go ahead, son. This is from our bees over in Albury."

Cody took a taste and grinned. "That's really good!"

I nodded, grabbing a jar. "We'll take one, thanks."

After a few more stops, we ended up at Earl's pie booth. Earl was in his element, chatting up customers and slicing fresh pies with his usual enthusiasm. He was also selling lemonade and some other food.

"Sean! Cody!" Earl greeted us with a wide grin. "How're y'all doin' this fine day?"

"We're good, Earl," I said, clapping him on the back. "Cody's been cleaning up at the games."

Cody proudly showed Earl his dragon toy. "Look! I won this shooting the pellet guns!"

"Well, ain't that something," Earl said with a chuckle. "You a winner, kiddo. And a good shot too. Remind me never to get on your bad side."

Cody grinned before his eyes wandered to the pies on the table. "Can we get a piece of pie, Dad? Please?"

I grinned. "Of course. Which one do you want?"

Earl held up a fresh apple pie, still warm from the oven. "This one's fresh outta the oven. I bet it's the best one I've made today. How'bout a slice, huh?"

I nodded, handing over the money. "We'll take it."

But Earl waved it off. "I ain't taking that money from you. Why, especially not from Dead-Eye Cody over there! It'd be best for me to keep a crack shot like that on my friendly side."

I laughed, then placed a few more bills on the counter. "Come on, Earl!" I said. "It's a stick-up, then! We want the whole pie!"

Laughing, Earl raised his hands and quickly boxed up the pie, winking at Cody. "Well, alright then! But you take care of this, Cody. It's your job to make sure your dad doesn't eat it all before you get home."

Cody laughed. "I will!"

With our pie in hand and Cody's dragon in tow, we made our way back to our stall, where Daisy and Caroline were busy with customers. Cody ran ahead, eager to show them the pie and his new toy.

I watched with a smile as he chatted away at the girls, and it warmed my heart to see him like this. We were a family, and it made me so very happy inside.

# Chapter 20

As the afternoon wore on and Cody was helping the girls at the stall, I took the chance to catch up with some of the townsfolk. The fair was in full swing now, with kids darting between booths, and the smell of food cooking from various stalls filling the air. I spotted Sheriff Fields over by the hot dog stand, laughing with a few locals. When he saw me, he waved me over.

"Sean! Looks like you're taking a well-deserved break," Sheriff Fields said, grinning as I approached.

I chuckled, nodding. "Yeah, figured I'd relax a bit. Cody's been having the time of his life running around."

The sheriff glanced over at Cody, who was 'helping out' while yapping Daisy's ears off. Tink followed him around, occasionally barking for attention. "Good to see him enjoying himself. It's great having you two here. You're fitting right in."

"It's been good for us," I agreed, leaning against the booth. "Cody's been having a blast today. It's nice seeing him so happy. He's also getting along with some of the other kids. I'm happy to see that; you never know how kids respond to each other, right?"

Fields nodded, looking thoughtful. "That's true. He seems like a good kid. Bet he's enjoying the break from city life, huh?"

"He is," I said, smiling. "Waycross suits him better. He likes the outdoors, the space to run around. It's been good for both of us." I grinned as we both watched Cody take Tink to some of the other kids. They were playing some kind of game I didn't understand, but it involved running around Tink and getting the dog all riled up until she barked and jumped at them.

"Well, he's having the time of his life," I said.

"Honestly, I figured he would if he's anything like his dad," the sheriff said, then patted me on the back. "Well, I'm glad you're here, Sean. I said it before, but I'm gonna say it again. This town needs good people like you. You've been a real positive presence."

"Appreciate that, Sheriff," I said, nodding. "It means a lot coming from you."

Fields grinned, tipping his hat. "Well, don't let me keep you. Looks like your boy's itching to show you something."

I glanced over to see Cody running toward me, Tink right on his heels, as well as the other kids, although they kept their distance from me, no doubt a little intimidated. "Dad! Look what I won!" Cody held up a few marbles, his face beaming with pride. "I won them from the other kids."

I ruffled his hair, grinning. "That's awesome, Cody! You're getting good at those games."

Cody puffed out his chest, clearly proud of himself, then glanced over his shoulder at the other kids. "I might give them back, though. Maybe the other kids will miss them…"

I smiled and nodded. "That'd be kind of you. Proud of you, bud!" I said.

With a broad grin, he ran off again, the other kids and Tink in tow. He handed the marbles back to the kids he'd won them from, and that was received with cheers and excited chatter. He was making some good friends here, and the kids themselves seemed kind.

Just then, I noticed Caroline making her way toward me, her face lighting up with a smile. Walking beside her was a man I hadn't seen before, but there was something familiar about him — the way he moved, the easy grin. He had the same warm eyes as Caroline, but there was a rougher edge to him, likely from long days working with his hands. He was a ginger, too, with a bushy red beard, and I was pretty sure the two of them were related.

Jack Bryce

"Hey, Sean," Caroline called out as she got closer, waving me over with a nervous smile. "There's, uh, someone I want you to meet."

By the way she fumbled with the sash of her dress and her green eyes darted back and forth, I could tell this was important to her — something that made her a little nervous. I smiled back, stepping toward her.

"This, uh, is my brother, Justin," Caroline introduced, patting him on the arm. "He runs the auto shop in town. I... I, uh, have been meaning to introduce you two."

Justin reached out his hand with a friendly grin. "Good to finally meet you, Sean. Caroline's been telling me about you."

I shook his hand, feeling the rough calluses from years of working with machinery and tools. "Good to meet you too, Justin. Caroline's mentioned you too. It's nice to finally match a face to the stories."

Justin chuckled, glancing over at his sister. "Yeah? All good things, I hope."

Caroline gave him a concerned look, way too nervous to get even this age-old and typical

248

banter. "Why would I…"

Justin laughed, shaking his head. "I'm only joking, sis. I know it's nothing but good stuff. Maybe about how you used to boss me around when we were younger." He grinned at me. "You wouldn't tell at first sight, but she has quite the temper."

I grinned, knowing full well what passions hid beneath Caroline's surface, but I wasn't going to elaborate on the topic to her brother, of course.

Caroline crossed her arms, a smirk playing on her lips. "Oh please, you were the one always getting into trouble, not me."

I chuckled, glancing between them. "I'm guessing you two were close growing up?"

Justin nodded, his smile softening a bit as he looked at Caroline. "Yeah, we were. Still are. She used to be my little shadow when we were kids, always wanting to hang out with the big kids." He turned to her with a playful grin. "But she was always a whole lot smarter than me and all those big kids together."

Caroline's cheeks flushed slightly, but she smiled fondly at her brother.

He stuck out his tongue. "Still, you were something of a snitch, though…"

Her green eyes widened. "A *snitch*!? Well, someone had to keep you in line. You were always making trouble, taking apart Dad's old radios, or trying to figure out how the lawnmower worked." She crossed her arms. "Taking his truck for a spin, even though you were *twelve*!"

Justin shrugged, grinning. "Yeah, well, look where it got me. Just a talent for machines."

I chuckled at their exchange. "Caroline mentioned you run the auto shop," I said. "That's gotta be a big job."

"It keeps me busy, that's for sure," Justin said, rubbing the back of his neck. "But I love it. Grew up with tools in my hands. Our dad was always tinkering with something in the garage, and I guess I picked up the habit. Plus, around here, everyone needs their car or truck fixed at some point. Plenty of farm machines here."

Caroline leaned in, her voice teasing. "Justin's being modest. He's built a great reputation in town. He's the guy everyone calls when something goes wrong with their car. Even when he's already up to his elbows in work, he'll find time to help. A lot of people from Blackhill prefer to call him over the big chain mechanic they have in town."

Justin waved her off, a bit embarrassed. "Hey, I just do what I can. Small towns are all about helping each other out, right? People here look out for each other. It's nice to be part of that."

"Sounds like you're doing more than your fair share," I said, impressed. "Running a business and still finding time to help everyone out — that's not easy."

He shrugged, glancing at Caroline. "Well, I learned that from our folks. They were always helping out the neighbors, even when things were tight. Mom and Dad are still in D.C. these days, but they check in on us all the time. Caroline's their golden child, though."

Caroline gave him a playful shove, easing up a little now that the conversation was going fine. "Oh, please. They worry about you just as much, especially with all the long hours you put in."

Justin smirked. "Maybe, but you're still the one who's always got her act together. I'm just the grease monkey."

Caroline shot him a look. "That's not true, Justin. You've built a successful business from the ground up. You work harder than anyone I know."

Justin chuckled, shaking his head. "Alright, alright, I'm not fishing for compliments here. But thanks, sis." He turned back to me, his tone shifting slightly. "How've you been settling in here, Sean? Looks like you and your kid are making yourselves right at home." He nodded in the direction of Cody, who was now deep in conversation with another kid near one of the game booths.

I smiled at the sight. "Yeah, we've been settling in pretty well. It's been a big change from the city, but a good one. Cody loves it here, and I've gotten to know a lot of folks around town."

"That's good to hear," Justin said. "Waycross is a good place for kids. Safe, lots of space to run around. I couldn't imagine growing up anywhere else." He paused for a moment, then added, "You think about sticking around for the long haul? I know you've been here a bit, but does it feel like home yet?"

I nodded slowly. "It's starting to. More and more every day, actually. Cody loves the outdoors, and it's nice to be part of a tight-knit community. Feels... right, you know?"

Justin smiled, clearly pleased. "That's what I like to hear. You'll find that the people here look out for each other. You ever need something, don't hesitate to ask. Same goes for your truck — if it ever gives you trouble, bring it by the shop. I'll take care of it. Won't pull your leg like they do in Blackhill, either."

"I'll keep that in mind," I said, shaking his hand again. "Appreciate it."

Just then, Cody came running back over, once again clutching his stuffed dragon from earlier. His face was flushed with excitement as he looked up at me. "Dad! Did you know there's some livestock being sold too!? Can we go check that out?"

I laughed, nodding. "Sure thing, bud. You wanna come with us, Justin?"

Justin glanced around at the bustling square, then smiled. "I've got a few more people to say hi to, but I'll catch up with you guys later. Enjoy the fair, Cody." He ruffled Cody's hair before turning back to me. "Good meeting you, Sean. Let's grab a drink sometime."

"Sounds good," I said, watching as Justin headed off to mingle with more folks.

Caroline smiled, watching her brother walk away. "I'm glad you two finally met. He's a good guy."

"Yeah, he seems like it," I agreed. "You guys seem close."

Caroline nodded, a soft smile on her face. "We are. He's always been there for me. It's... it's important to me that the two of you get along."

"Looks like we will," I said with a smile. Then, I glanced down at Cody, who was tugging on my hand, eager to explore more of the fair. "Well, let's go have a look at the animals, bud. Caroline, you good here?"

She waved me off with a smile. "See you in a bit."

The square was filled with all kinds of people — families, farmers, vendors — but Cody had a single-minded focus now: the animals. The pens were closer to the church, where there was a more serious part of the fair. There, farmers and ranchers sold their animals.

"Dad! Look, there are goats over there!" Cody exclaimed, pointing toward a pen where a few goats were lazily chewing on some hay.

I smiled at his enthusiasm and followed him over to the pen. As soon as we got there, Cody crouched down by the fence, sticking his hand through the slats to pet one of the goats. It was a smaller one, its fur rough under his hand, and it gave a curious bleat as Cody scratched its head.

"This one's so soft!" Cody said, his face lighting up as the goat nuzzled his hand. "Can we get one, Dad? Please?"

I chuckled. "A goat, huh? I don't think it's a smart move for us right now, but maybe in the future. For now, you can pet them as much as you want today."

Cody laughed but didn't look disappointed. He was too wrapped up in the moment, giving the goat all his attention. "I think it likes me," he said, grinning. "Do you think goats make good pets?"

I leaned against the fence, watching as he bonded with the animal. "They're definitely fun, but they're a lot of work too. You'd have to feed them, clean up after them, and make sure they have plenty of space to roam around."

Cody nodded seriously, still petting the goat. "I could do that. I'd be a good goat owner."

"I don't doubt it," I said, ruffling his hair. "Maybe one day, when we have more space."

Honestly, I was interested, but I wanted to move Daisy and Caroline in first and make us all comfortable before I would get us animals. Between getting the house ready and dealing with the magical stuff, I had enough on my plate already.

Satisfied with his interaction with the goat, Cody stood up, scanning the rest of the livestock pens. "Can we see the sheep next? They look so fluffy!"

"Lead the way, bud," I said, motioning for him to go ahead.

He dashed over to the next pen, where a few sheep were grazing peacefully. One of the farmers standing nearby gave us a nod, clearly used to the attention his animals were getting from kids all day. Since he was in between customers, he joined us with a grin.

"These sheep are so cool!" Cody said, his eyes wide as he watched one of the larger sheep munching on some grass. "Do they stay this fluffy all the time?"

The farmer chuckled. "They do for a while, son, but we shear them in the summer to keep them cool. That wool you see on 'em right now? We'll turn that into yarn soon enough."

Cody looked up at the farmer, fascinated. "You mean you shave them, like getting a haircut?"

"That's right," the farmer said with a nod. "It don't hurt 'em, and it helps keep them cool in the hot weather."

Cody's eyes brightened. "That's so cool! Can I pet one?"

The farmer smiled and waved him closer. "Sure thing, just be gentle."

Cody approached one of the sheep, reaching out slowly to run his hand through its thick wool. "It's so soft! I didn't know sheep were *this* soft."

I stood nearby, watching him interact with the

animals. Seeing Cody so happy, so full of energy and curiosity, made the day feel perfect. He loved animals, loved the outdoors, and here at the fair, he was in his element.

As Cody continued petting the sheep, he glanced over at me. "Dad, do you think we could live on a farm one day? Like with goats, sheep, and maybe even cows?"

I chuckled, leaning on the fence beside him. "I think we can, bud. It's a lot of work, though. You'd have to get up early every day to take care of the animals."

"I wouldn't mind," Cody said confidently. "I'd do it! It'd be fun."

As the afternoon wore on, we continued wandering the fair. Cody questioned the farmers and the stall owners, learning a thousand things — from how much a cow eats every year (over six thousand pounds of fodder) to which types of wood are best for carving small figurines (soft wood like basswood and butternut). Each time, I could see the wheels turning in his head, registering the information and storing it for later.

Eventually, we made our way back to our stall,

where Daisy and Caroline were finishing up the last of the sales. The fair was starting to wind down, the crowd thinning as families gathered their things and vendors began packing up for the day. Cody proudly showed off the little trinkets and prizes he had collected throughout the day, and we all laughed as he animatedly recounted every moment of excitement as we packed up the stall. Luckily, we had cleared out, so we only needed to pack the stall itself.

By the time we finished loading everything back into the truck and made our way home, evening was close. By now, even Cody's energy was waning. After packing up, I drove us home.

Later that evening, after dinner — with Earl's pie as the perfect dessert — the four of us gathered around a fire pit I improvised in my yard. The crackling flames flickered softly, casting a warm glow over the backyard as the night settled in. Cody sat next to me, his face lit up by the fire as he roasted marshmallows on a stick, his excitement from the day still buzzing inside him.

"This was the best day ever, Dad," Cody said,

holding his marshmallow over the fire. "I got to pet goats, win a dragon, and help at the stall. Can we come to the fair every year?"

I smiled, reaching over to grab my own stick. "Of course, bud. We can do it every year."

Daisy chuckled from across the fire, leaning back in her chair. "You were a big help today, Cody. You might have to start working full-time with me next year. Think you're up for it?"

Cody grinned, puffing out his chest. "Definitely! I can help sell stuff, and I'm really good at organizing the vegetables."

Caroline, sitting beside Daisy, smiled softly. "You're welcome anytime, Cody. You did an amazing job today." She popped a perfectly toasted marshmallow into her mouth, looking content.

Cody smiled, then was silent for a moment before looking up at me. "Dad," he said, his voice quieter now. "It… it feels nice here. I like it. I like spending time with you, Daisy, and Caroline." He paused, fidgeting with his stick. "It's different than Louisville. It's… just nicer."

Daisy reached over, tousling his hair. "We like

having you here too, Cody. It's nice to have family around."

Caroline nodded, her soft smile never leaving her face. "You fit right in, Cody. This place feels better with you here."

Cody smiled at that, but his eyelids were starting to droop, the day catching up with him. He yawned, trying to stay awake, but I could see he was fighting a losing battle. Eventually, he leaned against my side.

The girls and I kept talking for a while, winding down from the busy day as we shared what we had done and seen. Cody fell silent as he leaned against my side, and he was gone soon enough.

"He's out," Daisy said with a quiet chuckle.

I nodded, gently lifting Cody into my arms. "I'll take him inside. He's had a big day." I glanced over at Caroline and Daisy. "Be back in a bit."

Carrying Cody inside, I was struck by how peaceful he looked, completely at ease in my arms. I made my way to his room, laying him down on the bed and tucking him in under the covers. He stirred slightly but didn't wake up, his face soft and relaxed as he drifted deeper into sleep.

As I stood there, watching him for a moment, I felt so happy. Being a father was everything to me, and moments like this made it even more precious. Cody was my world, and providing him with a sense of stability, a place where he felt safe and loved, was the most important thing I could ever do.

I gently brushed his hair back, then quietly left the room, leaving the door cracked open just a bit as I made my way back to the fire pit where Daisy and Caroline were waiting.

When I returned to the porch, Daisy and Caroline were both sitting quietly, watching the last embers of the fire glow under the night sky. They looked up as I stepped outside, and Daisy patted the empty seat between them.

"Kid's out like a light, huh?" she asked with a grin.

I chuckled, sitting down between them. "Didn't take long. After the day he had, I'm surprised he made it through the marshmallows."

Caroline leaned her head back, letting out a soft sigh. "Today really was something. I can't remember the last time I enjoyed the fair that much."

Daisy nodded, stretching her legs out. "Yeah, feels different this year. Not just because of Cody, either." She glanced over at me. "It was just nice to do it together."

I nodded, letting my eyes drift around the yard. "Yeah, I feel that too. It was a family activity." I didn't mention, of course, that I missed Brooke a few times — sure, I had lots of fun and look back on a great day, but there were moments when I felt her absence. She belonged with us, and she should have been there.

Still, I was hopeful that she would be next year.

Caroline smiled, her hand resting on mine. "That's a good way to say it. A real family activity."

# Chapter 21

The next morning, the house was buzzing with a relaxed energy, but Cody was up early as usual, already full of ideas for the day. Over breakfast, he was watching Daisy closely, clearly eager to ask something as we enjoyed our morning coffee and began our day in a relaxed manner.

As he began fidgeting and rocking in his chair, I

shot him a wink. "Hey bud, you got something you want to ask Daisy?"

Daisy caught it and looked over. "Well, shoot, partner!" she said with a grin. "You know you can ask me anything!"

"Can I help on the farm today?" he blurted out, his voice brimming with excitement. "I want to see how you do everything, like picking vegetables and feeding the animals!"

I exchanged a look with Daisy. She understood — like I did — that taking on Cody for the day meant she would likely be doing less work than she would on a regular day of working. But the soft smile on her face said she wouldn't mind — in fact, I expected she would enjoy a day with Cody to get to know him a little bit better.

Daisy grinned at him, setting her coffee down. "You want to help out all day, huh? It's not just playing with animals; there's some hard work involved."

"I can do it!" Cody said confidently, turning to me. "Dad, is it okay if I go?"

I chuckled. "Well, if you're sure you're up for a full day of farm work and if Daisy's alright with having you tag along, then you've got my vote."

Daisy winked at Cody. "Alright then, sounds like I've got a farmhand for the day! But, you have to promise you'll follow directions, and I mean *all* of them, okay?" She waved her spoon at him and made a mock-serious face, narrowing her pretty blue eyes. "No lollygaggin'!"

Cody nodded so hard I thought his head might pop off. "Yes, I promise! I'll do whatever you say, Daisy!"

She raised an eyebrow at me with a smile. "Think he'll last the day?"

I laughed. "We'll see. Just don't let him talk your ear off out there."

"Oh, I can handle that," Daisy said, grinning. "But, Cody, if I tell you to take a break, you've gotta take a break. No trying to tough it out, deal?"

"Deal!" Cody said. "But I don't need breaks!"

Caroline smiled as she cleared her dishes. "Just wait until Daisy's got you hauling crates. You might change your mind."

Cody puffed up a bit, undeterred. "I can lift a lot, you know!"

"Well, yes you can," Daisy replied, giving him a playful pat on the shoulder. "We saw that at the fair yesterday, didn't we? Okay, finish up your breakfast, and we'll head out. There's a lot to get through."

Cody practically inhaled the rest of his food, then bolted up to his room to grab his little backpack. As soon as he was back downstairs, he hovered near the door, waiting like he was about to burst from the excitement.

"Hold your horses," Daisy said, laughing as she drained her coffee. "I haven't even got my boots on yet."

Caroline chuckled, watching the two of them with a smile. "I love how eager he is. And speaking of getting things done, I'm actually heading to the library for a bit. Got some work to catch up on."

I looked over at her, grabbing her plate. "Alright. You need a ride over there?"

She shook her head. "No, I'll walk. It's too nice a morning to pass up." She glanced over at Daisy and Cody. "We can head out together."

Daisy nodded. "Yup, yup! Sounds good." She

grinned at me. "And don't worry, Sean, I'll return him in one piece," she joked, giving me a wink. "Tired, but in one piece!"

Cody, still practically bouncing with energy, piped up. "Dad, I'm ready to go! Can we go now, Daisy?"

Daisy chuckled, reaching for her boots. "Alright, alright! Let me get my boots on, and we're out the door. Just make sure you're ready to work hard."

Caroline gave Cody a little wave as she put her own bag over her shoulder. "Have fun, Cody. We'll see who's more tired at the end of the day — me from the library or you from the farm."

"I'm not gonna get tired," Cody insisted, already heading toward the door as Daisy got her boots on.

"Alright, kiddo, let's hit the road," Daisy said, finally ready to go. She looked over at me and grinned. "Looks like you get a day off, Sean."

I smiled. "Well, a breather does sound nice. You don't let him wear you out, though."

Daisy laughed, holding the door open for Cody. "I think I can keep up. Come on, Cody, let's get you to work."

Caroline and I watched as Daisy, Cody, and Tink got ready, Cody talking a mile a minute about everything he planned to do on the farm. Daisy chuckled, giving him her full attention, nodding along as he listed his plans.

Caroline adjusted her own bag, smiling softly. "Alright, time for me to head out, too," she said, slinging the bag over her shoulder. "Lots to do at the library today."

I kissed all of them goodbye, then walked out onto the porch to wave them off, Tink running circles around them, eager to play with Cody. Daisy's farm was right next door, but Caroline was up for a slightly longer walk — I couldn't blame her, though; I loved the hike into town myself. It was a nice way to clear the head.

When they rounded the bend and were out of sight, I took a deep breath and relished in the silence for a moment. I loved having Cody around, but I also loved the quiet. Those two didn't go together, so it was nice to have a few hours.

With a smile, I headed back inside for another coffee to resume my easy start of the morning.

With the house finally quiet, I felt a calm settle over me that was rare these days. Only now did I realize how busy the past weeks had been. Now, with Daisy and Cody off to the farm and Caroline at the library, I found myself alone with my thoughts.

I lingered in the kitchen, coffee in hand, leaning against the counter as I took in the silence. As I slowly reflected on my life, I realized that I had been in Waycross for over five weeks, going on six. It felt like only a few days had passed, but so much had happened in that time.

The fast pace was something I hadn't expected to value so much before moving out here. But even though I had been busy, it was still a lot different from what it had been before. City life had been a constant buzz — a never-ending hum of traffic, noise, and annoyances. Even when things were "quiet," there was always some background noise in the city.

Here, the silence felt different. It was peaceful, unbroken by anything but the occasional birdcall outside or the soft rustling of leaves. In a way, it let me feel more grounded, connected to everything around me. I could just be still and not feel like I was supposed to be somewhere or doing something else. That meant that even though I was busy, the time I spent relaxing reinvigorated me that much more, leaving me with more energy.

But that kind of quiet also had a way of drawing up things I hadn't had time to think about. Since discovering the Sigils, life had taken on a different shape. They'd opened up possibilities I never would have imagined, and a kind of power I was still learning to wield responsibly. The Sigils didn't come with an instruction manual, but each one had its own unique energy, each one unlocking something new in the world around me — and within me.

Today, I had the chance to dive into some ideas I'd been holding back on for a while. Experimentation with magic was not something I wanted to do with the house full. But today, I'd have a chance…

I set my coffee down on the dining room table and let out a long breath, preparing to dive into something I'd been mulling over for a while. The

Portal Sigil combined with the Magnetic Sigil… It was an idea that had kept creeping into my mind ever since I'd mastered the basics of each on their own. I'd barely scratched the surface of what either one could do alone, let alone in tandem, but I was ready to make a start and see to what kind of place the Portal Sigil would take me if I were to combine it with the Magnetic Sigil.

First, I grabbed my backpack and pulled out some supplies from the drawer — rope, a pocketknife, some high-energy food, and an extra water bottle, just in case. Experimenting with Sigils was unpredictable at best, especially when I planned to test something as complex as opening a portal with the intent to go through it. I'd tested these Sigils individually, sure, but I knew that combining them would take things in a new direction altogether.

Having some gear at my side would give me a bit of insurance if things went south. As I gathered my things, I reflected on my experiences with the Portal Sigil so far. Every time I used it, I had felt the same distinct energy, like it was ready to bridge points that were separated by time and space. That wasn't the part that worried me.

The Magnetic Sigil, on the other hand, was still a bit of a mystery to me. I mean, it stood to reason that, when combined with the Wood Sigil, the Portal Sigil would open a portal to some kind of wooded plane of existence. And when I had combined the Portal Sigil with both the Wood and the Metal Sigils, it had led me to the village of Harrwick, which stood in the middle of an elemental plane of wood and metals.

Pretty predictable so far...

But what would a world look like that was magnetic in nature? To what kind of plane of existence would the Portal Sigil bring me if combined with the Magnetic Sigil? I wasn't a man of limited imagination, but I still struggled to come up with something plausible.

I would find out, though...

After one more sip of coffee, I gathered my Mossberg and made sure it was loaded, stuffing some extra shells — both double-aught and slugs — in my pockets. It was a trusty companion, and it was best to arrive prepared in this other world...

# Chapter 22 (Daisy)

As Daisy led Cody through the farmyard, she could see the joy radiating from the boy. They'd just been in the chicken coop, and the poor animals had gotten all jittery from the energy the boy brought.

Daisy had laughed inwardly at it. The enthusiasm and curiosity were just too cute.

Now, Cody was bouncing with every step, holding one of the eggs they'd just collected from the coop in both hands like it was a piece of rare treasure.

"Hold it gentle, now," she reminded him, smiling as he glanced up at her. "Eggs look strong, but they're tricky. Hold too tight, and you'll have scrambled eggs before you even crack 'em."

Cody grinned, lifting the egg carefully. "I got it! Look, it's not even a little cracked!" He trotted back to her, grinning ear to ear.

"You sure did get it just right," she said, ruffling his hair. "You ever helped with chickens before?"

He shook his head. "Nope! It's my first time, but I like it. The chickens are cute." He walked beside her toward the feed shed, where bags of grain and pellets were stacked in neat rows.

Daisy grabbed a small bucket and half-filled it with chicken feed before handing it to him. "Alright, Cody, this time you're the one feedin' 'em. Just watch out, they're gonna come runnin' the second they see that bucket. They're hungry little critters."

Cody's eyes grew wide with excitement, and he

took the bucket with both hands. "I'll be careful. Do I just pour it out, like this?"

She nodded, leaning against the fence. "That's it. Scatter it even, or else the big ones'll hog it all, and the little hens won't get any."

He focused, stepping carefully toward the chicken coop. "Here, chickens!" he called, shaking the feed just a little. Sure enough, they came clucking and flapping from the far side of the pen, eager for their breakfast. All of their grievances about Cody's chattiness disturbing the peace of their coop were instantly forgiven.

"Whoa! They're like little dinosaurs!" he exclaimed, laughing as the chickens pecked around his feet, jostling for the food. "Did you know chickens and dinosaurs are related?"

Daisy couldn't help but laugh. "No, I didn't, but I can see the resemblance. They get pretty wild when they're hungry."

When Cody had emptied the bucket, he ran back to her, still wide-eyed with excitement. "They ate all of it so fast! Do they ever get full?"

"Oh, eventually. But chickens will eat all day if you let 'em. They'd peck around in the dirt for snacks even after breakfast if they wanted to." She put a hand on his shoulder and nodded toward the garden patch. "Alright, ready for the next job? There's a little more to farming than feedin' chickens, you know?"

"Yeah! I want to help with everything!" he said, puffing his chest up a bit. "What's next?"

"Well, next we're gonna gather some veggies. But remember — some plants are strong, and some are soft, so you gotta be careful about where and how you pick 'em."

Cody looked at her with focused eyes. "I can do that. Let's go!"

They moved over to the vegetable patch, where Daisy handed him a small basket. She crouched down by a row of tomatoes, gesturing for him to do the same.

"Alright, tomatoes first," she said, gently picking one from the vine to show him. "See how I hold it? And you only pick the ones that are all red. The green ones ain't ready yet."

Cody inspected her technique, then carefully plucked a ripe tomato off the vine and held it up proudly. "Like that?"

"Exactly like that," she said, giving him an approving nod. "We're makin' a real farmer outta you."

As he filled his basket, he started asking her questions, the kind of curious questions that seemed never-ending but sweet. "Do you have to water the plants every day? How do you know when the plants are ready to pick? And do the tomatoes taste different than the ones from the store?"

Daisy answered each question, glad for his curiosity. "Yep, we water 'em most days, especially when it's hot. You can tell when they're ripe by their color and feel. And, yep, they taste better than store-bought tomatoes because they're fresh."

He nodded seriously, taking in each answer like it was a secret trick. "That makes sense. They're like… happier plants, then?"

She chuckled, nodding. "You could say that. They're well taken care of, just like anything that grows better when it's loved. And it's real nice to grow your own food too. It's hard work, but it'll leave you feeling a little… well, *more free*. More independent if that makes sense. Like you can take care of yourself and your own."

He seemed to mull over her words for a moment before giving a nod. "I think I understand. Like brushing your own teeth and putting on your own clothes."

Daisy clucked her tongue and made a gun with her thumb and index finger at him as she winked. "Exactly, mister."

He grinned, then looked down at his basket and back up at her. "Do you like working here every day? With all the animals and plants?"

Daisy smiled, a warmth blooming in her chest. "I do, Cody. It's a lot of hard work, but it's good work. You know, I grew up here, and I can't picture myself doin' anything else. Makes me feel like I'm taking care of something bigger than myself."

"That's cool," he said, his eyes wide. "I'd love to live on a farm someday."

"Well, you can come work with me any time you like," she replied, ruffling his hair. "You're a real natural at this. And besides, I like having a helper around. Makes the work feel a little more fun."

They moved on to gathering the carrots, and as Cody carefully pulled each one out of the ground, Daisy found herself watching him with a fondness that was more than just because he was Sean's kid. Cody was so genuine, so eager to help and learn. The way he smiled up at her every time he did something right made her heart ache a little, in a good way.

Daisy had always enjoyed kids, but with Cody, it was different. Spending this day with him made her wonder what it would be like to have a child of her own one day — someone to share this place with, to teach and care for, someone who could carry on the farm and the love she poured into it.

When they moved over to check on the sheep in the pasture, Cody spotted one of the lambs grazing nearby. "Can I pet it?" he asked, looking up at her with hopeful eyes.

Daisy grinned. "You sure can. They're friendly, just go slow so you don't spook 'em. Come from where they see you, too, not from behind."

Cody headed over carefully and in accordance with her instructions. The lamb didn't bolt, although it shot him a suspicious look. Then, Cody crouched down and reached out, gently stroking the lamb's soft wool. "It's so fluffy!" he said, laughing. "Do you shear them like the guy said at the fair?"

"That's right," Daisy said, crouching beside him. "In the summer, we shear 'em to keep 'em cool, and we turn the wool into yarn or blankets. It's just like a haircut, and they're all the better for it."

"You do that yourself?"

She chuckled and shook her head. "No, I sell the wool. I ain't much for knittin'. Besides, the farm keeps me busy enough as it is. I'm afraid I ain't got the time for much else."

Cody glanced over at her. "You'll have more time when I come help you! Would you like to learn how to knit then?"

Her heart warmed at his question. "I'd love that, Cody. You'd make a great farmhand." She paused, realizing just how much she meant it. She could see herself sharing this life with him — and with Sean, too. The idea of building something together here, a family, filled her with a warmth she hadn't felt before.

And maybe… just maybe… there could be more kids. She felt deep down that she would love that — a lot.

They spent the rest of the morning working side by side, checking on the animals and finishing harvesting everything that was ready. By the time they'd finished, Cody was carrying a basket full of carrots, tomatoes, and green beans. He looked up at her with a huge smile, his cheeks smudged with a little dirt.

"Did I do a good job, Daisy?" he asked, his voice filled with pride.

She smiled, reaching out to brush some of the dirt off his cheek. "You did more than a good job, partner. I think you could take the place over one day!"

# Chapter 23

With the house quiet and all my gear ready, it was time to begin. I sat in the middle of the living room, grounding myself with a few deep breaths, focusing inward.

I could sense my Spirit Grimoire, that intangible space within me where the Sigils had taken root since they'd first been absorbed after Greida expanded my powers. The Spirit Grimoire unfolded before me, revealing itself, and its familiar energy coursed through me, powerful but contained, like a door waiting to be unlocked.

This time, though, I wasn't opening a path to a place I'd been before. I arranged the Portal Sigil and the Magnetic Sigil together in the second slot, leaving the Wood and Metal Sigils in the first slot. Then, with everything so arranged, I called upon my magic.

The shift came naturally, almost like slipping on a glove that fit just right. The energy hummed in my veins, familiar and steady. Layering the Magnetic Sigil on top of the Portal Sigil added a subtle, thrumming vibration that traveled up my arm and settled deep in my chest. The two powers meshed, creating a path that opened at my command.

The portal shimmered into existence. It was an oval-shaped opening of swirling energies, shining with a blue glow, a little taller than I was myself.

This was it.

I rose and studied the portal. The surface of the portals I could conjure revealed a little insight into what was on the other side — in the case of the portal to Harrwick, I had seen trees and shining rocks that turned out to be ore deposits on the other side. Now, I just saw a blue-gray glow.

Maybe it was different this time... Or maybe this was just what a world of magnetism looked like.

Curiosity bubbled inside me. I wanted to see what it was like.

My pack and shotgun slung, I stepped toward the portal. I took a deep breath, then stepped through.

At once, the unmistakable pull of gravity cut out, replaced by an odd, floating sensation. I was weightless.

When I looked around, I found myself in an endless expanse of shimmering gray and blue, surrounded by fields of raw magnetic energy. There were no trees, no sky, no ground. Just layers upon layers of shimmering, pulsing currents stretching out in every direction, like rivers of invisible force flowing in patterns that were as fluid as they were alien. Still, there was something that created a kind of mist or haziness, because my sight did not expand endlessly in all directions, eventually turning hazy.

I gazed in wonder as the entire realm buzzed with energy. I could feel some kind of crackling power in the air, and every inch of my skin prickled at the sensation. It affected the flow of mana as well; it was no longer calm or rhythmic. Instead, it was charged, fast-moving, almost electric. It gave me the sense that I was part of the current, one with the forces that pulsed and twisted in the space around me.

As I floated in the middle of it all, I willed myself forward. Nothing happened, and I just kept on floating in front of the portal.

Then, I had an idea. I quickly arranged the Magnetic Sigil alone in a Spirit Grimoire slot, then called upon its energy, and sure enough, I could navigate using it. There was no physical effort, and I barely expended mana, but I could feel my power aligning with the magnetic fields, allowing me to glide forward with a slight push from within.

The sensation was strange and exhilarating — like swimming in a powerful river without being swept away. I could change direction on a dime, hover, slow down, or speed up with just a nudge of my will, and each adjustment felt like tuning into a different frequency, drawing on the Magnetic Sigil's power to manipulate the flow of the magnetic fields that suffused this realm of existence.

It was almost like flying, and I found myself grinning broadly at the sensation.

I held up my hand, and with a slight pull on the Sigil, one of the streams of energy reacted, bending toward me. It felt like a gentle tug against the core of my chest, pulling something closer without actually moving. The energy stream swirled and twisted as if aware of me, but it wasn't sentient. It was just responding to my manipulation, following my intentions in a way that was natural, instinctual.

My mana pulsed in time with the magnetic flow, and I realized that by syncing with the rhythm of the fields around me, I could amplify the power of the Sigil. The more I synced my energy to the environment, the more influence I could exert. I experimented a bit, drawing different streams closer to me, bending and twisting them in ways that made the currents dance around my hands and body. It was like holding a magnet near iron filings — they snapped into place, pulled by the force but never touching me directly.

In this world, magnetism wasn't a *secondary* force. It was the *only* native force, pure and raw, and I was part of it. With a flick of my hand, I could pull one current into another, creating an intricate web of fields that crisscrossed around me, responding to the smallest adjustments in my mana flow. I suspected I could launch an object so hard using these currents that it would never stop moving.

As I floated there, I began to wonder about the possibilities. If I could control the magnetic forces in this world so fluidly, what about back home? How could I use this experience to enhance what I could do in my own plane? The control I felt here was incredible, and I had the feeling that I was only scratching the surface. It was an untapped power, something that could make me a different kind of threat, an entirely new force on its own.

Curious to learn more, I ventured deeper into the plane, drawn forward by the sheer power that radiated through this world. The currents around me pulsed with energy, intensifying the deeper I went.

It wasn't long before I noticed how the magnetic forces were reacting to the metal I'd brought along. The shotgun strapped to my back began to vibrate slightly, responding to the invisible pull of the magnetic fields. My pack felt heavier, weighed down by the metal in my supplies. Every few minutes, I'd sense an unseen tug as something shifted in response to the field's invisible influence.

The strength of the pull was manageable, though — enough to keep me alert, but not enough to disrupt my concentration. I moved forward, adjusting the flow of my mana through the Magnetic Sigil, letting it align and amplify my control over my direction. Each movement felt natural, instinctive, like I was part of this world rather than just a visitor passing through.

But as I pushed deeper, something shifted. The currents became erratic, intensifying as though the entire plane was suddenly coming alive with a force I hadn't anticipated. I could feel the field's pull growing stronger, almost as if something was brewing.

Then, the energy currents in front of me began to twist together, pulling and knotting themselves into denser, more turbulent waves. I realized with a surge of clarity that these were no ordinary disturbances — they were magnetic storms forming, coalescing in the fields. They crackled with energy, pulling at the metal objects in my pack with an intensity that bordered on alarming.

I focused, channeling a surge of mana through the Magnetic Sigil, trying to steady myself against the sudden pull. My shotgun rattled in its sling, vibrating with an unsettling force. Even the smallest metal items — the keys in my pocket, the metal parts of my pack, the buckle of my belt — now felt like they were pulling at me.

I regained control, but if this kept intensifying, I might lose my grip.

I realized it was time to get out of here. I focused my energy, tuning into the path I'd come down, feeling out the currents that would lead me to the portal. Navigating with the Sigil was now much harder; the storms fought me with every movement, trying to drag me back, to pull me deeper into the plane's chaotic depths. I wrestled with the Magnetic Sigil's power, willing it to guide me, using every bit of my focus to maintain my course.

Finally, I spotted the faint glow of the portal I'd opened, still stable in the shifting currents of the realm. With one final push, I propelled myself forward, feeling the magnetic forces trying to pull me back even as I closed the distance to the portal. As I neared it, the current surged, but I thrust myself through the portal, leaving the magnetic plane behind.

The moment I crossed back into my living room, gravity returned, and I stumbled forward, feeling the magnetic tension dissolve instantly.

After stepping back into my living room, I shut the portal to the magnetic realm with a wave of energy. The magnetic fields and strange floating had been intense, but they'd given me a good sense of what was possible — and what was too risky.

But I was only starting to explore the potential here.

This next trial would combine the Metal Sigil and the Magnetic Sigil with the Portal Sigil. The thought had been hanging in the back of my mind since I first considered the Magnetic Sigil. What kind of world would that open a gate to?

I took a brief break, eating a little and having another cup of coffee in my kitchen. When I felt recovered, I went into the living room for the next round of experiments.

I pulled in my focus, tuning back into the Spirit Grimoire. Within seconds, the arrangement of the three Sigils came together, aligning smoothly in the intangible space of my Spirit Grimoire. A portal shimmered open in front of me, taller than I'd expected, the surface giving off a muted metallic sheen with hints of dark gray. It was odd but steady — so far, so good. With a quick adjustment of the gear on my shoulder, I stepped forward.

Crossing into the portal was almost seamless. One second, I was in my living room; the next, I was… here. The sensation was strange — less like stepping and more like moving through some dense but invisible curtain that held me for a brief second, only to release me on the other side.

When I opened my eyes fully, I realized I was standing in what seemed like an endless metallic landscape. At first, it looked almost like a field of jagged steel stretching out into the horizon, glinting with a sheen of gray-blue. But within seconds, I picked up the movement around me: shards of metal floated and twisted through the air, constantly shifting in erratic patterns.

The larger pieces drifted slowly, like they were caught in their own gravitational pull. Smaller, sharper bits moved faster, shooting across the metallic plane like bullets. I raised a hand instinctively to protect myself as a piece zipped past, the jagged shard close enough to feel the buzz of its magnetic pull.

This wasn't the safest of places.

I focused at once on the Magnetic Sigil, placing it alone in a slot, and tried to channel the Magnetic Sigil's energy to keep everything under control, but the sheer scale of what was pulling at me was overwhelming. Even when I focused, there were so many moving fragments that keeping them all in check seemed impossible.

Inching forward, I tried to test my control over the space. A small pulse of energy shifted the direction of a few shards, but the effect was limited, like trying to move a tide with a spoon. This place was all raw force, a vast magnetic charge that didn't care whether I controlled it or not.

Another shard came soaring, and I just managed to deflect it with a magnetic wave. Then, I focused on a smaller shard drifting nearby, but it was difficult to control them individually, as I controlled the waves and not the objects. My efforts pulled a bunch of shards to gather into a wave of deadly metal. With panic building in my stomach, I shot that wave of deadly projectiles in the opposite direction.

This wasn't a safe place *at all*…

The fields around me shifted abruptly. Without warning, a massive shard flew toward me, forcing me to jerk back. The portal shimmered a few steps behind me, still stable, but already, smaller shards were flying dangerously close to it. The energy seemed to be affecting the portal.

It was time to leave — while I still could.

I made a split-second decision. Turning sharply, I focused all my energy on moving back to the portal. For a moment, the force of the fields surged again, tugging at my pack, my metal gear, and everything I carried with me. The path back was harder, shards shooting across my line of sight, some of them snapping close enough to send up a spray of metallic sparks as they collided with one another.

My chest tightened as I kept navigating onward, but the pull was a lot stronger than I'd anticipated. It took a significant surge of mana to keep moving through the chaos, aligning my mana with the Sigils just enough to propel myself forward, using everything I had left to make it out. With a final burst, I launched myself toward the portal, crossing the threshold just as another shard shot past, skimming close enough to feel the vibration.

The moment I was through, I dropped my connection to the Sigils, watching as the portal closed in on itself, sealing away that chaotic realm.

# Chapter 24

When I stepped back into my living room, I felt the residual energy from the two planes humming through me like a faint, charged pulse that hadn't quite worn off. Closing the portal, I let the magic ebb away, grounding myself in reality for a moment and getting used to feeling... well, *normal*.

Once I had calmed down a little, I reflected on the strange experience.

Two planes, both unlike anything I'd ever seen — and neither meant to support life as I knew it. The first had been calm, like floating in a magnetic current, and I had experienced control there. The second, though... The chaos of those metallic shards and the raw power they carried was something I wouldn't soon forget.

Both worlds were stark and unfeeling, places of pure energy and matter, following their own violent rules. Even as I stood back in the safety of my own space, I felt a lingering edge of that strange, untamed force inside me, pulsing in tune with my Sigils.

I spent the rest of the afternoon relaxing and absorbing the details of those planes in my mind, letting them sink in and trying to make sense of the possibilities. The Sigils had opened these worlds to me, shown me new facets of energy, and hinted at powers I could bring back, yet not without risk. It was like scratching the surface of something vast and untamable. I wondered how far I could go, how much I could take in before the power might try to push back.

A few hours later, I heard voices outside, and then the sound of Cody's laughter broke the stillness, bringing me back to the present.

I looked out to see Daisy and Cody making their way up from the farm, arms loaded with what looked like fresh-picked carrots and a few tomatoes. Cody was chatting away as Tink ran alongside them, tail wagging.

When they reached the porch, Cody waved excitedly, holding up a small bundle of carrots. "Look, Dad! I picked these all by myself!"

"Nicely done, bud," I said, opening the door. "Did you leave any for Daisy, or did you clean out the whole field?"

Cody laughed. "There's plenty left! But Daisy said I did a good job. Right, Daisy?"

Daisy grinned, handing me the extra vegetables. "He did great, Sean. He might even be a better farmhand than you," she teased, nudging Cody playfully.

As they unloaded, I noticed Caroline coming down the path, a few books under her arm, smiling as she watched the scene unfold. She joined us on the porch, setting her things down on the bench. "Looks like you two had a busy day," she said, ruffling Cody's hair as he ran off to play with Tink.

With Cody occupied, I turned to the women. "Actually, I had a pretty interesting day myself," I began, nodding to the kitchen where we could talk privately.

Curious, Daisy and Caroline followed me inside, and we gathered around the kitchen table. Once we were settled, I leaned back, letting out a breath as I shared my story of the experiments. "I tried using the Portal Sigil today," I began, "combining it with the Magnetic Sigil first, then with the Metal Sigil as well."

Their eyes widened with interest, and Caroline leaned in. "Did it work? Where did you end up?"

"The first world was strange. Floating currents of magnetic force — felt like I was in the middle of an invisible storm, only instead of being blown around, I could control my direction using the Magnetic Sigil." I paused, remembering the currents. "It was intense, but it was… peaceful, in a way. No ground, no sky. Just currents moving in every direction."

Daisy's brow furrowed. "No life at all?"

I shook my head. "Nothing. Just the magnetic fields. It felt… isolated, like the plane didn't even register me. I was just moving through it."

Caroline considered that, her eyes thoughtful. "And the second plane?"

I sighed, leaning forward. "A lot more dangerous. I added the Metal Sigil to the combination, and I ended up in a plane filled with shards of metal. They were floating, like in the first plane, but everything was faster, more chaotic. The magnetic pull was erratic, and the shards were moving on their own, almost like they had a life of their own."

Daisy gave a low whistle. "Sounds like a place you'd want to avoid."

I chuckled. "Exactly. There was too much pull, too many moving parts. I didn't stick around long enough to test my luck. I'm pretty sure that if I stuck around, some of those shards would've seriously hurt me."

Caroline nodded slowly. "It's strange, isn't it? The Sigils open up these places, and they seem almost... made to keep life out."

I leaned back, considering her words. "It felt that way. Like they're worlds built on forces we can't fully control. Pure energy. There's a lot of potential there, a lot of power. But they're not places where anyone could survive for long."

We fell into silence, the weight of the possibilities settling over us. Finally, Daisy broke the quiet with a grin, patting my shoulder. "Well, we're glad you made it back in one piece. Don't go getting yourself lost in some shard-filled wasteland, alright?"

I laughed. "Don't worry. I've got no plans to set up camp in a place like that."

After our brief conversation in private, we got to preparing dinner. Cody was reading comics in the living room while the girls and I prepared the food using the fresh produce that Daisy and Cody had brought.

Dinner was a lively affair, with Cody eager to talk about his day. Between bites, he described every little detail of helping Daisy on the farm, right down to the way the chickens flapped and clucked whenever he fed them. He even mimicked

Daisy's "serious farmer face," making her laugh so hard she nearly dropped her fork.

"Hold it right there, mister," Daisy teased him. "A serious farmer face?"

Cody laughed, covering his mouth with his hand. "You did! You looked all serious when you told me not to mess around with the feed," he said, attempting her best stern look.

"Well, not sure if I can let that slide, mister. Still, serious farmer face or not, you did a great job," she said, winking at him.

Cody grinned proudly, but then he paused, glancing down at his plate. He seemed to lose a bit of his enthusiasm as he pushed his food around. I waited, sensing something was on his mind, and finally, he looked up at me with a frown.

"Dad," he said quietly, "do I really have to go back to Louisville tomorrow?"

The question hung in the air for a moment, and I could see the disappointment in his eyes. Cody loved it here — he'd gotten comfortable, found a sense of belonging with everyone around the table. I reached over, giving his shoulder a comforting squeeze.

"I know we had fun, bud," I said softly. "We all love having you here, too."

Caroline leaned in, smiling gently. "And guess what? We're all coming with you tomorrow, remember?"

"Yeah, we're goin' on a little road trip together," Daisy added, her tone light, though there was a hint of seriousness in her eyes. "We'll make sure you get home nice and safely."

Cody's eyes lit up a little. "Really? All of you?"

I smiled at his enthusiasm. I had asked the girls to come along, because I wanted them to get closer to Brooke. Seeing her in her own home might help. Besides, it would make the parting a little easier on Cody, and it would also give Brooke and me a chance to talk while Daisy and Caroline watched Cody.

"That's right," Caroline said, taking his hand in hers. "We're not about to let you and your dad have all the fun on the road."

Cody perked up a little at that, but his smile wavered. "It's just... different here. I like it better. There's more to do, and... well, it's just nicer."

Daisy gave him an encouraging nod. "Hey,

nothing wrong with that. But we're not going anywhere, and neither is Waycross. This place will be waiting for you next time you come back."

He considered her words, then sighed, his shoulders slumping a bit. "But what about Tink? I don't want her to miss me, either."

"She'll miss you, sure," Daisy said, "but she'll remember you every time you come back. And besides, we'll make sure she's happy. You think Tink would ever forget her best buddy?"

Cody shook his head, a small smile starting to creep back. "No, I guess not." He glanced around the table, his eyes settling on Caroline. "Do you think Mom'll come visit again, too?"

Caroline's smile softened, and she met his gaze with understanding. "I think she will. Maybe not tomorrow or next week, but she'll come around. She's got a lot on her plate, Cody, but she knows you're having a good time here. That's important to her."

Cody seemed to take that in, and he nodded, though I could see the hope in his eyes. "I hope she does. I wish she'd come live here. Then we could all live here."

He wasn't the only one who wanted that. I shot him a warm smile.

Daisy patted his shoulder. "I'll tell you what, next time you're here, we'll have another project for you on the farm. There's always work to do. Think you can handle it?"

Cody grinned, looking up at her with that gleam in his eye. "Oh yeah! I can be a real farmhand. I'll feed the chickens, pick the veggies, and help with all the hard stuff!"

I chuckled, ruffling his hair. "You'll be running the place if you're not careful."

Cody laughed, and the rest of us joined in. The dinner continued with more talk of Cody's farm adventures, each of us pitching in with ideas for his "next farm job" until Cody's face brightened, and his worries seemed to melt away.

As we cleared the table, he looked around at all of us, his earlier disappointment gone. "So… what time are we leaving tomorrow?"

I glanced at Daisy and Caroline, and they both nodded, as if reading my thoughts. "Whenever we're all ready," I said, clapping Cody on the back. "No rush. We'll take our time and make a day of it."

Cody's smile returned, wide and bright.

After dinner, we played games until Cody practically keeled over. He fought his tiredness tooth and nail, not wanting the day to end, but he had to surrender at last. I brought him to bed, then spent the rest of the evening with my women. Truth was, there hung a bit of a gloom over all of us, knowing that Cody would go back to Louisville tomorrow. We all enjoyed the energy he brought and his presence.

But it would also give me the chance to talk to Brooke and see her in her natural environment. And I had a feeling she wasn't doing as well as she made it out she was doing...

# Chapter 25

After breakfast, Cody got to fidgeting, packing and unpacking his backpack while Tink trotted after him. He'd fill the bag up, then reconsider, pulling things out and rearranging them with an intense focus. Every few minutes, he'd look over his shoulder toward the kitchen, where Daisy and Caroline were finishing up a batch of sandwiches and snacks for the road.

I leaned against the doorframe, watching him go through his routine. The kid looked like he was getting ready for an expedition instead of a simple trip home. He even had his little flashlight in there, the one I'd bought him for our hikes.

"You sure you're gonna need that flashlight, bud?" I asked with a soft smile.

Cody turned around, putting it down. "I guess not," he muttered. "I just wanna take some stuff so I can think about this place." He looked around the room, his gaze settling on Tink. "I just… I'll miss it."

Before I could answer, Daisy walked over, wiping her hands on a towel. She crouched down to his level, putting a hand on his shoulder. "Listen, partner, we'll be right here waiting for you when you come back. You and Tink can keep going on your hikes. It's just a short goodbye, okay?"

I smiled, appreciating the sweet effort. Cody nodded, but he still looked a little unsure. "It's just… what if it's a long time before I come back?"

I knelt down beside him. "Well, we'll do

everything we can to make sure you don't have to wait long. You had a good time this trip, didn't you?"

"Yeah!" Cody said, his face lighting up. "The best time! I got to help on the farm, play with Tink, and hang out with you, Dad." He paused. "And Daisy and Caroline, too." He shot them a shy smile.

"Well, we enjoyed it, too," Daisy said, and Caroline nodded her agreement. "We're looking forward to seeing you again," Caroline added.

I smiled and placed my hand on his shoulder. "Come on, bud," I said. "Everything's packed. Let's head over to the truck."

As we moved to load the truck, Cody's energy dipped a little. He kept glancing around the house and looking back at Tink, who'd been following him everywhere since he woke up. She seemed to know something was going on, staying close by, her tail low but wagging.

When he crouched down beside her, Tink flopped down on her belly, looking up at him with those big, knowing eyes.

"I'll miss you, Tink," Cody whispered,

scratching behind her ears. "But I'll be back soon. You just gotta wait for me, okay?"

Daisy leaned in, her voice gentle. "You know, Cody, Tink'll remember you every time you come back. She's good at that. And when you're here, you two are like a little team."

Cody looked up at her, nodding slowly. "I know. But what if she's lonely?"

Caroline joined us, placing a hand on his shoulder. "She'll have us, too. We'll make sure she's happy, and she'll be just as excited to see you when you come back."

After Cody said his last goodbyes to Tink, we finished loading the truck. The girls climbed into the back of the cab, while Cody slid into the front seat with me, his face brightening again as we pulled out onto the road.

Daisy leaned forward from the backseat, giving him a nudge. "You know, Cody, we're all heading to Louisville together today. This isn't goodbye yet. We're going to keep you company the whole way back. Ain't that great!?"

Caroline nodded in agreement. "That's right. It's not just a ride. We're making this a road trip! It's been ages since I've been out of state!"

Cody perked up, glancing over at me. "So... it's like a big adventure?"

"Exactly," I said with a grin. "We're all going together, and we've got enough snacks to last us through any adventure we might find."

Cody laughed, looking a little more at ease. "Then... let's do the license plate game! And the animal game! And all the games!"

"Oh boy," Daisy chuckled. "Alright, you start us off. But you better be ready to keep score!"

We drove down the winding country roads, playing game after game, and every time we passed a field, Cody would call out if he spotted a new animal. We hit the main road an hour later, and by then, he'd already racked up points spotting cows, sheep, and a stray deer that darted across the road up ahead.

Caroline leaned forward, pointing out the window. "Alright, Cody, see that? It's a black pickup. Five points if you can tell me what brand it is."

He squinted, then grinned. "It's a Ford! Just like Dad's! And it's got a hay bale in the back. Does that count for extra?"

Caroline laughed, nudging him. "I'll allow it. Extra points for the hay."

Daisy pulled a little packet of snacks out of the bag. "Alright, Cody, time to refuel. Think you can handle a cookie?"

Cody's eyes lit up as he took the cookie, munching on it thoughtfully as we kept driving. But after a while, he grew quiet again, and I could tell he was thinking about the day ahead.

As we continued down the road toward Louisville, I knew it'd be tough for him, and I truly hoped there would come a time when we would no longer need to do this.

Soon enough, Cody dozed off, and the car grew quieter. He was bundled in his seat, his head resting against the window, his breathing deep and even.

Daisy, watching Cody, turned her gaze to me and leaned forward. "You think Brooke's gonna be alright with us all droppin' in like this? I know we all agreed to go along, but it's gotta be a lot on her end too."

Caroline, seated beside her, nodded. "Yeah, it's

probably not the easiest situation. We all know how work's got her stretched thin. She looked tired when we saw her last."

I kept my eyes on the road, mulling over their words. They weren't wrong; Brooke had looked tired. Less so than before, but I knew she was still struggling. She'd put on a brave face, but she hadn't been able to hide those dark circles under her eyes or the tension in her shoulders.

"Yeah, I think you're both right." I shrugged. "I don't know, it feels a little like an intervention. This job is killing her."

Daisy's brow furrowed. "You ever think she might actually decide to make that career change?"

I nodded, though I wasn't sure what Brooke was ready for. "I hope so. We talked about it before, but... I can't push her. It has to be her choice. She's been thinking about stepping away from her job, finding something that'd give her a better work-life balance. Maybe spend more time with Cody. But it's easier said than done."

Caroline gave a gentle nod. "If she could work closer to Waycross, maybe even move out here eventually… It'd take a lot of stress off, don't you think? She'd be closer to all of us, and we'd be more than willing to help her."

"Yeah," I agreed. "And I'd love for Cody to be closer. This back-and-forth can't be easy on him, either. He wants to be with her, with us — he's kind of caught in the middle."

Daisy's voice softened. "I can't imagine it's easy for Brooke, either. She's gotta feel torn between giving Cody everything and staying on top of her own life."

I sighed, gripping the steering wheel a little tighter. "That's just it. Brooke always wants the best for him, but the demands from her job? They make it impossible to give him all her time. I keep hoping she'll decide that something's gotta give."

Caroline glanced at Cody, then back at me. "Maybe seeing him with us here will help. Show her it doesn't have to be just her and Cody against the world. She's got support, family… And if we can get her to visit more, maybe that can make a difference, too."

I nodded. "That's what I'm hoping, too. Maybe it's a big ask, but I think it'd be the best thing for Cody and for her. We just need to show her that there's a way forward here if she wants it."

"So, that's why we're all goin'?" Daisy asked.

"Yeah," I said. "She needs to feel like she's on the inside — like she belongs with us. Because I think that she does."

"I think so, too," Caroline said without hesitation, and Daisy nodded before she placed a comforting hand on my shoulder from behind. "Well, we'll be there for whatever she decides. You've got the patience and the vision for what Cody needs, Sean. She's lucky to have someone like you backing her up."

I smiled, grateful for their support. We all fell quiet, and I glanced over at Cody, fast asleep. Together we'd make sure he got what he needed, even if the road to get there wasn't simple.

# Chapter 26

We broke through the bustle of Louisville, and I drove us straight to our destination. When we pulled up in front of Brooke's apartment building, Cody woke up, blinking groggily before his eyes lit up, realizing where we were.

I was happy to see him smile. Despite everything, he had obviously missed Brooke a lot, and he was out of the truck in an instant, already heading for the door with his backpack bouncing on his shoulders.

"Hold up!" I said with a smile. "Wait for us."

We all left the truck, and Cody rang the bell. A moment later, Brooke buzzed us in, and we all went into the sterile lobby of her overpriced and overstyled apartment building.

"Yuck," Daisy muttered as she stared at some shapeless thing that was supposed to be art.

Caroline chuckled. "Can't say I'm a fan either."

I grinned as I kept my hand on Cody's shoulder while he led us toward the elevators. We passed a man in an expensive suit giving us a snooty look, and a woman wearing too much jewelry with a smile that looked like it was drug-induced.

As we piled into the elevator, Cody chattered away, his sleepiness quickly fading into excitement. He tugged on my sleeve, practically bouncing. "Dad, do you think Mom will want to see all the stuff I did at the farm?"

"She'll want to hear every story," I said, ruffling his hair. "And you've got plenty to tell her."

When the elevator doors opened on Brooke's

floor, Cody shot ahead, running to knock on her door. We followed, and I glanced at Daisy and Caroline, both of them looking calm but quietly aware that this wasn't just an average drop-off.

A moment later, the door opened, and Brooke stood there.

She was still beautiful — something about that black hair and those sparkling blue eyes. But the lines in her face told of tension, and the shadows under her eyes told of lack of sleep. She was looking worse than before, and I was immediately convinced that the work problem had not been resolved.

*At all.*

Her tired expression softened as she saw Cody. She pulled him into a hug right away, closing her eyes as he babbled excitedly about his trip.

"Oh, baby," she said, pulling him close. "I missed you so much."

"Mom, I got to feed chickens and pick vegetables!" Cody blurted, his excitement spilling over. "Daisy showed me how to tell if tomatoes are ripe, and Caroline let me try her pies! And I helped Dad with… everything!"

Brooke managed a smile, but she had to pull it from deep, and I could see how thin her patience was stretched. She looked up, noticing the three of us with Cody, and for a second, I saw the hint of surprise on her face, followed by a flash of unease.

"Hey," she said softly, her voice carrying a faint edge. "All of you came?"

I nodded, giving her a reassuring smile. "Yeah, figured we could all come. It's a bit of a drive, so we thought we'd stick together. Make it into a little road trip."

She narrowed her eyes for a moment, understanding more was going on, but that this wasn't the time to address it. She gave a small nod before motioning us inside. "Right. Come in."

Brooke's apartment was usually clean and organized, but now, stacks of papers covered the dining table, and dishes sat piled in the sink. The signs of her workload, the stress weighing on her, were everywhere, down to the rumpled throw blanket on the couch and the untouched laundry basket in the corner. Somehow, a sterile, modern place like this looked even worse when it was a little cluttered like a normal house.

Daisy and Caroline stepped in, taking in the scene without a word, but I caught the worry in Caroline's eyes. Brooke noticed this too, and quickly began clearing space on the table.

"Sorry, it's... been a busy week," she said, her voice strained as she moved some folders aside. "Things have been a little... overwhelming." She gave a nervous laugh. "If I knew you'd all be coming, I would've cleaned up a little!"

Cody, oblivious to the tension, dropped his backpack by the couch and started rummaging through it. "Mom! I brought you some of the vegetables we picked!" He pulled out a small bag of tomatoes, holding them up like they were gold.

Brooke took the bag from him, managing a small, grateful smile as she knelt to his level. "Thank you, Cody. These look amazing." She glanced up at me and the girls. "You must have had quite the adventure with him."

"He was great," Daisy said, her tone light but warm. "He's got a real knack for it, Brooke. You've got yourself a little farmer."

Brooke chuckled, brushing back a strand of raven hair, but I could tell it took effort for her to stay focused. Her eyes darted to the pile of work on the table, and her shoulders tensed. I could see the weight of it all bearing down on her, the silent pressure that never quite seemed to let up.

"Mom?" Cody asked, tugging on her hand. "Can Daisy and Caroline and Dad stay for the day? Maybe until dinner? Like all of us? I can tell you about everything."

She looked at him, then at me and the girls.

I shrugged and smiled. "We'd love to," I said. "And it looks like you could need the help around here."

"Yup, yup," Daisy agreed. "Sounds like fun!"

"Yeah, sounds great!" Caroline chimed in.

Brooke smiled, and for a moment, her expression softened again as she smiled at Cody. "Well, if they're up for it, then of course, sweetheart. They can stay the day."

I caught her eye as she stood, and in that brief exchange, I knew she felt the strain as much as I could see it. This needed to change.

"Cody," I said. "Why don't you watch some TV in mom's bedroom so we can catch up?"

He needed little more encouragement. With a

broad grin, he hopped to his feet and ran over to Brooke's bedroom to watch some television.

"Now," I told Brooke, "let's make some coffee. And let's talk."

She sighed and nodded. "Yeah... let's talk."

After Cody was settled in the bedroom, Daisy and Caroline helped Brooke make coffee, and we all sat down in the cluttered living room. As she wrapped her hands around her cup, Brooke took a long breath, glancing at each of us before finally focusing on her coffee.

"I'm going to be honest, Brooke," I said, breaking the silence. "You always look good..." She sputtered a laugh, probably her first in days. "But today," I continued, "you're pretty far on the 'tired and stressed out' end of the spectrum of good-looking."

Daisy and Caroline shot her sympathetic looks, smiling at my effort to lighten the mood a little.

"So, what's going on?" I asked. "We're friends here. Family. Don't hold back."

She took a deep breath, then shook her head. "Honestly, I don't know where to start," she said with a sigh, her voice low. "It's just… it's been one of those weeks, or maybe one of those months."

Daisy exchanged a quick look with Caroline, but neither spoke, leaving Brooke the space to continue. I leaned forward, resting my elbows on my knees, watching her carefully.

"Is this about Peter Mantle?" I asked. I knew the managing partner at her firm was trying to break her down, loading too much work on her.

She gave a tight nod, her fingers tightening on her cup. "Yeah, Peter. He's just gotten worse. More demanding. It's like… nothing is ever enough, you know? There's always something extra he wants me to do, always some 'urgent' report or last-minute project, and every time I think I'm getting on top of it, he throws something else at me."

Caroline leaned forward slightly. "Is there anyone else he's treating this way? Or is it just you?"

Brooke hesitated, then shook her head. "I don't know. Probably not. I mean, Peter's intense, but it feels like I'm always the one he's zeroed in on. I'm his go-to, I guess, which means everything lands on me."

"Peter tried to make a move on her," I explained to the other girls. "Brooke turned him down, and he's been hell-bent on treating her like shit ever since."

"What a dick," Daisy muttered.

Caroline frowned, crossing her arms. "That doesn't sound right. He shouldn't be in charge."

Brooke gave a bitter laugh. "Yeah, well, try telling him that. Any time I hint that I'm overwhelmed, he tells me I should be 'grateful for the opportunity.'" She sighed, looking down at her coffee. "I've tried to tell myself it'll get better, that it's just a busy season, but it never lets up. And it's not just the hours or the work. It's…" She paused, her voice wavering. "It's Cody. I hate that I'm not there for him like I want to be."

My chest tightened as I watched her struggle. She'd always taken her responsibilities seriously, but I could tell this was taking a heavier toll than she wanted to admit. "Brooke," I said gently, "you don't have to do this to yourself. You know that, right?"

She looked up, eyes tired but wary. "And what

am I supposed to do, Sean? Just walk away from it all? I can't just give up everything I've built."

Caroline placed a hand on Brooke's arm. "Maybe there's a way to have it without sacrificing everything else that matters to you."

Brooke closed her eyes for a moment, taking a deep breath. "I know, Caroline. But it feels like if I step back, if I say no to Peter, it'll all unravel. I'd be risking everything." She opened her eyes, glancing between us. "And then there's Cody. I already feel like I'm letting him down."

Daisy leaned forward, her voice soft but steady. "Brooke, I'm gonna be real with you. I see Cody around Sean, and I see how much he lights up when he talks about you. He doesn't need a mom who's perfect. He needs a mom who's happy."

Brooke looked away, her jaw tight. "I don't even know what that means anymore. It's been so long since I had… any balance. And then I see how you guys live in Waycross — the peace, the connection Cody's built with all of you… And it makes me feel guilty. Because he should be feeling that with me. But I just can't give him that right now."

I took a deep breath, trying to choose my words

carefully. "But you *can*, Brooke. We're here for you. All you have to do is accept the help. It doesn't need to hurt your pride."

Brooke held my gaze, her shoulders slumping a little. "Sean… I know you're all here for me and Cody, and that means so much. But I just don't know if I can let go enough to trust that everything will be okay. This job is all I've worked for. It's what's supposed to make me feel stable, secure, like I'm doing something right."

Caroline gave her arm a gentle squeeze. "But what's stability worth if it's leaving you so drained? And there are other options, Brooke."

Brooke nodded slowly, her expression softening as she took in Caroline's words. She let out a long breath, looking around the room, taking in the three of us who were here, showing up without hesitation. "I just wish I knew where to start," she murmured, more to herself than to any of us.

We gave her a moment of silence, and she took a deep breath, her hand resting on her coffee cup. She glanced at each of us before her gaze settled on me. "I don't know, Sean," she continued, her voice low. "I know you're all here to help, and I appreciate it, I do… but there's no easy answer."

Caroline offered her a soft smile. "Sometimes it's not about having it all figured out, Brooke. Maybe it's just about making a change for the better, even if it feels like stepping out without a safety net."

Brooke shook her head, her face tense. "But I can't just jump without thinking about what that means for Cody and me. What if it all backfires? I don't want to be reckless. There are bills I need to pay."

I leaned forward, trying to get her to meet my gaze. "Brooke, remember the gold and silver coins I gave you? Those were a backup, not just for emergencies but to help you find a way through this. They could buy you time, help you make a plan that doesn't involve working yourself into the ground."

She looked up, her eyes widening just slightly. "I remember. I thought you just… I don't know… you really meant for me to use them?"

I nodded. "Absolutely. I don't want you to stay trapped because you feel like you have no other choice. It's meant to be a real backup, something you can lean on while you figure out what'll work best for you and Cody."

Brooke swallowed, her grip on her coffee cup tightening. "It just feels like I've been trying to be the strong one for so long... and now, I'm not even sure I know how to let go of that."

"Brooke, accepting help is not losing," I said. "Doing things together doesn't mean you're not independent. You're a strong woman, but that doesn't mean you need to be alone all the time."

"I know," she muttered, close to crying. "I just... Ugh..."

Caroline leaned in closer, her tone gentle. "Brooke, just because you take a break doesn't mean you're giving up. It just means you're choosing a different way. You've got people here who want to help, who want to see you get that balance back. Maybe start there. Take the time to really think about what's best for you, not just the job."

Brooke's gaze lingered on Caroline, then shifted to Daisy, who nodded, her expression calm but resolute. "Cody lights up around you, Brooke. That's all he needs. He doesn't care if you're runnin' a high-powered superlawyer firm or teaching pottery classes, as long as you're there with him."

Brooke let out a short laugh, shaking her head. "I know. I know you're right." She looked back at me, her voice softer. "And it's not like I haven't thought about it. There are nights I'm working late and I can't help but think, 'What am I doing?' It's just…" She hesitated, her voice dropping. "I'm scared."

I nodded, meeting her gaze. "There's no shame in that. Change is terrifying. But you've got us. You've got people ready to support you if you want to make that choice."

Brooke sat there in silence, her fingers clenched around her coffee cup as she processed the words. She looked back and forth between us, hope and hesitation battling within her. "You all make it sound so… simple," she murmured, her voice barely above a whisper.

"It's not," I said gently, leaning forward. "It's not simple at all. But we're here, Brooke. You don't have to face this alone."

She looked down at her coffee again, her voice

wavering. "I've tried to keep pushing through, telling myself I could handle it, that it'd all be worth it in the end. But I don't know if I even believe that anymore. I keep thinking it's just a phase, just one more project... but it never ends. And each time, I just feel worse."

Caroline reached over, placing a comforting hand on Brooke's arm. "Brooke, it's okay to want something different. It's okay to change directions, especially when it's hurting you this much."

Brooke smiled at her sympathetically, then looked at me. "Is it just pride, Sean? You know me. Tell me straight what you think."

I shook my head. "Not *just* pride, Brooke. It's love too — for Cody, for yourself. But I know you, and if you want it straight, here it is: I think you should stop."

Brooke bit her lip, her hands trembling slightly. "I've never quit anything in my life. And this job... it's all I've worked for. It's all I have to show for the time I've put in, and... if I just let it go, what am I left with?" She paused, swallowing hard. "And what if I regret it?"

Daisy leaned in, her expression gentle but firm.

"What if you don't? What if you walk away, and it's the best decision you ever made? Life's too short to be miserable every day, Brooke. You've got so much ahead of you. This job doesn't define you."

Brooke looked at her, the resistance slowly giving way. "But it feels like I'd be throwing away everything. All the work, the years, the struggle... it's all tied up in this job. If I leave now, I feel like I'll have nothing left."

"You won't be left with nothing, Brooke," I said, leaning forward to meet her gaze. "You'll have your health, your peace... and you'll have us. That's worth more than any title on a business card. And if you ever feel like moving back into it, you can. I'm sure firms will line up to hire someone with your skills and experience if you decide you want to return to it."

She hesitated, shaking her head, almost as if she couldn't let herself believe it. "And if it doesn't work out? If... if I can't figure out something else?"

"That's what we're here for," Caroline said softly, giving her arm a squeeze. "You don't have to do this alone. And you have the coins Sean gave you, remember? That's your cushion."

Brooke gave a shaky laugh, wiping at her eyes. "I just kept thinking that I couldn't touch them, that they were... I don't know, too precious or something."

"Brooke," I said, keeping my tone calm but firm, "it's just money. It's there for you to use when you need it, not as some 'just in case' at the back of a drawer. This is that moment. Let those coins buy you time to regroup, to figure out what you really want."

She let out a long, shuddering breath, her eyes filled with doubt, but also a flicker of something else — hope. "But... quitting? Today? Could I really just walk away?"

Daisy nodded, a reassuring smile on her face. "You absolutely can. If that's what feels right to you, why wait another day? Take control of this now, not tomorrow."

Caroline jumped in, her voice gentle but supportive. "We'll take Cody out, let him have a little adventure around Louisville. That'll give you time to focus, to walk in there and put an end to this chapter."

I nodded. "It's your decision, Brooke. But if you want to quit, I can come with you."

Brooke looked at me, her gaze searching. "You'd come with me? Right now?"

"Of course," I replied, steady and certain. "You don't have to go through this alone, Brooke. I'll be with you every step of the way. You can quit this job, walk away from Peter's mess."

She was silent for a long moment, her eyes glassy, her hands trembling. "I want this, I really do... but I'm so scared. What if it all falls apart?"

I reached out, resting my hand over hers. "Then we'll face it together. But it's time you got back to a place where you feel whole, where you can be the mom Cody needs without sacrificing yourself for some job that only takes and never gives."

Brooke took a deep breath, then nodded, her shoulders slumping as she let go of the tension she'd been holding onto. "You know what?" she said. "You're right."

I smiled at her. "There's my girl," I said, feeling so proud of her.

She chuckled, then shot Daisy and Caroline a

thankful look. "You two are the best. Thank you."

Daisy grinned broadly. "Ain't a thing! You go get 'em!"

"Hm-hm," Caroline hummed. "Tell that asshole he can find someone else to push around."

With a broad smile, I rose, extending my hand to Brooke. "Come on," I said. "Let's go do it…"

# Chapter 27

Brooke and I walked down the gleaming corridor toward Peter Mantle's office.

Brooke's heels clicked with each step, and colleagues turned to watch us both. Since I wasn't wearing a suit — or even something business casual — I was the odd man out here. It had taken quite some persuasion from Brooke to even get me past the firm's overeager security. I had to fill in three forms...

As we walked, I could feel her pulse quicken beside me. We passed row after row of cubicles where the juniors sat until they managed to climb the ladder a bit. The smiles they shot Brooke were overly friendly, nauseatingly so. This was her world — or at least, it had been until now.

As we got toward the offices where the more senior employees were, several of Brooke's colleagues glanced up, some with surprised expressions, others with something that looked like curiosity or concern. It was obvious that word had spread about her workload and Peter's impossible demands. But nobody spoke.

As we turned the final corner, I saw him — Peter Mantle, right in front of his office, discussing something with another partner. He hadn't spotted us yet, but Brooke's hand tightened around her bag strap as she spotted him, her steps faltering for just a second.

"You've got this," I murmured, giving her a slight nudge forward.

She took a breath, nodding without meeting my

eye, and straightened up, her expression steeling as we moved closer. Just then, Peter turned around. He locked eyes with Brooke, his surprise quickly hardening into irritation.

"Brooke." His voice was clipped, the smile he wore purely for show. "Didn't expect to see you here today. And I see you've brought…" He glanced at me, barely acknowledging my presence before looking back at her. "A guest. Shouldn't you be focusing on your client reports rather than visiting with guests?"

Brooke stood her ground, keeping her gaze level. "Peter, I came here to talk to you." She glanced at me, drawing strength from my presence.

"About what?" he asked.

She took a deep breath, then said it. "I'm quitting."

Peter's smile dropped, his face shifting into a look of disdain. He crossed his arms, staring her down. "You must be joking."

"No," she said firmly, her voice steady but tense. "I'm not. I've decided to resign."

Peter scoffed, glancing briefly at his watch

before looking back at her. "Is this about your workload? I've told you, Brooke, that's part of the job. You wanted responsibility, wanted to move up in this firm — this is how it works."

Brooke took a step closer, and I could see her jaw tighten. "This isn't about just responsibility. It's about balance. My life has been completely off-balance since I started working here, Peter. I can't be the kind of mother I need to be or take care of my own health if I stay."

He laughed, shaking his head dismissively. "Motherhood. Right. Well, maybe you should've thought about the demands of this career before deciding to make your personal life a priority." His voice was low, condescending, as if she were wasting his time.

Brooke's face flushed, but she didn't back down. "That's exactly it, Peter. I *have* thought about it. I've thought about it every night for months. I've tried to keep up with your expectations, working weekends, skipping time with my son—" her voice faltered briefly, but she pushed through. "But it's not worth it anymore. I'm done."

He gave her a cold smile, shaking his head.

"And you think you'll be fine just... leaving?" He leaned in slightly, his voice dripping with condescension. "Brooke, do you understand what you're giving up? The opportunities, the connections? You don't get to walk away and expect to find that same respect and influence anywhere else. You'll be throwing everything away. You're sinking your own ship by doing this. No other firm will have you if you cave under the pressure."

She looked back at him, steady. "That's my choice. I've made my decision."

Peter's jaw clenched, his eyes flashing with anger as he took a step closer. The nonchalant mask he had put on was now slipping. His face darkened, and he crossed his arms. "Do you understand what you're saying?" he asked, his tone sharp. "You're really going to throw all of this away? All the hard work, the hours we've invested in you? Not to mention the opportunities you're going to miss if you leave now."

Brooke met his gaze but didn't respond right away, clearly steeling herself. She took a breath. "I've thought it through, Peter," she said. "I can't keep sacrificing everything else for this job. I need to be there for my son, and I need to have some kind of balance."

He scoffed, shaking his head. "Balance? Brooke, this is a *career*, not a hobby. Balance is a luxury — not everyone can afford it, especially at the level you're working." He raised an eyebrow, his voice dripping with disdain. "Do you think people who make partner talk about 'balance' when they're under pressure? You can have 'balance' when you retire a millionaire! At *fifty-five*! *That's* what this job will do for you, Brooke! You'll be set for life!"

It was bullshit, of course. He was promising golden mountains just so he could keep exploiting her — just like he did to everyone who wandered into his little web.

Brooke knew it. She held her ground, although I could see her fingers trembling slightly around her bag. "That's the problem, Peter," she replied. "I don't want to live my life under constant pressure for the sake of... what? A promotion? It's not worth losing my family over."

Peter's face hardened. "I expected more from you, Brooke. Honestly, it's disappointing to see you fold like this." His tone turned condescending, as if he were speaking to a child.

I could feel Brooke wavering slightly, and Peter noticed it too. He pressed forward, lowering his voice to a softer, almost persuasive tone. "Listen, maybe you're just burnt out. This project's been intense, I know that. But you don't walk away just because you hit a rough patch. This is where people prove what they're made of, Brooke. You show me you can do this, and your star will rise, Brooke. You could make managing partner once my term is up."

Brooke's face softened for a moment, and Peter seized on it.

"You've worked your way up from the bottom here," he continued. "You're not just some junior associate anymore. You're respected — reliable. People in this firm look up to you. And now you're going to walk away and leave everyone in the lurch? After everything we've given you? It's not just unprofessional — it's selfish."

I was getting close to punching him. He was a manipulative bastard, and he needed to be put in his place. But I knew Brooke — I knew her very well. If I intervened, it wouldn't feel to her like she came here on her own. And while she was willing to accept *some* help, she was the kind of woman who had to do something like this on her own.

She shook her head, struggling to keep her voice even. "Peter, you have no idea what it's been like. It's every weekend, every night. I can't even remember the last time I had a real moment with my son."

He smirked, clearly unimpressed. "You think *I* don't know? I've been there, Brooke. Everyone has to make sacrifices. I make sacrifices every day, and so does everyone else in this office. You knew what you were signing up for. This career isn't meant for everyone, but I thought you were better than this."

Brooke opened her mouth, hesitating, as her gaze flitted to me. I gave her a firm nod, and her resolve strengthened.

"Peter," she said, her voice firmer this time, "this job is taking everything from me, and I've let it because I thought it would all be worth it. But it isn't. I'm not walking away because it's *tough*. I'm walking away because it's *damaging*, and I can't keep pretending otherwise."

Peter's eyes narrowed. "Damaging? Don't kid yourself, Brooke. You have a position here that people dream of, and you're throwing it all away for a so-called 'balance' that doesn't exist." He looked her up and down, sneering. "Once you're gone, you'll realize just how little the world cares about your 'well-being.'"

I could feel her stiffen, but she held her ground. "I don't need your approval, Peter. I'm doing this for me and for my son, and if you don't understand that, then it's certainly better that I'm leaving."

Peter scoffed, throwing his hands out. "Fine. Go ahead. Run away. But don't expect to find anything better. You'll end up exactly where you started, probably regretting this little tantrum of yours."

Brooke looked him straight in the eyes, her expression finally calm. "I'd rather be starting over than staying here and giving up everything that actually matters to me."

Peter opened his mouth to respond, but she turned, leaving him standing there speechless. As we walked away, her colleagues' heads turned, and some even gave her nods of approval.

I gave her hand a squeeze as we walked and smiled at her. I was proud of her. She had finally done it.

After we left the office, Brooke took a deep breath as we walked down the steps, glancing back at the building like she was still trying to process what had just happened. Her grip on her purse loosened a bit, but there was still a touch of anxiety in her eyes.

She looked over at me, letting out a slow, shaky laugh. "Did that... did I really just do that? Walk out? Tell Peter Mantle I was done?"

"You did," I said with a grin, giving her hand a reassuring squeeze. "And you handled it like a pro. I've never been prouder of you, Brooke."

Brooke let out a short, breathy laugh, then shook her head in disbelief. "I can't believe I actually stood there and said all that." She paused, and her smile wavered. "Though it doesn't feel real yet. I'm still half-expecting him to come after me and try to force me back inside."

I chuckled. "Not a chance. If he tried, he'd have to get past me."

She laughed, a little more freely this time. "Maybe I need you as my official guard, Sean. Keep Peter out of my life for good."

I smirked. "Anytime. But I think you've got it covered. You didn't need me in there — you handled him like a boss."

She hesitated, then nodded slowly. "Maybe. But I won't lie — I'm terrified of what comes next. Everything I knew, everything I worked for... it's just gone."

I squeezed her hand. "Gone? Hardly. You've got your health, Cody, and a fresh start. This is just the beginning."

She gave me a look, the beginnings of a smile forming. "I don't know if I'd call it a fresh start just yet. But... maybe you're right."

As we walked, I spotted a small, low-lit bar on the corner and pointed it out. "How about we celebrate? Toast to this new chapter?"

She glanced over at the bar, then at me, hesitating for a moment before nodding. "Yeah... actually, that sounds good. I think I could use a drink right about now."

We headed inside, finding a booth in a quieter corner of the bar. The place had a calm vibe, with dim lighting and a low hum of conversation around us. Once we settled into the booth, the waitress came over, and Brooke ordered a glass of wine. I got a whiskey.

When our drinks arrived, I raised my glass. "Here's to freedom and fresh starts."

Brooke clinked her glass with mine, a small but genuine smile on her face. "And here's to having the best support I could ask for. I'd have never made it without you."

We took sips of our drinks, and she leaned back, her gaze drifting out the window. "You know, I've been here so many times with my colleagues. Celebrating wins, networking, all that. But it never felt… like this."

"Because this time, it's not just about work," I said. "It's about you."

She nodded, the tension in her shoulders finally easing a bit. "It's strange, though. I've been saying for years that I'd leave if things got to be too much. But I never thought I'd actually do it." She looked at me, almost as if needing confirmation. "I really did quit, didn't I?"

"You did," I said. "And you didn't just quit. You walked away for the right reasons. For Cody, for yourself."

Brooke took a slow sip of her wine, processing that. "Yeah. It just… I guess it hasn't sunk in yet. I keep wondering what I'll do next. This job was everything — my career, my security. And now I've got… nothing."

I shook my head. "You've got way more than nothing, Brooke. You've got options, you've got support, and you've got your family. That's more than most people get."

She was silent for a moment, then let out a deep breath. "Maybe you're right. I guess I just… never thought I'd have to start over."

I leaned forward, meeting her gaze. "You're not starting over, Brooke. You're building something new, something better. And you're not doing it alone. I'm here, and so are Daisy and Caroline. And Cody? He's just happy to have you back."

She looked down, her voice softer. "I didn't think he'd notice how bad things were getting. But he did, didn't he?"

"Of course he did," I said. "He loves you. He's aware of this in his own way."

Brooke managed a small smile, a mix of pride and sadness in her eyes. "I just... I want him to know he's my priority, even if I got lost in work for a while."

I reached across the table, resting a hand on hers. "He already knows. All that's left is for you to be there, really be there. You've given up so much for him already. Now, it's time to live the life you deserve."

Brooke squeezed my hand, her gaze lingering on mine. "Thank you, Sean. I mean it. I've never felt this much support... or relief. It feels like I've been carrying this weight forever, and now..." She paused, searching for the right words. "It's finally gone."

"Well," I said with a grin, raising my glass again, "then I'd say that's definitely worth celebrating."

We clinked glasses, sharing a smile that was no longer tinged with worry or doubt — just a sense of hope for what lay ahead.

After Brooke and I finished our first round, I could sense that she wanted to celebrate more, and I wholeheartedly agreed with the sentiment. So, I excused myself and stepped outside to call Daisy.

When Daisy picked up after the second ring, her voice was upbeat, the kind of tone she had when things were going well. "Hey, Sean! How's it going over there?" she asked.

"Better than expected," I said, glancing back at Brooke through the bar's window. "She went through with it, Daisy. She quit."

Daisy let out a short, triumphant laugh. "That's incredible! I mean, I knew she'd get there, but still, hearing she actually did it... that's huge."

"It is. You can see the relief, but she's still a little shocked." I paused, looking back at Brooke through the window, still sitting in the booth, sipping her wine. "I think it's hitting her just how much her life's about to change."

"Well, it's about time she has a change that's good for her," Daisy said. I could almost hear her smiling. "Listen, Sean, how 'bout this? Caroline and I can take Cody back to Waycross tonight.

You two have the night to yourselves — no rush, no worries about getting home."

"You sure?" I asked, surprised. "Cody can be a handful. And it's a long drive back."

"Oh, we've got it covered. Caroline and I have been keepin' him busy. He's got ideas about Tink and the chickens and seems thrilled to have us listening to every single one." She laughed. "I think he's planning on training Tink to herd sheep next. Kid's got ambition."

"Sounds like he's in his element." I grinned, shaking my head. "Alright, if you're sure, then yeah, that would be perfect."

"Absolutely. You go enjoy your night," she said, a hint of teasing in her voice. "And tell Brooke we're all cheering for her."

"Thanks, Daisy. Really appreciate it," I said.

"Anytime, Sean. Have fun. We'll see you back in Waycross when you're ready. No rush." With that, she hung up, and I smiled at how sweet she was, knowing exactly what was needed.

I slipped my phone back into my pocket and headed inside. Brooke looked up when I sat down, curiosity flickering across her face as she picked up on my grin.

"Good news," I said, taking a sip of my drink before meeting her gaze. "Daisy and Caroline are going to take Cody back to Waycross for the night. Just you and me, no rush."

Her eyes widened, then a smile broke through. "Really? They offered to do that?"

"Yep. Cody's on board, too. He's apparently got big plans for Tink and some farm projects." I chuckled. "He sounded happy, so we've got nothing to worry about."

Brooke shook her head, clearly surprised. "I'm so lucky he has you — and them. I don't think I could've done this without knowing he'd be okay with you all around him."

"Well, we're glad to have him, Brooke." I met her gaze, letting her see I meant it. "And tonight's all yours. We can do whatever you want. Celebrate, relax, talk. No pressure."

She exhaled, leaning back and looking around the bar. "You know, I don't even remember the last time I went out just to enjoy myself. It's always been work dinners or networking events. But this? Just sitting here, talking about what's next without someone breathing down my neck... it's freeing."

I raised my glass. "Then let's toast to that. To whatever's next, and to being free."

She clinked her glass with mine, her smile turning softer. "To what's next." She took a sip, then looked down, swirling her wine. "And, I don't know... I'm realizing I haven't really thought much about 'what's next.' I've spent so long just grinding, pushing for this career, that I almost forgot there's a whole life out there."

"Maybe now you'll have the time to figure that out," I said. "What do you want to do, if not this?"

Brooke hesitated, as if she hadn't even let herself consider the question. "Remember I used to want to teach?" she said, her voice barely above a whisper. "Before law, before all of this... I used to think that was what I would do. I've been thinking of it again of late. It's funny, I haven't even admitted that out loud in years."

"Teaching, huh?" I grinned. "Yeah, I remember. I think you'd be great at it. Hey, and Waycross could use a good teacher."

She laughed, a real, easy laugh. "A small-town

teacher? Can you picture that? I'm not sure the PTA would know what to do with me."

"They'd be lucky to have you," I said. "It doesn't have to be Waycross, although I'd like that, but I think a change like that could be good for you."

Brooke nodded slowly, her gaze thoughtful as she mulled it over. "Maybe," she said softly. "For now, I'll just take this as it comes. Just take a day to… enjoy." She raised her glass again. "So, here's to new starts, wherever they might lead."

"To new starts," I echoed, clinking my glass against hers again.

Brooke took a drink, then swirled the wine in her glass, looking at it thoughtfully. She glanced up at me, a small smile forming. "I can't believe I'm saying this, but… I think I'd like living somewhere quieter. Like Waycross. Not just for Cody's sake, but for mine."

I leaned back, surprised but glad to hear her say it. "Yeah?" I grinned. "That happens to be just what I think." I winked at her. "So, what happened to the Brooke who liked mocking small-town life?"

Brooke chuckled, shaking her head. "I did do that, didn't I?"

"'Rural recluse,' I believe you called it," I said with a chuckle. "But you got it all wrong, you know. I found more to care about out there than I ever thought I could in the city."

She was quiet, mulling that over. "I can see that now. There's just... something different in Waycross. Cody feels it too. He lights up there in a way I haven't seen here in a long time." She looked down, swirling her wine again. "I think he feels more at home there than anywhere else."

"Well, it's not hard to see why," I said. "You know he's got a whole team rooting for him there. Tink, the chickens, Daisy, Caroline — he's got a whole setup."

Brooke smiled at the mention of them, glancing up. "They're pretty great, aren't they? I'll admit, I was a little skeptical at first, but they've been incredible. Even to me. And Cody just adores them."

"Daisy and Caroline are the best," I agreed. "You know they'd do anything for him. Or for you, for that matter."

Her eyes softened as she met my gaze. "I don't think I ever thought I'd say this, Sean, but I really do feel welcome around them. I mean, they've just been... good to me. It's like I can finally breathe when I'm around them, like they just get it. At first, I thought it would be weird..."

"Why?"

"Well, you're in a relationship with them. I thought there would be... well, jealousy."

"If everyone is communicating and being honest, there is no need for it. They enjoy it, Brooke — they like sharing me with each other. They like the large family."

She blushed a little. "I can see that. They're sweet. I like them."

"I'm glad you feel that way. They feel the same about you," I said, watching her closely. "And I do, too. It's good to have you closer." I paused, then added, "If you're serious about moving, that would mean the world to Cody — and to me, Brooke."

She held my gaze, her expression turning thoughtful. "I *am* serious, Sean. This feels like a second chance for me — to be there for Cody, to have a real life." She hesitated, then laughed a little, nervously. "And to be there with you. If that's… something you'd want."

I felt warmth spread through me at her words. I reached out, resting my hand over hers. "Brooke, you have no idea how much I'd want that. Having you close… not just for Cody, but for me too. It's everything I didn't know I was missing."

She smiled, her fingers brushing over mine. "I don't know what it'll look like, Sean. I mean, we've been in and out of each other's lives for so long, and now… this." She shook her head, as if she still couldn't quite believe it.

I nodded. "That's the thing about this life, Brooke. It's never been simple. It's always had its complications, but I don't think we've ever been as sure as we are now."

She looked at me, her eyes searching mine. "And Daisy and Caroline? You're right, they're important to you. I get that. And I can accept that. They're already part of Cody's life, too."

Hearing that from her felt like something big, something solid, settling into place. "They're important, yeah. But I know you, Brooke. And I think you know yourself. You're ready for this. You, me, Cody… and them. It could work, don't you think?"

She smiled and nodded slowly, a small smile creeping onto her face. "It feels *right*, Sean. And… I want that, too. I want that for Cody and for us." She glanced down, almost shy, then back up at me. "And for me. I've missed this — missed us."

I felt a smile tugging at my lips. "Then maybe we should stop overthinking it."

Brooke's gaze softened, and there was something in her eyes I hadn't seen in a long time. "Maybe we should," she murmured.

Slowly, I leaned in, her breath warm as our faces were inches apart. She looked up, her eyes meeting mine, and she tilted her head slightly. When her lips met mine, it was gentle but certain, a connection I hadn't realized I'd missed so much until now.

When we pulled back, she let out a small, nervous laugh. "So… maybe I should think about it, right? Let the dust settle. Maybe I can look for a place close by?"

I wanted her to live with me — in my house. But

I wasn't going to push her. "Sounds good," I said, feeling satisfied with this important step. "You think about it. Our door is always open."

Her hand rested on mine for a moment, and then I saw that familiar light blaze in her blue eyes as she tucked a strand of raven hair behind her ear.

"What do you say we get out of here?" she asked, a mischievous light in her eyes.

"Music to my ears," I replied with a grin.

# Chapter 28

We stumbled into Brooke's apartment mid-kiss. Both of us wanted this. Badly. We were feeling, touching, remembering, and we tolerated only a moment of our bodies' separation as we at least made sure the door was locked behind us.

"God, I missed this, Sean," Brooke breathed.

"Me too," I muttered, barely able to finish the

sentence as we kissed again.

It was as if the time of our separation melted away, and I was back in the arms of my passionate, ambitious love. Brooke's kisses were hungry, her tongue eagerly exploring my mouth, and I could feel the heat radiating off her body.

"God, I've wanted this," she whispered between kisses, her breath hot against my face. Her hands roamed my torso, pulling me closer as if to satisfy an insatiable craving.

My heart pounded in my chest, my blood rushing through my veins like molten lava. The intoxicating scent of her perfume clouded my senses, and a primal desire took hold of me. I wanted her more than anything — not just for the physical release but for the connection — I wanted to light the fire again.

"Brooke," I moaned, my voice thick with lust. "I want you so bad."

Her eyes gleamed with mischief as she dropped to her knees in front of me. "I want to taste you again, Sean," she purred, her fingers deftly unbuckling my belt and sliding it off. She unbuttoned my pants and pulled them down along with my boxers, allowing my rock-hard cock to spring free. She did so in seconds — hungry, passionate, needy.

Just how I liked her.

"Fuck," I muttered under my breath, my mind reeling from the sight of her on her knees, her blue eyes locked onto mine.

"Let me show you how much I missed you," she said, her voice sultry and low.

With that, she wrapped her lips around the head of my cock, swirling her tongue around it before taking me deeper into her warm, inviting mouth. She sucked, her cheeks hollowing, and I groaned at the familiar pleasure. Brooke was a devil in the sheets.

"Brooke...you're amazing," I breathed, my fingers tangling in her silky black hair as she continued to work her magic on me. "I've missed this so much."

"Me too," she murmured, pulling back momentarily and gazing up at me with those piercing blue eyes. "I've missed us." And with that, she returned her attention to my throbbing cock.

The sensation of her warmth and wetness sent shivers up my spine, and I reveled in the feeling of our connection reigniting. With each bob of her head, I could feel my desire for her growing stronger.

"God, I missed this cock too!" she mumbled, her voice muffled by my cock. "I love you, Sean."

"Brooke," I groaned, my fingers tightening in her hair. "I love you too. So much."

Her eyes met mine again. I could barely contain myself as I watched her continue to work her magic, never breaking eye contact. My heart swelled, realizing how much we had both been craving this moment, this rekindling of passion that once burned so brightly between us.

"Brooke," I panted, feeling my arousal building. "I want to see you naked again. I need to see all of you."

A thrill flickered in her eyes at my command, and she immediately let go of my cock, her hands deftly undoing the buttons on her blouse. Her firm breasts sprang free, bouncing slightly as she shrugged off the garment. She then wriggled out of her pencil skirt and lace thong, leaving only her stockings and heels on.

"Is this what you wanted?" she asked with a sultry smile, her body displayed before me in all its glory.

She was beautiful — older than Daisy or Caroline, but a blessed combination of genes, disciplined workouts, and an active lifestyle left her the perfect MILF. I nodded, unable to speak, as she once more lowered her head to my throbbing erection.

"Remember how it felt when you would cum inside me?" she teased, her tongue dancing around the tip of my cock. "I miss that feeling, Sean. I want it again."

Her teasing made the pressure in my loins reach a tipping point, and she sensed it, pulling back as she looked up again, her eyes smoldering with desire. "Fuck me here on the floor, Sean," she purred. "Do it now. Please."

My heart raced as I took in the sight of Brooke's naked body, bathed in the dim light of her apartment. The way her stockings hugged the curves of her legs and her heels accentuated her toned calves was maddening, and I knew I wouldn't even make it to the bedroom.

With a lustful growl, I pushed Brooke down onto her back on the floor, my mind still swimming at our reunion. I felt something primal awaken within me; a need to reclaim my woman. I positioned myself between her thighs, rubbing my cock against her slick entrance, delighting in the sensation of our bodies pressed together once again.

"Please, Sean," she begged, her blue eyes filled with desperation. "I need you inside me."

"God, Brooke," I whispered, awestruck by the intensity of the moment. "You have no idea how much I've missed this... missed you."

"Show me," she urged, her voice shaking with anticipation. "Make me feel whole again."

I could no longer postpone it. With a groan, I pushed, and the moment I slipped inside Brooke's wet pussy, I felt her delicious and familiar warmth again.

Her moan echoed through the room as she wrapped her legs around me, pulling me deeper into her warmth. "God, Sean... I've wanted this for so long," she whispered, her eyes glistening with sincerity. "I missed you so much."

"Brooke, I—" The words caught in my throat, choked by the intensity of our connection. I began to move within her, each thrust driving us both closer to the edge. My gaze locked on her heaving breasts.

"Fuck, yes, Sean! Harder!" she cried out. She reached down between us, rubbing her clit as I continued to quicken my pace.

I grinned and pounded her faster, watching her please herself like the vixen she was between the sheets. I knew then, as I renewed my claim on her, I was not going to let her go again.

"God... Please, Sean, I need your cum inside me," she panted, her fingers working feverishly on her clit. "Fill me up! Make me yours again."

Hearing those words sent shivers down my spine, and I could feel my orgasm approaching. But I fought against it, wanting to prolong this intense reunion for as long as possible.

I let out a growl and pounded deeper, harder, making her squirm and yelp, her eyes rolling up in their sockets. "Fuck!" she gasped. "Yes! Sean, oh God!"

Her nails digging into my back jolted me, a reminder of the fire that had always burned between us. I knew this was how it was supposed to be; she and I as one.

"Sean... I'm... I'm so close," she panted, her voice shaking with need. Her legs wrapped around my waist, pulling me in even tighter.

"Let go, baby," I encouraged her, overcome by the sight of her flushed face and trembling lips, which I kissed as I plunged deeper. "Cum for me."

"Sean, fffuuck... I... I love you!" she cried out, her words punctuated by the intensity of her orgasm. I watched as waves of pleasure wracked her body, her eyes rolling back in sheer bliss.

With a gasp for air, I gave in to my own climax, filling her up with a primal growl, pumping rope after rope of warm cum into her welcoming body as she held me close, taking it all until we were both spent.

Panting, I collapsed beside her on the floor, a little surprised at how intense our reunion had been but enjoying every moment of it.

"Wow," I breathed, my heart still racing from the passion we'd just shared.

Brooke chuckled softly, our eyes meeting as we lay side by side on the floor. "I missed this, Sean."

"Me too," I admitted, reaching over to pull her into my arms. We held each other tightly, our bodies still tingling from the afterglow of our lovemaking.

"Thank you for tonight," she whispered, her breath warm against my skin. "I'm so happy that this happened."

"Brooke," I said softly, feeling a surge of emotions within me, "I've never stopped loving you."

For a few moments, we simply lay there, basking in the warmth of our rekindled connection. But then, I noticed a sudden quietness from Brooke, her gaze focused on the ceiling.

"Hey," I said, my fingers brushing a stray strand of hair from her face. "What's the matter?"

For a moment, she hesitated, as if weighing her words carefully. But then, with a deep breath, she finally spoke. "Sean," she began, her voice quivering slightly, "I... I don't want to wait. And I don't want to stay here in this apartment or even in Louisville for another day."

Her words caught me off guard, but I listened intently as she continued, my heart pounding in anticipation.

"I want to move to Waycross with you. I want us — you, me, and Cody — to be a family again. And I want Daisy and Caroline to be there, too." Her eyes searched mine, searching for my reaction, her vulnerability on full display.

I felt a surge of warmth and happiness enveloping me at her confession. My chest swelled with joy, and I wrapped her tighter in my arms, pressing a tender kiss on her forehead.

"Brooke, I can't tell you how happy that makes me," I whispered, my voice thick with emotion. "Of course, I'd love for you to come to Waycross with me."

"Really?" She looked up at me, her blue eyes shimmering with unshed tears.

"Really," I confirmed, brushing away a tear that managed to escape down her cheek. "I still love you, Brooke. And I want nothing more than for us to be a family again."

"Thank you, Sean," she breathed, relief washing over her face as she settled back into my embrace.

As we each basked in the happiness of this moment, we lay on the floor, our naked bodies pressed together. And as we held each other close, I thought about what lay ahead for us. Rebuilding. Reuniting.

# Chapter 29 (Brooke)

The morning light crept through the blinds, gently waking Brooke from the deepest, most restful sleep she'd had in a long time.

Since she and Sean broke up, actually…

She blinked, half expecting the usual rush of thoughts to flood her mind — what emails she needed to answer, what deadlines were coming up, what work awaited her at the firm. But instead, there was only quiet. The stillness of the room filled her with a calm she hadn't felt in... well, longer than she could remember. There was no tightness in her chest, no early morning tension weighing her down.

As she lay there, she let her gaze wander around the room, taking in each small detail with fresh eyes. Sean was no longer in bed — he'd always been an early one. Maybe he had gone out to get them some fresh coffee and rolls like he used to?

Slowly, her mind drifted over the events of the past few days, replaying everything she'd done and said, all the choices she'd made. Each one, from leaving her job to deciding to move in with Sean in Waycross, felt like peeling back a layer of herself that had been hidden away. And now, here she was — bare, open, and somehow unafraid of what the future held.

The thought of moving to Waycross, of starting fresh, brought a smile to her lips. It was still sinking in that she'd actually walked away from her job, that she'd had the strength to finally say enough was enough. But as freeing as that felt, the reality of it brought a twinge of anxiety.

Her mind turned, almost instinctively, to all the practical things she'd need to manage in the coming weeks. There were bills — her lease payment, utilities, the monthly expenses that added up to a small mountain when she thought of it all at once.

She'd have to contact her landlord, find a way to get out of her lease or, at the very least, sublease the place. Even if she pulled that off, the apartment had collected so much of her life — furniture, Cody's things, countless little knick-knacks. She'd have to sort, pack, and decide what to keep, what to let go of. It felt like a massive job, one she hadn't fully allowed herself to acknowledge until this moment.

And there were still other costs she couldn't ignore: insurance, groceries, subscriptions, and other obligations she couldn't instantly cancel. Her stomach knotted up just thinking about how she'd manage it all without her steady paycheck. Sure, she had some savings, but those wouldn't last forever. She took a breath, feeling her nerves prickling up as her thoughts kept spiraling.

But then, she remembered the coins.

Sean had told her they were there to ease any transition, and she trusted him — knew that if he said it, he meant it. She'd never leaned on anyone before, but maybe this time, it was okay to let herself do that. And with those coins, she could take a real, steady approach to this move. There was time, enough to cover expenses and get settled, to get herself and Cody into a routine in Waycross.

Brooke let out a long breath, releasing the tension that had built up. "It'll be okay," she murmured softly, smiling as she lay back against the pillow, letting herself believe it.

For so long, she'd felt like she couldn't let go, couldn't walk away from all the hours, the years of pushing herself to climb that ladder. But now, she saw how that ladder had been leaning against the wrong wall.

She could picture it so clearly now — life with Sean, Cody, and everything that came with living easy in Waycross. She imagined mornings like this one, waking up to the sun pouring in, Cody laughing as he ran around outside, Tink chasing after him. She could see herself gardening with Daisy, baking with Caroline, watching Cody learn and grow in ways he never could in the city. This wasn't the life she'd once planned for herself, but as she thought about it, she realized that maybe this was better. So much better.

And fresh air. Just an endless supply of it.

The idea of raising Cody in Waycross filled her with a new kind of hope. He deserved a life with more space to roam, where he could grow up surrounded by nature, by the peace that Waycross offered. He wouldn't have to miss out on his childhood because she was stuck in some office, buried in endless paperwork. He'd have the chance to be close to family, to build memories that weren't colored by stress and exhaustion. And she'd be there, fully present, not just squeezing in moments between late nights and early mornings.

She hadn't allowed herself to think like this for so long — to imagine a life without rushing from one task to the next, without sacrificing moments with Cody for deadlines that no longer meant anything. She'd spent years believing she was working toward something meaningful, only to find that what truly mattered had been waiting for her all along. It was humbling, in a way, realizing that what she'd needed wasn't more success, more validation, but simply the freedom to be herself, to live fully and freely with the people she loved.

Thinking about her future here made her heart swell. She felt light, almost like a weight had been lifted, like she'd been handed back a part of herself she thought she'd lost forever.

And she had Sean to thank for it.

# Chapter 30

The next three days were a whirlwind as Brooke and I set about wrapping up her life in Louisville. There was so much to go through — sorting, packing, organizing, deciding what stayed and what would make the journey to Waycross. Every day was full, and every day had a purpose. Cody had taken on the role of "pack supervisor," darting between rooms with an uncontainable excitement that kept us both going, even when the exhaustion set in.

"Mom, do you really need this?" Cody asked, holding up an old book Brooke hadn't cracked open in years.

Brooke laughed, taking it from him. "Probably not, huh? Let's donate it."

He nodded, already moving on to the next box. "Are you gonna keep that lamp?" he asked, pointing at a tall, stylishly sleek designer floor lamp in the corner.

Brooke shrugged, looking at it thoughtfully. "I'm not sure. What do you think?"

Cody grinned. "Nah. It doesn't go with our new place, does it?"

"Guess not," she said, laughing as she marked the lamp for donation.

Meanwhile, I focused on the heavier work. I tackled the furniture, loaded up bags of clothes, and set things up in the truck while they packed up Cody's room. Every time I passed his door, I heard snippets of conversation — Cody narrating what he'd do with each toy once he got to

Waycross, and Brooke laughing along, indulging his plans.

After about an hour, I poked my head in. "Hey, how's it going in here?"

Cody held up a stuffed dinosaur. "This is Ringo, Dad. He's gonna sit on my new bed. And Rocky" — he held up a smaller stuffed bear — "he'll keep him company."

Brooke rolled her eyes playfully. "Apparently, everything has a designated spot already. Cody's decided on the whole layout."

I chuckled. "Sounds like he's got it all figured out."

Cody nodded, very serious. "I do! And Dad, can we make a place for Tink, too? Like, maybe a little bed next to mine?"

"Absolutely," I said. "We'll make sure she's all set."

The next morning, we tackled the kitchen. Brooke sorted through dishes and appliances, trying to keep just the essentials.

"Are you taking the blender?" I asked, watching as she held it up, considering.

"I think I'm going to pass on it. I'm done with

kale smoothies. I'll just eat fresh food and live healthier instead. You want it?" she teased.

"Nope," I said, grinning. "I'm good. What about these mugs? You've got a collection here."

Brooke glanced over and shook her head, laughing. "I never realized how many I had. Let's keep a few and donate the rest."

Cody was busy loading the "keep" mugs into a box. "I call dibs on the one with the dog on it!" he announced, holding up a mug with a cartoon puppy. "It's for my hot chocolate."

"Deal," Brooke said, ruffling his hair. "Now go grab the spoons, pack supervisor."

As he scampered off, she turned to me with a smile. "It's almost strange, you know? Going through all this stuff, seeing what matters and what really doesn't."

"Big change," I agreed, handing her a stack of plates. "But I think you'll like it once we're back in Waycross. Less stuff, more space."

She nodded, setting the plates down. "I think so, too."

That afternoon, we tackled Cody's toys. He was surprisingly decisive, already understanding that some toys would be staying behind since he had outgrown them.

"Okay," he announced, holding up a toy truck, "this one goes to Jamie. He always liked it."

Brooke smiled. "That's thoughtful, Cody. I'm sure Jamie will appreciate it."

Cody grinned, proudly setting the truck aside in the "friends" pile. "I'm making Waycross room!"

By the end of the third day, the essentials were packed up, with boxes stacked in neat piles, ready to go. We'd donated what we could and managed to sell a few bigger items Brooke didn't want to keep, leaving the apartment empty. It was strange seeing the place so bare, but it made leaving feel more real.

Finally, on the fourth day, I pulled up to the apartment to pick them up. Cody was ready to go, bouncing on his heels as he clutched his backpack, which was stuffed with his favorite things. Brooke was gathering the last few items in the kitchen when I walked in.

"Got everything?" I asked, looking around at the bare walls and empty shelves.

Brooke gave a final glance around, then nodded.

"Yeah, I think we're all set."

Cody ran over to me, already eager to load up. "Let's go, Dad! I wanna get to Waycross!"

Brooke laughed, picking up her bag. "He's been counting down the minutes all morning."

Once everything was packed into the truck, the three of us climbed in, with Cody in the middle, eagerly peering out the window as we pulled away from the apartment building.

"So," I said, glancing down at him, "are you ready for the big move?"

"Totally!" Cody said, nodding. "And I have everything I need right here." He pointed at his backpack. "Got Rocky, got Ringo, and I even brought my flashlight!"

Brooke chuckled. "Flashlight, huh? Planning any late-night adventures?"

"Maybe," he said, grinning. "You never know."

As we drove out of Louisville, Brooke kept glancing out the window, watching the city fade behind us. I could tell she was experiencing a mix of emotions — excited for what was ahead but still processing everything she was leaving behind.

After a while, she let out a sigh, looking over at

me. "It feels surreal, leaving it all behind."

I nodded, understanding. "Big change. But Waycross is ready for you, Brooke. And Cody's excited to have you there."

Cody chimed in, "Yeah, Mom! It's gonna be awesome! We'll go to the fair, and you can help on the farm!"

Brooke smiled, her expression softening. "Alright, Cody. I'm looking forward to it, too. Let's make it an adventure."

# Chapter 31

Dinner that evening was as lively as I'd ever seen.
Cody had taken a spot between Daisy and
Caroline, who'd already listened to every story
about his adventures in Louisville and the items
he'd brought for his new home — here, with us.
My heart jumped every time he spoke of Waycross
like home.

Brooke seemed at ease, laughing along with the others as we shared the first real meal since arriving back in Waycross. She was sitting beside me, and she looked like she was seeing a whole new side of life — her cheeks flushed, her smile real and unguarded. Sure, it would all take some getting used to, and I was certain it wouldn't all be easy, but the start was good.

"Okay, so what's this about Tink learning to herd sheep?" Brooke asked, raising an eyebrow with a grin. She looked over at Cody, who was happily stuffing his face with a dinner roll.

Cody swallowed and gave her a wide-eyed look. "Oh, yeah! Daisy says I can help train her! Tink's pretty smart already, but we're gonna teach her to, like, do stuff just by pointing."

Daisy winked. "She's a natural, just like her trainer here," she said, ruffling Cody's hair. "She'll be rounding up chickens like a pro in no time, won't she?"

"Yep! And then maybe we can teach her to find all the toys I lose, too," Cody announced proudly.

The whole table broke into laughter, and Brooke reached over to squeeze his hand. "I'm sure she'd be a great toy-finder."

"She is," Cody said. "She found Ringo for me! He was under the bed for… for…" He glanced at me. "For months!"

"So, wait," Brooke said, chuckling as she leaned in toward Cody, "you're telling me this Ringo the Dinosaur got stuck under the bed for *how long*?"

Cody's face was dead serious as he replied, "Well, maybe not *months*. A week, maybe?" He shot me another look, and I gave an exaggerated 'that'll be about right, pal' nod. "Yeah! And when I found him, he was covered in dust! He looked like a mummy." He scrunched up his face, mimicking the poor toy's fate.

Daisy clapped a hand to her mouth to stifle her laughter. "Poor Ringo! Survived the dinosaur extinction just to get trapped under a bed."

"Hey, that's not funny!" Cody protested, though his grin betrayed him. "He's my best buddy, right after Rocky. They both had to come here. And Dad even let me keep them in the truck on the way back!" He looked at me proudly, like I'd just pulled off the parenting feat of the year.

I chuckled. "That's right, bud. Couldn't leave

your crew behind."

Caroline, who had been quietly observing the conversation, leaned over, adding with a playful smirk, "So, Cody, did Ringo and Rocky get along with Tink on the drive back?"

Cody thought about it for a second, then nodded, laughing. "Yeah, but Tink kept trying to sniff them. I told her they're not food, but she didn't listen!"

"Hey, she can be curious," I said. "She probably just thought Ringo was a funny-looking squirrel."

Brooke laughed, looking over at me. "You're really encouraging all his ideas, aren't you?"

"Every last one," I replied, grinning. "The kid's got vision."

Daisy was slicing the last of the pie, but she couldn't resist throwing in, "With all these big plans, Cody, we're gonna need you to handle all the farm projects by the time you're ten."

"Oh, I can do that!" Cody declared, puffing out his chest. "I know how to feed the chickens and pick the best tomatoes and... and... I could maybe even build a... chicken house." He glanced at me. "What's it called again?"

"A coop," I said.

"Isn't that, like, a car?"

Daisy laughed and ruffled his hair. "Sure, it is! You keep it up, and you'll be runnin' this place before long." She grinned at the rest of us. "And ole Daisy can finally get some R&R and have a man around to do the work." We all laughed at that.

And as we enjoyed the meal together, I looked around, feeling a sense of completeness I hadn't felt in years. This was it. Everyone I cared about, together, sharing this moment. Brooke had that relaxed glow about her, like she was finally letting go of all that stress she'd carried around for so long, and it made me feel like maybe things were just starting to fall into place.

Caroline must've noticed, too, because she leaned over and gave Brooke a gentle nudge. "You're looking more at ease than I've ever seen you, Brooke. How's it feel?"

Brooke smiled, taking a breath before replying. "Honestly? Like I can finally breathe." She glanced over at me. "It's just… different here. It feels real."

Daisy raised her glass, her eyes bright with

sincerity. "Well, welcome to Waycross, officially. We're all happy you're here to stay this time."

Brooke lifted her own glass, giving a soft, grateful smile. "To Waycross. And to a whole new start."

Everyone raised their glasses, and for a minute, we all just looked at each other, that unspoken connection hanging in the air. But just as we were about to dig back in and finish the meal, there was a loud knock at the door.

We all froze, exchanging quick glances. I couldn't recall the last time someone had shown up unannounced this late.

And late visitors usually weren't good news.

"Expecting anyone?" Daisy asked, her brow raised in curiosity.

I shook my head. "Not a clue."

"Maybe it's a ghost," Cody whispered, his eyes wide, looking around like we were in the middle of a mystery novel.

I chuckled, then stood up, heading toward the door. The others kept their voices low, but I could still feel their curiosity following me across the room. When I opened the door, I found myself looking at a stranger.

A woman, maybe around her late twenties. She had striking pink hair that fell in soft waves around her shoulders, but she wore a hoodie under her leather coat and had pulled the hood up. Her green eyes were sharp, taking everything in as if she were already two steps ahead of us. She gave a slight smile, one eyebrow raised.

The eyebrow was pink, too…

"Good evening. I'm looking for the Mage of Waycross. Would that be you?" She had a French accent.

Her question was direct, and her voice held a certain edge, like she was used to being in control. I crossed my arms, studying her for a moment before I replied. "Who's asking?"

She gave a small, amused shrug, tilting her head as she replied, "Well… me."

**Finished and eager for early access to my next book? Check out my Patreon: patreon.com/jackbryce**

## THANK YOU FOR READING!

If you enjoyed this book, please check out my other work on Amazon.

Be sure to **leave me a review on Amazon** to let me know if you liked this book! Like most independent authors, I use the feedback from your review to improve my work and to decide what to focus on next, so your review can make a difference.

**If you want early access to my work, consider joining my Patreon (https://patreon.com/jackbryce)!**

If you want to stay up-to-date on my releases, you can join my newsletter by entering the following link into any web browser: https://fierce-thinker-305.ck.page/45f709af30. You can also join my Discord, where the madness never ends... Join by entering the following invite manually in your browser or Discord app:

https://discord.gg/uqXaTMQQhr.

**Jack Bryce's Books**

Below you'll find a list of my work, all available through my author page on Amazon.

### Mage of Waycross (ongoing series)

Mage of Waycross 1

Mage of Waycross 2

Mage of Waycross 3

### Sky Lord (completed series)

Sky Lord 1

Sky Lord 2

Sky Lord 3

### Frontier Summoner (completed series)

Frontier Summoner 1

Frontier Summoner 2

Frontier Summoner 3

Frontier Summoner 4

Frontier Summoner 5

Frontier Summoner 6

Frontier Summoner 7

Frontier Summoner 8

Frontier Summoner 9


## Country Mage (completed series)

Country Mage 1

Country Mage 2

Country Mage 3

Country Mage 4

Country Mage 5

Country Mage 6

Country Mage 7

Country Mage 8

Country Mage 9

Country Mage 10


## Aerda Online (completed series)

Phylomancer

Demon Tamer

Clanfather


## Warped Earth (completed series)

Apocalypse Cultivator 1

Apocalypse Cultivator 2

Apocalypse Cultivator 3

Apocalypse Cultivator 4

Jack Bryce

Apocalypse Cultivator 5

## **Highway Hero (completed series)**

Highway Hero 1

Highway Hero 2

Highway Hero 3

## A SPECIAL THANKS TO...

My patron in the Godlike tier: Lynderyn!

My patron in the Archmage tier: James Hunt!

My patrons in the High Mage Tier: Brian M., David D., Eduardo P., and Walter Kimberly!

All of my other patrons at patreon.com/jackbryce!

Scott D., Louis Wu, and Joe M. for beta reading. You guys are absolute kings.

If you're interested in beta reading for me, hit me up on discord (JauntyHavoc#8836) or send an e-mail to lordjackbryce@gmail.com. The list is currently full, but that might change at any moment!

Made in United States
Troutdale, OR
12/29/2024

27365620R00243